cooking
with
marie

ON ANY
OCCASION!

BRIGHT SKY PRESS

Box 416, Albany, Texas 76430

Text copyright © Marie Hejl
Photographs © Jim Hejl, Jr.

10   9   8   7   6   5   4   3   2   1

Library of Congress Cataloging-in-Publication Data

Hejl, Marie, 1978-
Cooking with Marie. On any occasion! / by Marie Hejl.
p. cm.
Includes index.
ISBN 978-1-933979-10-6 (jacketed hardcover : alk. paper) 1. Cookery, American. 2. Entertaining.
I. Cooking with Marie (Television program) II. Title. III. Title: On any occasion!

TX715.H445 2008
641.5973—dc22

2007035679

Book and cover design by Cregan Design,
Ellen Peeples Cregan and Tutu Somerville

Printed in China through Asia Pacific Offset

cooking
with
marie

ON ANY
OCCASION!

by **MARIE HEJL**
PHOTOGRAPHY by JIM HEJL, JR.

BRIGHT SKY PRESS

To my
late grandmother
Jean Nunn Tunis,
who taught me
to treasure
every occasion

tableofcontents

introduction

I lead a busy lifestyle...busier than I ever thought I would. I am a lawyer during the week and host a cooking show on the weekends. Despite my passion for cooking, I'll be the first to admit I don't have time to cook every day of the week. As a result, it's not at all uncommon for me to eat out or order in.

That said, there are those *certain* times—the truly special occasions—when I know that a homemade dish brings so much more to the table than even an order-to-go from the best restaurant in town.

The problem, as I see it, is that cooking for other people, especially on special occasions, can often be a little intimidating. Imagine hosting a dinner for your boss, making *the* cake for your best friend's birthday party or—oh my gosh—planning your first holiday dinner!

Fear no more.

The recipes you need are here. These recipes are good, and easy, and they'll turn out right the first time. With this book, my hope is that you will try your hand in the kitchen *on any occasion*. Surprise yourself. Delight your family and friends. Above all, have fun.

Before we begin, I'd like to thank my friends and family who encouraged me to cook, create and improve these recipes. More important, thank you for filling my life with so many memorable occasions. I will always cherish these special moments in time.

Marie Hyl

October 2007

BREAK-INTO-THE- daybreakfasts

A popular Spanish-radio program begins: *"Buenos Dias! Buenos Dias! Buenos Dias!"* I like it because it reminds me of those rare, perfect mornings when something sweet or savory is cooking in the kitchen.

On other mornings—okay, *most* mornings—I join the masses at a nearby coffee shop. The caffeine feels good. Add a muffin, and I'm a happy girl.

But it isn't breakfast the way I remember it.

Breakfast was the first meal I learned to cook. My dad taught me to make pancakes as soon as I could reach the stove. He taught me three lessons: (1) Never overmix the batter; (2) For fluffier pancakes, let the batter sit for 10 minutes; and (3) Make sure the griddle is hot before you cook.

I still follow those basic lessons today. As with most things, once you get the basics, you can be creative. Hence the origin of my Mix-'em-Up Buttermilk Pancakes. Why settle for plain pancakes when you could toss in bacon, blueberries or chocolate chips?

Here, I provide the basics, but leave you room to mix things up. In my opinion, the ability to make a recipe your own is what makes a great chef. So, *Buenos Dias y Buena Suerte!*
That is: Good Morning! And Good Luck!

SUNRISE COFFEE CAKE

SERVES 8

I love this coffee cake because it is good as is, but it's also perfectly suited for unique additions. I've made it with blueberries, chocolate chips and pecans. I've added a drizzle of blackberry jam to the middle before baking. When I made it for my brother Chris and his college roommates in Chicago, I substituted cheap beer for the almond extract. Kidding! But really, have a little fun with this recipe. You'll be pleasantly surprised.

1½ cups all-purpose flour

¾ cup sugar

2½ teaspoons baking powder

¾ teaspoon salt

¼ cup canola oil

¾ cup fat-free milk

1 large egg

2 teaspoons vanilla extract

1 teaspoon almond extract

TOPPING:

½ cup packed brown sugar

¼ cup all-purpose flour

1 teaspoon ground cinnamon

3 tablespoons cold unsalted butter

Preheat oven to 375°. Grease a round 9-inch cake pan with nonstick cooking spray or soft butter.

In a large mixing bowl, combine the flour, sugar, baking powder and salt. Add oil, milk, egg and extracts. Beat on high speed for 1 minute. Pour into the prepared pan. In a food processor, mix the topping ingredients until mixture has the texture of cornmeal. Sprinkle over batter.

Bake for 25-30 minutes or until a toothpick inserted into center of cake comes out clean. Cool for at least 10 minutes. Cut into wedges and serve.

VARIATION: To add blueberries, chocolate chips or chopped pecans to the coffee cake, first pour half of the batter into the cake pan, then sprinkle with ¾ cup of one of those three items; top with the remaining batter and then the topping.

MARIE'S SUGGESTED OCCASIONS:
* SPECIAL BREAKFAST FOR HOUSEGUESTS
* BRUNCH BUFFET AT A WEDDING OR BABY SHOWER
* HOUSEWARMING GIFT FOR NEW HOME OWNERS
* SURPRISE TREAT FOR YOUR COLLEAGUES AT WORK

MIX-'EM-UP BUTTERMILK PANCAKES

MAKES 12 TO 16 MEDIUM PANCAKES

Not much sounds better than a warm stack of homemade buttermilk pancakes. But don't let that stop you from turning plain-Jane flapjacks into your own signature creation. My mom likes my banana-nut version: I add three or four thin slices of fresh banana and a sprinkle of small pecan pieces to the uncooked side of the pancake while it is on the griddle.

My sister-in-law, Laura, loves it when I add a few blueberries. And my brother Jim raves over my latest creation—crumbled bacon pieces and a spoonful of syrup spread around the inside of his pancakes! If you're on a health kick, add a sprinkle of ground flax seed or toasted wheat bran. Or if you're not, indulge with chocolate chips!

2 cups all-purpose flour

2 teaspoons baking powder

1 teaspoon baking soda

$\frac{1}{2}$ teaspoon salt

3 tablespoons sugar

2 large eggs

3 cups low-fat buttermilk

4 tablespoons unsalted butter, melted
 and cooled

Additional butter for griddle

OPTIONAL ADD-INS:

Sliced fresh bananas and chopped
 pecans

Fresh blueberries

Sliced fresh strawberries

Maple syrup and crumbled cooked
 bacon

Chocolate chips

Toasted wheat bran

Ground flax seed

TOPPINGS:

Butter, maple syrup, fresh fruit, yogurt,
 honey *or* jam

In a large bowl, combine the flour, baking powder, baking soda, salt and sugar with a rubber spatula. In a separate bowl, gently whisk the eggs. Add buttermilk and melted butter; whisk again. Add wet ingredients to dry and mix with the spatula (don't overmix; lumps are okay).

Heat a griddle or skillet over medium heat. After 3-5 minutes, sprinkle water on the heated pan; if the water "dances," it's hot enough to use. Place a small pat of butter on the pan and spread the butter around the surface.

Using a $\frac{1}{4}$-cup measuring cup or small ladle, pour batter onto the skillet to form a pancake. Sprinkle with your choice of add-ins if desired. When the uncooked side starts to bubble and the sides of the pancake begin to dry, the pancake is ready to flip. Use a pancake turner (a large flat spatula) to flip. Cook for 2-3 more minutes or until the underside is golden brown.

Transfer pancakes to plates; serve immediately with toppings of your choice.

MARIE'S SUGGESTED OCCASIONS:
* SPECIAL BREAKFAST FOR OVERNIGHT HOUSEGUESTS
* BREAKFAST IN BED ON MOTHER'S OR FATHER'S DAY
* BRUNCH FOR OUT-OF-TOWN WEDDING GUESTS
* HEARTY BREAKFAST BEFORE AN EARLY FOOTBALL GAME

MELT-IN-YOUR-MOUTH SCONES

MAKES 8 SCONES

Scones have always been one of my favorite breakfast or brunch items. For sweet scones, I like using dried cranberries with a light glaze flavored with orange zest. For a savory version, I enjoy bacon, cheddar and chives. Homemade scones are naturally rustic, as the original triangular-wedge shape morphs slightly during baking. To me, these slight imperfections serve as a subtle reminder that this breakfast was not produced in a factory, but rather, made with your heart and your own two hands.

2 cups all-purpose flour

1/4 cup sugar

2 teaspoons baking powder

1/2 teaspoon baking soda

1/2 pound cold unsalted butter, cut into cubes

3/4 cup dried sweetened cranberries

2/3 cup low-fat buttermilk

GLAZE:

1/4 cup fat-free milk

1 cup confectioners' sugar

1 tablespoon unsalted butter

1 navel orange

Preheat oven to 375°. Line a baking sheet with parchment paper.

In a food processor, combine the flour, sugar, baking powder and baking soda. Add butter; pulse until the mixture has the texture of cornmeal. Pour into a large bowl; stir in cranberries. Add buttermilk; mix until no dry flour is visible (dough will be sticky).

Turn the dough onto a lightly floured surface. Pat into a 1-inch-thick round; cut into eight wedges. Place on the prepared baking sheet. Bake for 18-20 minutes.

Meanwhile, in a saucepan, stir milk and confectioners' sugar a few times. Add butter; cook over medium-low heat, stirring continuously until mixture is smooth. Using a handheld grater, grate the zest of the orange directly into mixture (avoid grating the bitter white pith). Reduce heat to low; continue stirring to keep glaze smooth.

Transfer warm scones to a wire rack set over a sheet of parchment paper. Drizzle glaze over the top, letting excess drip onto parchment paper; let the glaze harden. Serve warm or at room temperature.

VARIATIONS: Substitute chocolate chips or chopped nuts for the cranberries.

For savory scones, omit the cranberries and glaze; reduce sugar to 1 tablespoon; add 1/3 cup crumbled cooked bacon, 3/4 cup shredded sharp cheddar cheese and 1 tablespoon minced chives.

MARIE'S SUGGESTED OCCASIONS:
* SPECIAL BREAKFAST FOR HOUSEGUESTS
* BRUNCH BUFFET AT A WEDDING OR BABY SHOWER
* HOUSEWARMING GIFT FOR NEW HOME OWNERS
* SWEET TREAT AT AN AFTERNOON TEA PARTY

EVERYTHING EGG-WHITE OMELET

SERVES 1 (MULTIPLY FOR MORE!)

Open your refrigerator. Do you have eggs? If so, you can make this omelet. I call this recipe the "Everything" Egg-White Omelet, but "Anything" is probably more appropriate. As long as you have a basic egg base, you can add almost anything for filling.

A spinach-mushroom-jalapeño-cheese combo is my favorite, but don't let my likings limit you. Love bacon? Throw in some crumbles. Have a leftover baked potato? Sauté pieces in olive oil and toss them in. Also, if you'd rather use the full egg (yolk and white), go for it!

2 tablespoons unsalted butter, *divided*

3 to 4 egg whites

2 slices deli turkey *or* ham, cut into bite-size pieces

½ cup baby spinach

2 large mushrooms, chopped

8 to 10 slices pickled *or* fresh jalapeños, optional

2 tablespoons shredded cheddar *or* provolone cheese

2 slices avocado, chopped

1 slice tomato, chopped

1 tablespoon minced red onion, optional

Kosher salt and freshly ground pepper to taste

In a medium skillet, melt 1 tablespoon butter over medium heat. Whisk egg whites; pour into skillet and cook until partially set. Using a spatula, lift edges, letting uncooked eggs flow underneath. Repeat until entire omelet is cooked. Then flip the omelet so the top gets browned.

Meanwhile, in another skillet, melt remaining butter. Add turkey; cook until lightly browned. Transfer to a small bowl. In the same pan, cook the spinach, mushrooms and jalapeños if desired over medium heat until spinach is wilted and mushrooms are soft. Toss with turkey.

Transfer omelet to a microwave-safe plate; place the turkey mixture and then tomatoes on one side of omelet. Sprinkle with cheese. Fold the other half of omelet over the filling. Microwave for 30-45 seconds to melt cheese. Top with avocado and onion if desired. Season with salt and pepper. Serve immediately.

MARIE'S SUGGESTED OCCASIONS:
* EASY AND HEALTHY "BREAKFAST FOR DINNER"
* SPECIAL BRUNCH FOR HOUSEGUESTS
* PROTEIN-, VITAMIN- AND FIBER-PACKED BREAKFAST

USE-UP-YOUR-BANANAS BREAD

MAKES 1 LOAF

Baking was my first hobby—before cooking, that is. I'm not sure how I became so interested in baking, but part of it was out of necessity. I remember when I was fairly young hearing my mom say, "Oh, no, the bananas are brown! Can you make a banana bread, Marie?" As a result, banana bread has always been a functional food for me: It solves the quickly browning-bunch-of-bananas problem.

That aside, banana bread is a universal favorite—perfect as an afternoon snack or a quick breakfast on the way out the door. Add chopped walnuts for a dose of healthy vitamins and oils. Functional, quick and healthy? Baked goods just don't get much better than that!

2 tablespoons plus 2 cups all-purpose flour, *divided*

¾ cup sugar

¾ teaspoon baking soda

½ teaspoon salt

2 large eggs

3 very ripe bananas, mashed

½ cup unsalted butter, melted and cooled

2 teaspoons vanilla extract

1 cup coarsely chopped walnuts

Preheat oven to 350°. Grease the bottom and sides of a 9-inch x 5-inch x 3-inch loaf pan. Dust with 2 tablespoons flour and tap out excess.

In a large bowl, combine the sugar, baking soda, salt and remaining flour. In a separate bowl, whisk the eggs; stir in the bananas, butter and vanilla. Add to the dry ingredients and stir just until combined. Fold in walnuts (batter will be thick and chunky).

Pour into the prepared pan. Bake for 50-60 minutes or until golden brown and a toothpick inserted into center of loaf comes out clean. Cool for at least 15 minutes before removing from pan. Serve warm or at room temperature.

MARIE'S SUGGESTED OCCASIONS:
* SPECIAL BREAKFAST FOR HOUSEGUESTS
* BRUNCH BUFFET AT A WEDDING OR BABY SHOWER
* HOUSEWARMING GIFT FOR NEW HOME OWNERS
* HEALTHY TREAT AT AN AFTERNOON TEA PARTY
* WEDDING SHOWER GIFT, MADE IN A PAN REQUESTED BY THE COUPLE

WARM 'N' CUDDLY BLUEBERRY MUFFINS

MAKES 1 DOZEN

The best blueberry muffins I've ever had were at a bed-and-breakfast in Bar Harbor, Maine. As I walked downstairs from a long night's sleep, the heavenly aroma of fresh-baked real-Maine blueberry muffins greeted me. I followed the aroma through the grand old house onto a screened porch, where the other guests were enjoying muffins and coffee while trading travel stories. Every time I make this recipe, it takes me back to that special moment.

2 cups all-purpose flour

1 tablespoon baking powder

½ teaspoon salt

1½ cups fresh *or* frozen blueberries

1 large egg

1 cup sugar

4 tablespoons unsalted butter, melted
and cooled

1 cup (8 ounces) sour cream

2 tablespoons fat-free milk

Preheat oven to 350°. Grease a standard 12-cup muffin tin with soft butter or nonstick cooking spray.

In a large bowl, combine the flour, baking powder and salt. Add blueberries and toss until coated. In a separate bowl, whisk the egg. Add sugar, butter, sour cream and milk; whisk until combined. Fold into the dry ingredients with a spatula until combined (do not overmix, as overmixed muffins will be tough).

Spoon into the prepared muffin cups. Bake for 25-30 minutes or until light golden brown. Cool for 5 minutes before removing from pan.

HELPFUL HINT: If you're using frozen blueberries, you don't need to thaw them first. Just toss the frozen berries with the dry ingredients. Whether you're using fresh or frozen berries, this step helps prevent your muffins from turning blue.

MARIE'S SUGGESTED OCCASIONS:
* BRUNCH-STYLE WEDDING OR BABY SHOWER
* EASY AND PORTABLE GIFT FOR NEW NEIGHBORS OR OFFICE MATES
* ON-THE-GO WEEKDAY BREAKFAST
* TEATIME SNACK FOR FRIENDS

MAMA'S FAMOUS MIGAS

SERVES 4

My mom grew up in Aransas Pass, a small fishermen's village on the Texas coast. Every summer our family goes back to visit and spend time at the nearby beach. These visits bring back memories for my mom...when we pass the surf shop owned by one of her former classmates, or the sturdy building where they sheltered from a hurricane.

She also tells stories about my favorite topic—the food. Her family didn't own a freezer, so they had to eat an entire container of ice cream in one sitting. She laughs about that. With a little less humor, she talks about eggs. Her family raised chickens, so fresh eggs were a staple. Understandably, she can hardly eat an egg today if it isn't mixed with other ingredients. Hence, her famous migas!

8 large eggs

Kosher salt and freshly ground pepper to taste

2 tablespoons unsalted butter

$1/4$ cup diced yellow onion

1 to 2 fresh jalapeños, thinly sliced *or* minced

3 white mushrooms, thinly sliced

3 slices deli ham *or* turkey, cut into bite-size pieces

1 medium tomato, seeded and chopped

16 to 20 tortilla chips, broken into bite-size pieces

1 cup (4 ounces) shredded cheddar cheese

4 to 8 flour *or* corn tortillas, warmed

Salsa

In a bowl, whisk eggs with salt and pepper; set aside. In a large skillet over medium heat, melt butter. Add onion and jalapeños; cook until onion is translucent, stirring often. Add mushrooms and ham; cook for 2 more minutes or until mushrooms are soft and ham is lightly browned. Add tomato; cook and stir 1 minute longer.

Pour eggs into skillet. Stir from the bottom up with the other ingredients, and then begin to scramble the eggs as they cook. About 1 minute before the eggs are done, add the chips and cheese; stir well.

Transfer to a serving bowl. Serve immediately with tortillas and salsa.

MARIE'S SUGGESTED OCCASIONS:
* SUNDAY BRUNCH AFTER A LONG WEEKEND
* PRE-GAME BREAKFAST BEFORE A LONG WEEKEND
* AUTHENTIC BREAKFAST FOR SOUTHERN GUESTS

MINI AUTUMN PUMPKIN BREADS

MAKES 3 LOAVES

This is my favorite quick bread. ("Quick bread" means you don't use yeast, which—because it requires waiting and kneading—is not quick.) Aside from being easy to make, there are two things I love about this bread. First, although pumpkin is often considered a fall or winter ingredient, I bake this bread year-round, and everyone enjoys it. Second, since the recipe makes three small loaves, I can save one for myself, keep one in the freezer for surprise guests and give one away! All this with no extra effort? I'm sold.

4 large eggs

2 cups sugar

1 cup packed light brown sugar

1 cup canola oil

$2/3$ cup evaporated milk

1 can (15 ounces) pumpkin

$3 1/2$ cups all-purpose flour

2 teaspoons baking soda

1 teaspoon baking powder

1 teaspoon salt

1 tablespoon ground cinnamon

1 teaspoon ground nutmeg

$1/4$ cup confectioners' sugar

Preheat oven to 350°. Grease three 5 3/4-inch x 3-inch x 2-inch loaf pans with nonstick cooking spray or soft butter.

In a large mixing bowl, beat eggs, sugars, oil and milk. Blend in pumpkin. Combine the flour, baking soda, baking powder, salt, cinnamon and nutmeg; add to pumpkin mixture and beat until combined.

Pour into the prepared pans. Bake for 45 minutes or until a toothpick inserted into center of loaves comes out clean. Cool for at least 15 minutes. Using a butter knife, gently loosen sides of bread from pan. Invert pan so that bread falls out; turn right side up. Slice and dust with confectioners' sugar (use a handheld sifter to get an even coating).

MARIE'S SUGGESTED OCCASIONS:
* BREAKFAST FOR HOUSEGUESTS, SERVED WITH BUTTER OR CREAM CHEESE
* PERFECT FOR SURPRISE GUESTS (FREEZE, AND THEN WARM SLICES IN THE MICROWAVE)
* GIFTS FOR FRIENDS, OFFICE MATES OR NEW NEIGHBORS
* SWEET SNACK AT A TEATIME SHOWER

THE AUSTIN BREAKFAST SANDWICH

SERVES 1 (MULTIPLY FOR MORE!)

Austin, Texas, is my hometown. Other than vacations and one summer in Florida, I've never left. I'm happy here. We have lakes, green hills, boutique shopping, nice people...and more music, bars and entertainment than anyone has time for. For the most part, Austin is a fit city. It's also the home of Whole Foods Market and the original Central Market, so we're spoiled with fresh food.

We like to be different, often reminding people to "Keep Austin Weird" on T-shirts, bumper stickers and the like. To me, this open-faced sandwich is Austin in fast-food form: It's hearty and healthy, quick and easy, colorful and fresh, kinda crazy and very tasty. Enjoy!

½ **whole-grain English muffin**

1 **tablespoon unsalted butter**

1 **tablespoon extra virgin olive oil**

1 **large egg**

2 **slices deli turkey** *or* **ham**

1 **slice mozzarella** *or* **provolone cheese**

1 **large slice tomato**

3 to 4 **chunks firm avocado**

Kosher salt and freshly ground pepper to taste

Preheat oven to 375°. Spread English muffin half with butter; place on a foil-lined baking sheet. Toast for 5 minutes or until golden brown.

Meanwhile, in a small skillet over medium-high heat, heat oil. Break egg directly into pan, being careful not to break the yolk. Fry until the white becomes opaque and the yolk begins to set. Using a thin metal spatula, flip egg, again being careful not to break the white or yolk. Fry for 2 more minutes.

Remove muffin from oven. Top with meat, cheese and fried egg. Return to the oven for 5 minutes or until cheese is soft and meat is lightly browned on edges. Top with tomato and avocado. Season with salt and pepper. Serve immediately.

MARIE'S SUGGESTED OCCASIONS:

* SPECIAL BREAKFAST FOR HOUSEGUESTS
* HEARTY SNACK BEFORE EARLY TAILGATING
* PROTEIN-, VITAMIN- AND FIBER-PACKED BREAKFAST

POST-YOGA GRANOLA

MAKES 9 TO 10 CUPS

Although the name of this recipe makes it sounds like I'm a yoga pro, that's not actually the case. I've been a few times–to that one where they make it really hot?–and loved it. But it's not a workout I do on a daily basis. If I did, I think I would enjoy a light breakfast like this afterward.

The real memory that spawned this recipe was my brother's wedding. His dear bride-to-be, Laura, asked for this granola on the morning of their big day. Hey–that's just what I would have wanted! I knew she was a keeper.

4 cups old-fashioned oats

1 cup oat bran

2 cups chopped almonds

³/₄ cup canola oil

³/₄ cup honey

1 tablespoon vanilla extract

2 teaspoons almond extract

1 cup nonfat dry milk powder

Preheat oven to 375°. Line two baking sheets with nonstick foil.

In a large bowl, combine the oats, bran and almonds. In a separate bowl, whisk the oil, honey, extracts and milk powder. Pour over oat mixture and stir until well combined (mixture will be sticky, so use your hands to stir if necessary!).

Spread in an even layer on the prepared baking sheets. Bake for 20 minutes. Remove from oven and stir. When you return the baking sheets to the oven, switch positions so the one that was on the bottom rack is now on the top, and vice versa. Bake 10-15 minutes longer or until oats are golden brown. (Be careful not to overbake!)

Cool completely on pans; oats will become crisp as they cool. Store in an airtight container for up to 3 weeks, enjoying as desired with flavored yogurt and fresh fruit, or just by the handful.

MARIE'S SUGGESTED OCCASIONS:
* BREAKFAST ON YOUR WEDDING DAY
* TREAT FOR THE WEDDING PARTY ON A SPA DAY
* LIGHT BREAKFAST AFTER WORKING OUT WITH FRIENDS
* HEALTHY MID-MORNING SNACK

TORTILLA ESPAÑOLA (SPANISH OMELET)

SERVES 6 TO 8

Although the traditional Tortilla Española is made with potatoes and onions, I opted to eliminate the potatoes from this recipe for a couple of reasons. First, not having to peel, wash and cook the potatoes saves time. Second, potatoes are high in carbohydrates. I'm not suggesting that you eliminate carbs from your diet, but a lot of people tend to watch their carbs these days, even if they're not on an official "low-carb" diet.

Regardless of how you feel about potatoes, you'll love what I added in their place: Deli turkey, vitamin-packed spinach and button mushrooms, all of which require almost no preparation. Hooray!

2 to 3 tablespoons extra virgin olive oil, *divided*

1/2 yellow onion, thinly sliced

1 teaspoon salt, *divided*

6 ounces sliced deli turkey, cut into bite-size strips

2 cups baby spinach

1 cup white button mushrooms, sliced

6 large eggs

Freshly ground pepper to taste

OPTIONAL GARNISHES:

1 small jar store-bought salsa

1 small bunch fresh cilantro

1 slightly firm avocado, cut into large chunks

1 cup homemade *or* **store-bought pico de gallo**

1 cup crumbled queso fresco

1 small jar sliced pickled jalapeños

In a large skillet, heat 1-2 tablespoons oil. Add onion and 1/2 teaspoon salt; cook over medium heat for 5 minutes or until onion is translucent. Add turkey, spinach and mushrooms; cook for 3 minutes or until spinach is wilted and mushrooms are soft. Transfer to a large bowl. In a separate bowl, whisk the eggs, pepper and remaining salt. Fold in the turkey mixture.

Place the skillet over medium heat; heat 1 tablespoon oil. Add egg mixture; cook for 5-6 minutes, loosening the edges occasionally with a rubber spatula, letting the uncooked eggs flow underneath. Adjust the heat if necessary to avoid browning the underside of the omelet (underside should be golden, not brown). Using two spatulas, flip the omelet so the topside cooks in the bottom of the pan. Cook until set, about 5 minutes.

Loosen edges of the omelet with a spatula and gently slide onto a large plate. Let stand for 10 minutes. Cut into wedges and serve at room temperature with desired garnishes.

HELPFUL HINT: If you have trouble flipping the omelet, try flipping it into a separate skillet by placing the second skillet on top of the first, and then turning them both over together at the same time. If you choose this method, make sure you grease the second skillet with a bit of olive oil before flipping the omelet into it.

MARIE'S SUGGESTED OCCASIONS:
* HEARTY BRUNCH ON A LAZY SATURDAY
* EASY AND HEALTHY DINNER
* TEX-MEX BREAKFAST FOR HOUSEGUESTS
* MID-MORNING SNACK (WITH A BLOODY MARY?) BEFORE TAILGATING

MAKE-MY- middaymeals

For me, the ideal lunch is something that is easy to make and gives me extra energy for the rest of the day. Veggies are key, as is protein. When it comes to carbs, I choose whole grains when possible.

Lest we forget: Flavor. Although most of my lunch options are geared toward the health-conscious, almost all recipes include a slice or sprinkle of cheese, bacon crumbles or a pat of butter.

Butter?! Yes, butter.

I believe in eating healthy most of the time. It makes me feel good. You'll never see my car at the drive-through window, but that's only as a matter of preference. Thanks to my parents, I grew up eating real, whole foods. As a result, my taste buds balk at anything that isn't.

Back to butter. Butter is a real food—full of fat, but not hydrogenated oil or things I can't pronounce. I'm not a dietitian or doctor. I'm just a regular girl who wants to feel good about what I put into my body...and *great* when I slide on a little black dress!

I hope my lunch recipes will inspire you, if you don't already, to think about what you eat on a daily basis.

EASY CHICKEN CHALUPAS

SERVES 4 TO 6

When I was growing up, my dad always had a big pot of beans on the stove or in the refrigerator. He ate them almost every day for breakfast, while the four of us kids preferred pancakes or cereal. Come lunchtime, however, everyone enjoyed his homemade beans spread over a crispy tortilla and topped with all kinds of goodies. I usually don't have time to make beans from scratch. So here, I opt for canned beans, which—don't tell my dad!—are just as good.

8 to 12 white *or* whole-wheat flour tortillas

1 precooked rotisserie chicken

2 cans (15 ounces *each*) black beans

2 cups shredded iceberg lettuce

8 to 10 cherry tomatoes, quartered

¹/₂ cup chopped fresh cilantro

1 cup (4 ounces) finely shredded cheddar cheese

1 jar store-bought salsa

1 cup (8 ounces) light sour cream

2 slightly firm avocados, cut into bite-size chunks

1 lime

Kosher salt and freshly ground pepper to taste

Preheat oven to 400°. Arrange tortillas on foil-lined baking sheets. Bake for 4 minutes on each side or until golden brown. Place on a serving platter; keep warm. Reduce oven to 250°. Remove chicken from bones; remove skin. Shred chicken with your hands or a fork. Place in a baking dish; keep in the oven until ready to serve.

Pour beans with liquid into a saucepan over medium heat. Using a potato masher, mash the beans to create a thick bean paste (similar to refried beans, but without the fat). Keep beans warm over medium-low heat, stirring occasionally so they don't burn. If beans become too thick, stir in 1-2 tablespoons water. Transfer to a bowl when ready to serve.

Place the lettuce, tomatoes, cilantro, cheese, salsa and sour cream in separate serving bowls. Place avocados on a small platter; squeeze lime juice over avocados to prevent browning. Season with salt and pepper.

For buffet-style serving, place tortilla platter at the beginning of the line. Follow with the bowl of mashed black beans, the dish of shredded chicken, and then the bowls of lettuce, tomatoes, cilantro, cheese, salsa and sour cream. Finish with the avocado platter. In assembly-line fashion, spread beans over tortillas. Add chicken and desired toppings.

VARIATION: For a healthier option, only use the white meat of the chicken. Then you'll need to buy two rotisserie chickens instead of one.

MARIE'S SUGGESTED OCCASIONS:
* CASUAL DINNER PARTY
* FIESTA-THEMED WEDDING SHOWER WITH HOMEMADE MARGARITAS
* QUICK AND HEALTHY WEEKNIGHT MEAL
* EASY WEEKEND LUNCH FOR FAMILY OR GUESTS

YUM, A REUBEN

SERVES 1 (MULTIPLY FOR MORE!)

A friend of mine, Tyson Cole—who is regarded as one of the best sushi chefs in America—once taught me about the importance of flavor and texture in the eating experience. Although a Reuben sandwich is nothing like sushi, I think one of the reasons it is such a classic American sandwich may be because of its unique yet perfectly complementary blend of flavors and textures. Think about it: In one single bite, a Reuben is sweet, sour, soft, gooey, salty, slightly peppery, chewy, buttery and crispy. Yep, I think Tyson's right—I'm hungry just thinking about it!

1 tablespoon unsalted butter

2 slices rye bread

4 thin slices corned beef

2 tablespoons light Thousand Island dressing

2 ounces sauerkraut with 1 spoonful of liquid from jar or can

2 slices Swiss cheese

In a small skillet, heat ½ tablespoon butter over medium heat; swirl melted butter to coat bottom of pan. Place one slice of bread in the pan; cook until lightly toasted. Remove toasted bread from pan and place on a microwave-safe serving plate, toasted side down. Repeat with the remaining butter and second slice of bread.

After toasting the second slice, place corned beef in the warm skillet. Cook for about 1 minute on each side or until heated through and lightly browned. Spread Thousand Island dressing over the non-toasted side of each slice of bread. Place corned beef on top of the dressing on one slice.

Add sauerkraut with liquid to the warm skillet; cook just until warm, about 1-2 minutes. Spoon over corned beef. Top with Swiss cheese. Place second slice of bread on top of cheese. Microwave for 30-45 seconds or until cheese is melted. Cut in half and serve immediately.

MARIE'S SUGGESTED OCCASIONS:
* WARM AND HEARTY WINTERTIME LUNCH
* LAZY SATURDAY LUNCH
* LUNCH WITH NEW FRIENDS OR NEIGHBORS

WARM GOAT CHEESE, SPINACH AND BACON SALAD

SERVES 2 (MULTIPLY FOR MORE!)

There is a popular café in Austin that serves a salad topped with baked goat-cheese medallions. "Baked goat cheese" was a complete mystery to me. Goat cheese is a soft spreadable cheese, so won't it melt in the oven? Finally, I figured out the secret: Chill the cheese before baking to increase the melting point! I should have known. And now that I do, I make this salad all the time, especially in the winter when I want something warm with my greens but am not in the mood for mucho meat.

1 package (8 ounces) goat cheese
(cylindrical shape, about 2 inches
in diameter)

4 slices bacon

1 egg

1 cup fat-free milk

1 cup plain dried bread crumbs

Kosher salt and freshly ground pepper
to taste

5 tablespoons extra virgin olive oil,
divided

1 to 2 tablespoons white balsamic
vinegar

3 cups baby spinach

4 cherry tomatoes, quartered

Preheat oven to 400°. Slice cold goat cheese into ½-inch-thick rounds. Freeze for 20 minutes (this will help the cheese hold its shape when baked). Meanwhile, cook the bacon. Cool slightly, then chop into small crumbles; set aside.

Crack egg into a bowl; add milk and whisk together. Place bread crumbs in a separate bowl; season with salt and pepper. Remove cheese from the freezer (cheese should be very cold and firm, but not fully frozen). Dip each cheese round into egg mixture, then coat well with bread crumbs. Place on a foil-lined baking sheet. When finished coating all of the cheese rounds, drizzle with 1 tablespoon oil. Bake for 5 minutes.

In a small bowl, whisk vinegar and remaining oil; season with salt and pepper. In a large bowl, combine the spinach, tomatoes and bacon. Drizzle with vinaigrette and toss to coat evenly.

Remove cheese rounds from oven. Set oven to broil. Return the baking sheet to the oven and broil the cheese rounds. Keep the oven door open and an eye on the cheese to make sure it doesn't burn. When the rounds are light golden brown, remove from the oven. Divide spinach mixture between two large plates or deep bowls; gently place warm goat cheese on top of each salad. Serve immediately.

VARIATION: Substitute finely ground pecans or pistachios for the bread crumbs. Both make a delicious coating for the goat cheese.

MARIE'S SUGGESTED OCCASIONS:
* ELEGANT LUNCH FOR HOUSEGUESTS
* LUNCH FOR THE WEDDING PARTY
* SUNDAY BRUNCH WITH THE IN-LAWS

MOUTHWATERING MUFFALETTA

SERVES 1 (MULTIPLY FOR MORE!)

Marinated artichokes are one of my favorite ingredients, and I always keep a jar in the pantry. In this recipe, when diced and combined with black olives, the artichokes turn a typical turkey sandwich into an elegant Mediterranean-style meal.

1 tablespoon unsalted butter

2 slices sourdough bread

2 slices provolone *or* Swiss cheese

4 marinated artichoke hearts

6 pitted black olives

4 thin slices deli turkey

In a small skillet, heat ½ tablespoon butter over medium heat; swirl melted butter to coat bottom of pan. Place one slice of bread in the pan with one slice of cheese on top. Cook until bread is lightly toasted and cheese is melted. Remove bread from skillet and place on a cutting board. Repeat with remaining butter, bread and cheese.

Meanwhile, dice artichokes and olives; place in a small bowl and stir gently to combine. Add turkey to warm skillet; cook for 1-2 minutes or until heated through. Place turkey on the non-toasted side of one slice of bread; gently spread artichoke mixture over the top. Place second piece of bread over top, with cheese facing down. Cut in half and serve immediately.

VARIATION: This sandwich also works wonderfully open-faced—omit the top slice of bread, and serve with a knife and fork!

MARIE'S SUGGESTED OCCASIONS:

* WARM AND HEARTY WINTERTIME LUNCH
* MINI MUFFALETTAS (CUT INTO WEDGES) FOR A WEDDING SHOWER
* LUNCH DATE ("YES, I CAN MAKE SOMETHING BESIDES A GRILLED CHEESE")
* LUNCH WITH NEW FRIENDS OR NEIGHBORS

"VOTE FOR BACON" BLT

SERVES 1 (MULTIPLY FOR MORE!)

Bacon has been through an interesting evolution during my lifetime. What was once a breakfast staple—even a symbol of excellence, thanks to filet mignon—moved to the "DO NOT EAT" list in the fat-free era of the early 1990s, and then was acceptable again in the protein-only craze several years later. I'm guessing that, today, with our current national obesity crisis, poor bacon is back on the hit list.

This back-and-forth popularity pendulum reminds me of what our nation's political parties have experienced over the same time period. Well, my fellow Americans, I will be the swing vote that brings bacon back. Yes, without compromising a commitment to healthy eating, you, too, can "Vote for Bacon, in Moderation!"

2 tablespoons unsalted butter

2 slices whole-wheat bread

4 slices bacon

2 tablespoons light blue cheese dressing

2 lettuce leaves

2 slices tomato

2 slices provolone cheese

In a small skillet, heat 1 tablespoon butter over medium heat; swirl melted butter to coat bottom of pan. Place one slice of bread in pan; cook until lightly toasted. Remove to a serving plate, toasted side down. Repeat with remaining butter and bread. Meanwhile, cook bacon.

Place second slice of bread on serving plate, toasted side down. Spread blue cheese dressing over non-toasted side of each slice. On one slice, layer one lettuce leaf, both tomato slices, both slices of cheese and all of the bacon; top with second lettuce leaf and second slice of bread, dressing side down. Cut in half and serve immediately.

MARIE'S SUGGESTED OCCASIONS:
* LUNCH FOR MOMMIES DURING PLAYGROUP
* ON-THE-GO WEEKDAY LUNCH
* LAZY SATURDAY LUNCH IN FRONT OF THE TV

Q&A with marie

QUESTION:
I don't like to cook bacon because it makes a mess of my stove and smells up the house. How do you cook it?

ANSWER:
I agree with you. Cooking bacon can make a real mess—oil splatters on the stove area and even your clothes—and it does make the whole house smell. Plus, you have to be fairly attentive when you are cooking bacon because it takes a while and is easy to burn. Finally, the leftover grease is no fun to dispose of.

But since I like bacon, I've discovered a way I can cook it with no mess. I use Hormel's Microwave-Ready Bacon. It comes in a 12-ounce box containing four packages of four slices each. You microwave the bacon right in the package, which has an insert that absorbs the grease. This convenient product eliminates the things I don't like about bacon, while still allowing me to enjoy the great bacon flavor in a variety of dishes.

WHEN-A-SALAD-WON'T-DO SANDWICH

SERVES 1 (MULTIPLY FOR MORE!)

Often after a vacation or extravagant dinner, I know I need a few extra serving of veggies. But I also know that a straight-up salad just won't cut it. That's when I turn to this sandwich. When I bite into the lightly buttered toasted wheat bread, filled with rich avocados, juicy tomatoes, hearty mushrooms, crisp lettuce and ooooh, that smoky cheese, my taste buds are completely fooled! Salad? This is a sandwich. And a good one, too.

1 to 2 tablespoons unsalted butter

2 slices whole-wheat bread

1 tablespoon light mayonnaise *and/or* mustard

1 large white button mushroom, sliced

3 slices avocado

2 slices smoked white cheddar cheese *or* cheese of your choice

2 slices tomato

2 lettuce leaves

In a small skillet, heat ½ or 1 tablespoon butter over medium heat; swirl melted butter to coat bottom of pan. Place one slice of bread in pan; cook until lightly toasted. Remove to a serving plate, toasted side down. Repeat with remaining butter (again using ½ or 1 tablespoon) and bread. Place on serving plate, toasted side down.

Spread mayonnaise and/or mustard over non-toasted sides of bread. On one slice, stack mushrooms, avocado, cheese, tomato and lettuce; top with second slice. Cut in half and serve immediately.

MARIE'S SUGGESTED OCCASIONS:
* VEGETARIAN LUNCH
* TEATIME WEDDING SHOWER
* LUNCH FOR MOMMIES DURING PLAYGROUP
* PACK-AND-GO LUNCH FOR LATER

SPICY SPINACH AND MUSHROOM QUESADILLA

SERVES 1 (MULTIPLY FOR MORE!)

Both of my parents worked as full-time home builders when I was young. Fortunately, for many of those years, they worked from our own home and toted my three brothers and me around with them to various job sites.

My mom, whose Hispanic roots have influenced our family in a number of ways, taught us all to appreciate a good cheese taco. Instead of grilled cheese sandwiches, we grew up on lightly fried corn tortillas stuffed with cheese, and if we were lucky, sautéed onions and jalapeños. Now that I'm older and more health-conscious, I make my cheese tacos—quesadillas, in Spanish—with whole-wheat tortillas, less oil and more vegetables.

2 tablespoons extra virgin olive oil, *divided*

1 tablespoon diced white onion

1 jalapeño, diced (seeded if desired)

4 white button mushrooms, sliced

1 cup baby spinach

2 white *or* **whole-wheat flour tortillas**

¹/₂ cup shredded mozzarella cheese

Cilantro sprigs, chopped tomato, diced red onion *and/or* **sliced avocado for garnish, optional**

In a medium skillet, heat 1 tablespoon oil over medium heat; swirl skillet so oil coats the bottom of the pan. Add onion and jalapeño; cook until onion is translucent and jalapeño is lightly browned and soft. Transfer to a small bowl. In the same skillet, cook mushrooms until lightly browned and soft. Add spinach; cook until wilted, about 1-2 minutes. Add to bowl with onion mixture.

Add remaining oil to the pan; swirl again to coat the bottom. Place one tortilla in the pan; top with cheese. Using tongs, evenly place vegetables over cheese. Place second tortilla on top; gently press down with a spatula. Cook for 2-3 minutes, continuing to press down as cheese melts. With the spatula, carefully flip. Cook for about 1 minute or until second tortilla is lightly browned.

Remove from skillet and place on a cutting board. Using a sharp knife or pizza cutter, cut into quarters. Serve immediately with desired garnishes.

MARIE'S SUGGESTED OCCASIONS:
* GAME-WATCHING PARTIES
* EASY LUNCH FOR TEENS
* MEXICAN LUNCH
* PARTIES, SERVED IN INDIVIDUAL WEDGES

BIG HEALTHY GREEK SALAD

SERVES 2 (MULTIPLY FOR MORE!)

I'll admit it...I'm that annoying girl who goes to a pizza place and orders a Greek salad. I can't help it; it's my favorite. After you try this one and take a big bite of marinated artichoke hearts, olives and feta cheese—lightly coated with a tart balsamic vinaigrette—you just might join my annoying club.

1/4 cup extra virgin olive oil

1 to 2 tablespoons white balsamic vinegar

Kosher salt and freshly ground pepper to taste

4 cups mixed greens

8 cherry tomatoes

1 jar (6 to 6 1/2 ounces) marinated quartered artichoke hearts, drained

10 pitted kalamata olives

4 small white button mushrooms, thinly sliced

1/4 cup crumbled feta cheese

Toasted whole-wheat pita triangles *or* warm bread

In small bowl, whisk oil and vinegar; season with salt and pepper. In a large bowl, combine the greens, tomatoes, artichokes, olives and mushrooms. Drizzle with vinaigrette and toss to coat evenly. Divide between two large serving plates or flat bowls. Sprinkle with feta cheese. Season with additional salt and pepper if desired. Serve with pita triangles or bread.

MARIE'S SUGGESTED OCCASIONS:
* COMPANY POTLUCK (BE SURE TO MAKE ENOUGH!)
* VEGETARIAN LUNCH
* EASY WEEKEND LUNCH
* LUNCH FOR NEW FRIENDS OR NEIGHBORS

CURRIED CHICKEN SALAD SANDWICHES

SERVES 4 TO 6

My late grandmother Jeannie and I used to love to eat chicken salad sandwiches on her porch. We made a fairly basic version—with chicken, mayonnaise, pickles, celery and walnuts—served on sourdough bread. Then my good friend Wendy taught me how to make the version that her grandmother taught her to make. What a find! This recipe is absolutely delightful. More important, it will always remind me what a pleasure it is to cook and share recipes with family and friends.

1 precooked rotisserie chicken

2 to 4 tablespoons light mayonnaise

1/4 cup dried sweetened cranberries

1/4 cup quartered red seedless grapes

1/4 cup coarsely chopped unsalted pecans

1/4 cup minced celery

Juice of 1/2 lime

1 tablespoon yellow curry powder

Kosher salt and freshly ground pepper to taste

8 to 12 slices white *or* whole-wheat bread

Remove chicken from bones; remove skin. Chop chicken into small bite-size pieces. Place in a large mixing bowl; add 2 tablespoons mayonnaise. Add more mayonnaise if needed and depending on your preference.

Add cranberries, grapes, pecans and celery; stir gently until all ingredients are coated. Add lime juice, curry powder, salt and pepper; stir again. (Finished salad should have a light yellow color from the curry.) Spread onto four or six slices of bread; top with another slice of bread. Cut on the diagonal for an elegant presentation.

MARIE'S SUGGESTED OCCASIONS:
* PACK-AND-GO LUNCH
* PICNIC IN THE PARK
* WEDDING OR BABY SHOWER, SERVED AS TEA SANDWICHES
* HOUSEWARMING PARTY

TURKEY AND SPINACH WHOLE-WHEAT WRAP

SERVES 1 (MULTIPLY FOR MORE!)

Remember when fast-food wraps were all the rage? And then we discovered—because of the dressing and various fillings—wraps could, in fact, be higher in fat and calories than a cheeseburger! Wait...don't turn the page! This wrap is different. The whole-wheat tortilla and variety of veggies offer an excellent dose of vitamins and fiber. Turkey provides a low-fat source of protein, while reduced-fat mayonnaise or naturally fat-free mustard adds extra flavor.

1 tablespoon light mayonnaise
or mustard

1 whole-wheat tortilla

3 slices roasted deli turkey

1/2 cup baby spinach

3 slices tomato

1 large white button mushroom,
thinly sliced

4 slices avocado

Sliced banana peppers, jalapeños *or*
pickles, optional

Spread mayonnaise down the center of tortilla; top with turkey, spinach, tomato, mushrooms and avocado. Finish with peppers or pickles if desired. Roll up and serve.

MARIE'S SUGGESTED OCCASIONS:
* LIGHT AND HEALTHY LUNCH ON-THE-GO
* LUNCH FOR TEENS
* EASY WEEKNIGHT "TV DINNER"
* LUNCH FOR MOMMIES DURING PLAYGROUP

COOKED SHRIMP CEVICHE WITH MIXED GREENS

SERVES 2

Ceviche is a Latin American dish typically consisting of uncooked seafood, which is marinated in lime or other citrus juices, mixed with onions, peppers, tomatoes and cilantro, and served with chips or crackers. I absolutely love good ceviche, but I hesitate to make it at home. This recipe removes the raw factor. "Cooked ceviche"–somewhat of a contradiction in terms–will quell the fear of contamination, whether held by the chef or the guest.

If you leave the tails and the last segment on the shrimp, it makes for an elegant presentation. If using this as an appetizer, it will serve 4.

1 lime

1 orange

2 lemons

2 tablespoons extra virgin olive oil

1 teaspoon sugar

Kosher salt to taste

12 large shrimp, peeled and deveined (tails on)

1 red bell pepper, roasted, peeled and diced

1 yellow bell pepper, roasted, peeled and diced

1 tomato, seeded and diced

1 Serrano pepper, minced (seeded if desired)

1 tablespoon finely chopped cilantro

1/2 red onion, diced

SALAD:

2 cups mixed greens

1/4 cup extra virgin olive oil

1 to 2 tablespoons white balsamic vinegar

12 pitted green olives

Grate the zest of the lime, orange and one lemon into a bowl. Add juice from the lime, orange and both lemons to the bowl. Add oil, sugar and salt; whisk to combine.

In a large pot, bring salted water to a boil. Add shrimp; cook for 3-4 minutes or until light pink and opaque. Remove shrimp from water and place in the citrus marinade; toss to coat evenly. Marinate for at least 15 minutes but not more than 1 hour.

In a large bowl, combine the roasted peppers, tomato, Serrano pepper, cilantro and onion. Add shrimp and marinade; toss to coat. In a separate bowl, toss the greens with oil and vinegar. Season with salt and pepper. Place desired amount of dressed greens on a serving plate. Spoon ceviche over greens; garnish with green olives.

MARIE'S SUGGESTED OCCASIONS:
* LIGHT AND SUMMERY BRUNCH FOR SPECIAL GUESTS
* LOW-CARB, BUT VITAMIN- AND PROTEIN-PACKED, WEEKDAY LUNCH
* ELEGANT DISH TO SERVE AT A SMALL POOLSIDE PARTY WITH FRIENDS

HOW TO ROAST A BELL PEPPER:

There are two ways to roast a bell pepper, depending on what type of equipment you have. If you have a gas stove, light the fire to medium and place a whole bell pepper over the open flame. Use tongs to turn the pepper as it blackens on each side (you want most of the skin to turn black). If you don't have a gas stove, do the same thing using your broiler in the oven.

Once the skin is blackened, place the hot pepper in a plastic bag. The steam in the bag will loosen the skin on the pepper, which will allow you to peel it more easily. After about 15 minutes, remove pepper from bag and peel off the skin; it should come off fairly easily. Cut the pepper in half, remove the stem and scrape out the seeds. Then dice the pepper and it's ready to use.

teasers&pleasers

Appetizers! My favorite course to cook and eat, for so many reasons. For one thing, I am *el queen* of sampling—often to my brothers' or a date's dismay. ("Hey, could you pass me a bite of your steak....ooooh yeah, put some crab on top and dip it in that yummy sauce!") Fortunately, with appetizers, I can go on my own little tasting spree without poking my fork onto someone else's plate.

Another reason I adore appetizers is because, if I'm having them, it probably means that I'm with a group of fun friends, maybe having an after-work cocktail at a fabulous new restaurant, or lounging at a last-minute get-together at someone's home.

Finally, most American entrées are enormous. More food for cheap is always better, right? Maybe if you're Homer Simpson. My ideal meal is one where I can leave a restaurant sans doggie bag and without having to loosen my belt.

If eating appetizers for dinner seems odd, think of it as part of the tapas-party trend. Tapas are a Latin American tradition, where everyone shares a tableful of "small plates" paired with a variety of wines. For me, *es una fiesta perfecta!*

KEEP-'EM-COMING CRAB CAKES

SERVES 4 TO 6

If you've eaten brunch, lunch or dinner with me, you probably know that crab cakes are my favorite dish. If crab cakes are on the menu, I order them. It's somewhat of an obsession. To me, the perfect crab cake consists of crabmeat, plus just enough of the "other" ingredients to hold the seafood together, pan-fried in a bit of olive oil until the top of the cake is browned and the center is soft. This recipe does the job. So enjoy these as an appetizer or, like I do, for brunch, lunch or dinner!

3 tablespoons freshly grated Parmesan cheese

3 tablespoons light mayonnaise

2 tablespoons minced green onions (green portion only)

2 tablespoons plain bread crumbs (more if desired)

1 tablespoon minced fresh lemon basil, sweet basil, cilantro *or* parsley

1 teaspoon Old Bay Seasoning

Freshly ground pepper to taste

1 large egg

1 pound fresh lump crabmeat (check for shells, but do not wash)

¼ cup extra virgin olive oil

GARNISH:

1 to 2 cups mixed greens

Extra virgin olive oil

Salad vinegar (balsamic, white balsamic *or* tarragon)

Kosher salt and freshly ground pepper to taste

12 pitted green olives

In a medium bowl, toss the first eight ingredients until combined. Add crab and toss gently to coat. Using your hands, form balls of crab mixture into small round patties, about ½ to ¾ inch thick, and 1 ½ to 2 inches in diameter.

Place patties on a parchment paper-lined baking sheet. Place in the freezer for 15-30 minutes (this will help the cakes keep their shape when cooked).

In a skillet, heat 2 tablespoons oil. Cook crab cakes in batches, two to three at a time, for 3-4 minutes on each side or until nicely browned. Use remaining oil as necessary.

In a bowl, toss the greens with oil, vinegar, salt and pepper. Place in the center of a serving plate. Arrange crab cakes around the greens. Garnish with olives.

MARIE'S SUGGESTED OCCASIONS:

* COCKTAIL PARTY
* TAPAS-STYLE DINNER
* SNACKS AT A WEDDING SHOWER
* LIGHT BUT HEARTY LUNCH
* SERVE BEFORE A FORMAL DINNER PARTY

PARTY CHICKEN SKEWERS WITH PEANUT SAUCE

MAKES ABOUT 2 DOZEN

One of my good friends once said, "At a party, people will eat anything on a stick!" She's exactly right. So, if you decide to make these for a party, you might want to double (or triple) the recipe to make sure you have enough. I made these yummy chicken skewers for a recent art party, and they were the first dish to disappear. Be sure to have extra sauce and marinated chicken on hand. Keep extra bamboo skewers in water (otherwise, they'll burn in the broiler).

1 pound boneless skinless chicken breasts

2 tablespoons reduced-sodium soy sauce

2 tablespoons teriyaki marinade

Juice of 1 lemon

2 tablespoons extra virgin olive oil

2 cloves garlic, minced

1 teaspoon yellow curry powder

Freshly ground pepper to taste

24 to 30 bamboo skewers (4 to 6 inches long)

SAUCE:

¹/₃ cup natural crunchy peanut butter

¹/₃ cup unsweetened coconut milk

2 tablespoons reduced-sodium soy sauce

2 tablespoons teriyaki marinade

3 teaspoons cayenne pepper

2 teaspoons light brown sugar

Cut chicken into strips and then bite-size pieces; place in a ziplock bag. Add soy sauce, teriyaki marinade, lemon juice, oil, garlic, curry powder and pepper. Seal bag; mix so all of the chicken is coated. Marinate for 20 minutes or up to 1 hour. Meanwhile, soak the skewers in water for at least 20 minutes.

In a saucepan, combine the sauce ingredients. Warm over low heat, stirring occasionally.

Set oven to broil. Remove chicken from marinade and discard marinade. Thread one chicken piece onto the end of each skewer. Place on a foil-lined baking sheet, eight to ten skewers at a time. Broil for 3 minutes. Remove from the oven and turn over carefully (skewers will be hot!). Broil for 3-4 more minutes or until browned.

Remove sauce from the heat and pour into a small bowl. Serve immediately with chicken skewers.

MARIE'S SUGGESTED OCCASIONS:
* CHIC ART PARTY
* HOUSEWARMING PARTY
* GAME-WATCHING PARTY

Q&A with marie

QUESTION:
I worry about serving the peanut sauce at a large party because of the seriousness of peanut allergies. Do you have a solution?

ANSWER:
Yes. I have the same concern. My solution, which has worked very well so far, is to label each dish by placing a basic white name card in front of the dish. On the card, I include the name of the dish and sauce, and if it contains peanuts, I'll add an asterisk followed by bold writing that says "*CONTAINS PEANUTS."

PURPLE CABBAGE BOWL AND VEGGIE PLATTER

SERVES 20 TO 24

I know what you're thinking: "Veggie platter? Oh, that's original." I agree with you that a veggie platter is a basic appetizer, which makes an appearance at almost every party. That's precisely why I wanted to include it in this book!

People like a good veggie platter—it gives them a lighter option to mix in with all the other possibly not-so-healthy snacks. It's great for vegetarians or those watching their weight, especially those who prefer not to call attention to their dietary desires. And let's not forget the host! A veggie platter is often the easiest appetizer to make, adds a variety of bright colors and takes up a good amount of space if—whoops!—you didn't realize how big your serving table is.

What I like about this veggie platter is the presentation. Instead of simply setting out a premade platter in a plastic container, display the veggies on an elegant platter with a large, bright cabbage bowl in the center.

1 large head purple cabbage

2 cups broccoli florets

2 cups cauliflowerets

2 cups baby carrots *or* 3 carrots, peeled and sliced into sticks

2 cups cherry tomatoes

2 yellow summer squash, sliced into thin rounds

2 zucchini, sliced into thin rounds

Light blue cheese *or* ranch salad dressing *or* dip

To prepare the cabbage bowl, peel outer leaves off cabbage until you reach the fresh, bright purple leaves. Using a large sharp knife, slice off the bottom core so the cabbage has a flat base. Set cabbage on its base and begin to work on the top. Using a small sharp paring knife, hollow out a portion of the top of the cabbage. Be sure to leave a thick edge around the hollow portion so the dressing or dip doesn't leak out the sides. Continue to hollow out the center until you have gone about 2 inches deep.

Place cabbage bowl in the center of a large platter. Arrange veggies around the bowl. If you have extra veggies, keep them in a container in the refrigerator and refill the platter as needed. When your guests are about to arrive, pour dressing or dip into the cabbage bowl. Be careful not to fill it too high, or it might drip down the sides or overflow when people dip into it. Refill bowl as needed during the party.

VARIATION: Feel free to use other vegetables. Celery sticks, white button mushrooms, Belgian endive leaves, green onions or bell pepper strips are all fabulous options.

MARIE'S SUGGESTED OCCASIONS:
* HOUSEWARMING PARTY
* WEDDING OR BABY SHOWER
* GAME-WATCHING PARTY

IT-WAS-NOTHING
CHICKEN LETTUCE WRAPS

SERVES 8 TO 10

This is one of those recipes that looks intimidating because there are many—and many slightly unusual—ingredients. But really, thanks to the precooked chicken and repeat use of ingredients, and as long as you have your shopping list in order, it's surprisingly simple. Of course, there's no reason to tell your guests that! Just say, "Oh, this? It was nothing." And then smile casually as you present this mouthwatering appetizer.

COOKING SAUCE:

2 teaspoons cornstarch

1 teaspoon sugar

2 tablespoons oyster sauce

2 tablespoons water

1 tablespoon hoisin sauce

1 tablespoon reduced-sodium soy sauce

1 tablespoon dry sherry

1 teaspoon sesame oil

FILLING:

2 precooked rotisserie chickens

1 teaspoon cornstarch

2 teaspoons dry sherry

2 teaspoons reduced-sodium soy sauce

2 teaspoons water

2 tablespoons canola oil

1 teaspoon minced fresh ginger

2 cloves garlic, minced

2 green onions, minced

1 Serrano pepper, thinly sliced

8 white button mushrooms, minced

1 can (8 ounces) bamboo shoots,
   drained and minced

1 can (8 ounces) water chestnuts,
   drained and minced

16 to 20 iceberg *or* butter lettuce leaves

In a medium bowl, combine the cooking sauce ingredients; set aside. Remove chicken from bones; remove skin. Chop chicken into small bite-size pieces. In another bowl, combine the cornstarch, sherry, soy sauce and water until smooth. Add chicken and stir to coat. Marinate for 15 minutes.

Heat a wok or large skillet over medium-high heat; add oil. Stir-fry the ginger, garlic, onions and Serrano pepper for 1-2 minutes. Add mushrooms, bamboo shoots and water chestnuts; stir-fry 2 more minutes. Add chicken with marinade. Stir cooking sauce and add to wok; cook until thickened and hot. Transfer to a large serving bowl.

Place lettuce leaves on a plate or platter. To serve, spoon warm chicken mixture into lettuce leaves and wrap up.

MARIE'S SUGGESTED OCCASIONS:
* CHIC ART PARTY
* COUPLES' WEDDING SHOWER
* SERVE BEFORE A FORMAL DINNER PARTY

Q&A with marie

QUESTION:
I want to make this dish, but I'm really not in the mood to search for all of those ingredients. Am I out of luck?

ANSWER:
Not at all! Get whatever is on this list that you can find. If the sauces are causing you trouble, stick with simple soy sauce and a teriyaki marinade. Sure, it won't be quite as flavorful, but I'm certain your guests will enjoy it.

GOAT CHEESE-STUFFED MUSHROOMS

MAKES 1 DOZEN

When I first heard about goat cheese, I was a little suspect. Unknown cheeses—especially if they are particularly pungent—can be pretty overwhelming. My suspicions were for naught. Goat cheese has a mild, salty flavor and wonderfully rich, creamy texture. It's versatile, too: I've seen it used in ravioli, dotted across pizzas, baked on salads and spread over slices of toasted baguette.

In addition to its many uses, goat cheese also tends to be lower in carbohydrates but higher in calcium than comparable cow's milk cheese, such as cream cheese. So even if you are a little hesitant, or if you happen to love goat cheese already, give this recipe a try!

1 tablespoon extra virgin olive oil

12 large white button mushrooms, stems removed

1/4 cup minced green onions

1/4 cup plus 2 tablespoons grated Parmesan cheese, *divided*

1/4 cup soft bread crumbs

1/4 cup minced pecans

1 tablespoon minced fresh thyme

Kosher salt and freshly ground pepper to taste

4 ounces goat cheese

In a large skillet, heat oil. Sauté mushroom caps over medium-high heat for 2-3 minutes. Turn caps over; sauté 2-3 more minutes or until lightly browned and slightly soft. Drain on paper towels.

Add onions to skillet; sauté over medium heat until tender. Remove from the heat; stir in 1/4 cup Parmesan cheese, bread crumbs, pecans, thyme, salt and pepper. Crumble goat cheese into mushroom caps; top with crumb mixture and press down slightly. Sprinkle with remaining Parmesan cheese.

Set oven to broil. Arrange mushrooms on a foil-lined baking sheet. Broil (with oven door open) for 2-3 minutes or until lightly browned. Serve warm.

MARIE'S SUGGESTED OCCASIONS:
* CASUAL OR FORMAL DINNER PARTY
* COCKTAIL PARTY
* TAPAS-STYLE DINNER
* BUFFET AT WEDDING SHOWER

Q&A with marie

QUESTION:

With all due respect, I read your encouraging words about how much you have grown to love goat cheese. Unfortunately, I've tried it several times, and I still despise it. Do you have any substitute suggestions?

ANSWER:

In fact, I do! If you don't like goat cheese (or don't have any on hand), you have a couple of options. For example, I've made these with cream cheese (mixed with cooked ground sausage for extra flavor) and feta cheese. Although I haven't personally tried it, I bet a good seasoned ricotta would work well, as would Brie.

If blue cheese or Roquefort is your favorite, you might try that; however, because the flavor of these cheeses is so striking, they might clash with the thyme. Consider substituting a more neutral herb, such as parsley.

HOLY GUACAMOLE

SERVES 4

I call this "Holy" guacamole because in Texas, homemade guacamole is an especially treasured appetizer. When I make it before dinner, it's usually gone in about 15 minutes. Although I recommend using fresh tomatoes, peppers and cilantro, if you happen to be in a rush, you can mix some of your favorite salsa with the avocados instead. Still add the lime juice, though, which will prevent the avocados from turning brown.

Use one or two jalapeños, with or without the seeds, depending on your heat preference. Serve baked tortilla chips to reduce calories and fat. Or, if you are watching your carbs, serve the guacamole over a bed of lettuce.

2 large soft avocados, peeled and pitted

¹/₂ cup diced seeded tomato

¹/₄ cup chopped fresh cilantro

1 to 2 jalapeños, diced

Juice of 1 lime

Kosher salt to taste

Tortilla chips *or* shredded lettuce

In a large bowl, mash avocados using a fork or potato masher (or your hands!). Add the tomato, cilantro, jalapeños, lime juice and salt; stir to combine. Serve immediately with tortilla chips or atop a bed of lettuce.

MARIE'S SUGGESTED OCCASIONS:

* GAME-WATCHING OR TAILGATE PARTY
* SERVE BEFORE A MEXICAN-STYLE DINNER
* SIMPLE SNACK AT A PARTY BY THE POOL
* TOPPING FOR CHALUPAS, FAJITAS OR QUESADILLAS

Q&A with marie

QUESTION:
I always like to do as much as I can before guests arrive.
Is this a good appetizer to make a few hours before the party?

ANSWER:
Nope! Avocado has a tendency to turn brown once exposed to air. The lime juice
will help prevent browning, but not over a period of hours. My recommendation is
that you make this dish as your first few guests are arriving, or just a few
minutes before you plan to serve it. In this case, fresher is definitely better!
If you are feeling stressed about having to make it at the last minute,
try putting all of your ingredients and utensils in one area.
This way, when it comes time to make the guacamole, you're all set.

YUMMY HUMMUS WITH BAKED PITA TRIANGLES

SERVES 4 TO 6

My dad adores homemade hummus, and he's the one who taught me to make it. The one major change I made from his recipe is the number of garlic cloves. He uses so much garlic, I literally cannot talk to him after he's eaten it! If you are a garlic lover like my dad, feel free toss in a few more cloves than I recommend in my recipe. But be careful if you are planning to mingle with others afterward...and don't say I didn't warn ya!

4 whole-wheat pita breads

¹/₄ cup extra virgin olive oil

Kosher salt to taste

HUMMUS:

1 can (15 ounces) garbanzo beans, drained and rinsed

3 cloves garlic

¹/₄ cup tahini (sesame seed paste)

Juice of 1 lemon

6 to 8 tablespoons extra virgin olive oil

Kosher salt to taste

Preheat oven to 350°. Cut each pita bread into six triangles. Place 12 triangles on a foil-lined baking sheet. Brush with oil and sprinkle with salt. Bake for 6 minutes or until lightly browned. Remove from oven. Turn triangles over; brush with oil and sprinkle with salt. Bake for 6 more minutes or until fully toasted. Repeat with remaining pita triangles. Cool before serving.

Place the garbanzo beans, garlic, tahini, lemon juice, 6 tablespoons oil and salt in a food processor; blend until smooth. Add more oil if mixture is not smooth enough. Transfer hummus to a serving bowl. Top with a generous drizzle of oil and sprinkle of salt. Serve immediately with baked pita triangles.

VARIATION: Instead of pita triangles, serve the hummus with a thinly sliced baguette or fresh veggies, such as radishes, sliced zucchini, and carrot and celery sticks.

MARIE'S SUGGESTED OCCASIONS:
* VEGETARIAN APPETIZER
* COCKTAIL PARTY
* LIGHT SNACK BEFORE A CASUAL DINNER PARTY

FRESH TOMATO-BASIL BRUSCHETTA

MAKES 2 DOZEN

When I was traveling in Italy a few years ago, I discovered bruschetta. (There, they say "bru-SKET-uh.") The moment I bit into the crispy baguette and tasted the fresh tomatoes, basil and garlic, I was hooked. From then on, I insisted on getting this appetizer whenever I could find it. Each restaurant served it a little differently...sometimes the garlic was more pronounced, sometimes there were onions, and some breads were crisper than others. All that to say, be creative—if you think of a flavor that might mix well with the others, go for it!

1 large clove garlic, halved

24 slices (½ inch thick) baguette

6 tablespoons extra virgin olive oil, *divided*

1 bag (12 ounces) vine-ripe cherry tomatoes, quartered

1 tablespoon white balsamic vinegar

10 fresh basil leaves, roughly chopped

Kosher salt to taste

Basil sprigs for garnish

Preheat oven to 350°. Rub cut sides of garlic over one side of each slice of bread. Place on a foil-lined baking sheet. Using 3 tablespoons of oil total, brush each side of bread. Bake for 10 minutes or until lightly browned, turning once.

Meanwhile, in a bowl, combine the tomatoes, vinegar, basil, salt and remaining oil. Taste, and add more salt or vinegar if necessary. (I like to make mine a little more salty and tart than you would normally expect because the bread really softens the flavors.)

Remove bread from oven. Cool for 3-4 minutes so you can handle it without burning your fingers. Spoon a generous portion of the tomato mixture onto each slice; spoon remaining juices from the bowl over the top. Serve immediately, garnished with basil sprigs.

MARIE'S SUGGESTED OCCASIONS:
* REFRESHING SNACK BY THE POOL
* CHIC ART PARTY
* TAPAS-STYLE DINNER
* WEDDING OR BABY SHOWER

EVERYONE LOVES SPINACH-ARTICHOKE DIP

SERVES 4 TO 6

Get excited about this recipe. I don't know one person who doesn't like it. That said, who could have guessed such a popular appetizer is so unbelievably easy to make? Just check out the instructions—four sentences! I actually considered writing, "Dump everything into a dish and microwave until done," because really that is all you are doing, but I suspected you might prefer some formality. This is a cookbook, after all.

½ cup light sour cream

½ cup light mayonnaise

½ cup grated Parmesan cheese

½ cup shredded mozzarella cheese

1 to 2 teaspoons minced garlic

1 package (10 ounces) frozen chopped spinach, thawed and squeezed dry

1 can (14 ounces) water-packed artichoke hearts, drained and roughly chopped

Tortilla chips *or* fresh veggies

In a large bowl, combine the first seven ingredients and mix thoroughly. Transfer to a shallow microwave-safe dish. Microwave, uncovered, on high for 4-6 minutes, stirring occasionally. Serve immediately with tortilla chips or veggies.

MARIE'S SUGGESTED OCCASIONS:
* GAME-WATCHING PARTY
* HOUSEWARMING PARTY
* COCKTAIL PARTY
* SERVE BEFORE A CASUAL DINNER PARTY

APPLE-BLUE CHEESE SALAD BOATS

MAKES 2 1/2 DOZEN

Belgian endive is the key to this recipe. Each individual leaf, after being carefully removed from the base of the plant, forms the "boat" for the flavorful filling. If you haven't had Belgian endive (or didn't know what it was when you ate it), it's a tangy, slightly bitter, crispy vegetable of the lettuce variety. Healthwise, it is high in minerals, low in sodium and has just one calorie per leaf!

When you are picking the plant for this recipe, remember that a good Belgian endive should be a creamy white color, with a tightly closed head and light green or yellow points. As long as you keep it chilled, you can buy it a couple of days in advance of when you plan to use it.

1 large red apple, cored and diced

3 ounces blue cheese, crumbled

1/2 cup coarsely chopped pecans

3 tablespoons sweet vinaigrette

1 tablespoon fresh lemon juice

Kosher salt to taste

5 large Belgian endives
(about 6 inches long)

In a medium bowl, combine the apple, blue cheese, pecans, vinaigrette and lemon juice; stir gently. Season with salt. Break off leaves of endive, being careful to keep the long leaf structure intact; wash leaves and gently pat dry. Mound a small spoonful of apple mixture onto the core end of each leaf. Serve immediately.

MARIE'S SUGGESTED OCCASIONS:
* COCKTAIL PARTY OR CHIC ART PARTY
* LIGHT SNACK BEFORE A CASUAL DINNER PARTY
* HEALTHY CHOICE AT A TEATIME WEDDING SHOWER

Q&A with marie

QUESTION:
I'm co-hosting a wedding shower brunch with several of my friends in mid-November. I agreed to bring an appetizer. Would this one work?

ANSWER:
These salad boats are perfect for what you described, for several reasons. First, you can make the filling at home, put it in a plastic container for easy transport and then assemble the appetizers when you arrive. This way, you won't have to worry about what is happening to your final presentation on the drive over! Second, all of the ingredients are nice for a late-fall or winter occasion. Apples, pecans, blue cheese and endive are very common in "winter" salads. Finally, these appetizers—basically finger-food salad—are ideal for a buffet-style brunch with lots of options. They're so easy to make and eat, allow for a unique presentation and taste delicious!

ONE QUICK SIDE NOTE:
If you were going to a *baby* shower, my answer might not be the same. Remember that some pregnant women prefer to avoid soft cheese, so either make some without the blue cheese, or be sure to alert your expecting friends.

GARLIC-ROASTED SHRIMP COCKTAIL

SERVES 4 TO 6

Basic shrimp cocktail has always been one of my favorite appetizers. My late grandmother Jeannie, one of the best hostesses I've ever known, served this easy appetizer quite often. To add my own twist to her old favorite, I roast the shrimp with minced garlic, kosher salt, freshly ground pepper and good olive oil. The added flavors and roasted texture turn an average appetizer into classy cuisine—with almost no extra effort!

2 tablespoons extra virgin olive oil

2 cloves garlic, minced (about 1 tablespoon)

$1/2$ teaspoon kosher salt *or* to taste

Freshly ground pepper to taste

$1^1/2$ pounds shrimp (16-20 count), peeled and deveined

1 jar store-bought cocktail sauce

2 to 3 tablespoons prepared horseradish, optional

Lemon wedges and parsley sprigs for garnish

Preheat oven to 450°. In a large bowl, whisk oil, garlic, salt and pepper. Add shrimp and toss to coat. Arrange in a single layer on a baking sheet. Roast for 3 minutes. Turn; roast 2-4 minutes more or until shrimp are firm and opaque.

If you prefer to serve the shrimp warm, arrange on a serving platter with a bowl of cocktail sauce. Stir in horseradish if desired to spice it up. Garnish with lemon and parsley.

If you prefer to have the shrimp cold, transfer to a shallow dish and refrigerate until chilled, about 2 hours, before serving.

HELPFUL HINT: When peeling the shrimp, leave the last segment of the shell and the tail on for an elegant presentation. The tail also makes it easier for guests to pick up the shrimp.

MARIE'S SUGGESTED OCCASIONS:
* FLAVORFUL ADDITION TO A GREEN SALAD
* COCKTAIL PARTY
* TAPAS-STYLE DINNER
* SERVE BEFORE A CASUAL OR FORMAL DINNER PARTY
* LIGHT MIDDAY SNACK BY THE POOL

NEW YORK-STYLE BRUSCHETTA

MAKES ABOUT 2 DOZEN

I will never forget my first trip to New York City. It was right after I finished my junior year in college. For a young girl from Texas, New York City was a jaw-dropping experience. I did everything a tourist should do—saw a Broadway play, took a boat to the Statue of Liberty, spent too much money on a pair of shoes, ate lunch in Central Park and stayed at fine hotels.

I also had my first lox bagel sandwich. The toasted bagel, topped with a layer of cream cheese and a stack of smoked salmon, was heavenly. This bruschetta recipe was inspired by that memory. "I Heart NYC." And yes, I do own the T-shirt.

10 to 12 ounces thinly sliced smoked salmon, chilled

1 baguette, sliced into bite-size rounds

1 package (8 ounces) cream cheese, softened

10 cherry tomatoes, thinly sliced

1 small jar of capers, optional

Place salmon on a cutting board. Using a sharp knife, slice salmon into bite-size squares that will fit on top of the bread rounds. Spread a teaspoonful of cream cheese onto each bread round. Top with a square of smoked salmon and a slice of cherry tomato. Add capers if desired.

MARIE'S SUGGESTED OCCASIONS:
* BRUNCH WITH THE IN-LAWS
* WINE AND CHEESE PARTY
* COCKTAIL PARTY
* SERVE BEFORE A FORMAL DINNER PARTY

Q&A with marie

QUESTION:
I see capers or caper sauce on restaurant menus all the time. I'm dying to know—what are capers?

ANSWER:
Capers are tiny green unopened flower buds (or berries) that come from the caper bush, common in the Mediterranean. Capers are usually pickled and slightly peppery in flavor. They're pungent, so use them sparingly. Or, serve them in a small bowl with a little spoon or fork. This way, your guests can add a few capers to their bruschetta, depending on their own personal preference.

My preference is to add them to just about anything—sandwiches, salads, sauces and more. They are essentially fat-free, but their peppery-salty flavor adds a little bite of irreplaceable delight!

IS-IT-HOT-IN-HERE STUFFED JALAPEÑOS

SERVES 10 TO 12

My family always had a garden in the backyard. We grew tomatoes, peppers and herbs every year, along with some other fruits or vegetables on occasion. My two younger brothers, Matt and Chris—who we endearingly called los brazos—were usually given the duty of collecting whatever was ripe. (Los brazos, which literally means "the arms" in Spanish, is slang for "the working men.") True to form, the boys went out with large baskets and came back with an assortment of goodies for my mom and me to use.

Although the tomatoes were hit or miss—too green, too ripe or half-eaten by bugs—the peppers were consistently good. So I grew up eating fresh peppers with just about anything, and that's why I adore these spicy snacks. If mild is your style, be sure to remove the white pith and seeds from each pepper before stuffing it.

22 large jalapeños

1 pound bulk pork *or* beef sausage

1 package (8 ounces) cream cheese, softened

3/4 cup grated Parmesan cheese, *divided*

Preheat oven to 425°. Slice the jalapeños in half lengthwise; remove the pith and seeds (unless you want really hot appetizers!).

In a skillet, brown the sausage over medium heat. In a large bowl, combine the cream cheese and 1/2 cup Parmesan cheese; add sausage and mix until blended. Stuff into jalapeño halves. Place on a foil-lined baking sheet. Sprinkle with remaining Parmesan cheese.

Bake for 10-15 minutes or until peppers and stuffing begin to brown.

MARIE'S SUGGESTED OCCASIONS:
* BACKYARD BARBECUE
* GAME-WATCHING PARTY
* FIESTA-THEMED WEDDING SHOWER
* HOUSEWARMING PARTY

SALMON CAKES WITH WASABI DIPPING SAUCE

SERVES 8

Although I adore crab cakes, I also love this variation with salmon and especially the wasabi dipping sauce. Salmon is often easier to find at your local grocery store and possibly more affordable than lump crabmeat. Plus, salmon offers a variety of health benefits, including healthy fats and oils as well as vitamins and minerals. Feel good as you dive into these!

1 salmon fillet (2 pounds), bones and skin removed

1 tablespoon extra virgin olive oil

Kosher salt and freshly ground pepper to taste

1/2 cup minced green onions

1/2 cup dried bread crumbs

1/4 cup light mayonnaise

2 large eggs, lightly beaten

2 tablespoons fresh lemon juice

SAUCE:

1 cup (8 ounces) sour cream

1 cup light mayonnaise

2 tablespoons wasabi paste (purchased in a tube)

Kosher salt to taste

4 lemons

Preheat oven to 400°. Place salmon on a foil-lined baking sheet. Brush with oil; season with salt and pepper. Bake for 15-20 minutes or until salmon is cooked through. Cool. Using a fork, flake salmon into small pieces.

In a large bowl, combine the onions, bread crumbs, mayonnaise, eggs and lemon juice; mix gently. Season with salt and pepper. Add salmon and mix again. Using your hands, form mixture into small cakes, about 1/2 to 3/4 inch thick, and 1 1/2 to 2 inches in diameter. Place on a baking sheet. Refrigerate until firm, about 20 minutes, or freeze for 10 minutes.

For the sauce, in a medium bowl, whisk the sour cream, mayonnaise and wasabi. Taste, and add salt and additional wasabi if desired. Chill until serving. To make the garnish, thinly slice the lemons; gently remove pulp from the inside of each slice so you are left with only a thin, round lemon rind. Set aside.

Set oven to broil. Broil salmon cakes for 6-8 minutes or until golden brown on top. Serve with wasabi dipping sauce; garnish with twisted lemon rind.

MARIE'S SUGGESTED OCCASIONS:
* CHIC ART PARTY
* BRUNCH WITH THE IN-LAWS
* AFTERNOON WEDDING OR BABY SHOWER
* SERVE BEFORE A FORMAL DINNER PARTY

Q&A with marie

QUESTION:
I love sushi, so I eat wasabi often. But I'm a little embarrassed that I have no idea what it is. Can you help?

ANSWER:
Wasabi is a spice that comes from a knobby green root of the Japanese plant wasabia japonica. More than you wanted to know? Basically, wasabi is very similar to American horseradish. Both have a powerful, fiery flavor. If you get too much, it shoots up toward your nose—often making your nose sting and eyes water. This type of heat is different than heat from, say, hot peppers. Heat from jalapeños or Serranos is generally felt in your mouth and down into your body when you swallow. I love both!

first impressions

During the second half of my first year in law school, I began interviewing for summer internships along with the rest of the students. I heard a story—I still don't know if it's true—about one extraordinarily bright student. With outstanding grades and a fantastic resumé, he was highly recruited by all the top firms.

When he arrived in New York for yet another interview, he followed his regular procedure: Found the limousine driver holding a card with his name, dropped his bags at the driver's feet and strutted to the car. No handshake. No hello. No thanks.

As the story goes, when they arrived at the office, the driver stepped out of the car, removed his costume hat and kindly introduced himself as the managing partner of the firm.

The moral of the story, which I assume you can guess, also applies to food. The first course you bring to the table is an introduction to the occasion your guests are about to experience. Preparation, presentation and good manners set the tone. A warm smile exudes confidence and makes everyone feel welcome.

Remember the story of the young law student next time you host an event. There is only *one* first course; make it good.

ELEGANT TOMATO-MOZZARELLA FANS

SERVES 4

Over my many years of cooking, I have learned that the presentation of food is almost as important as the taste. These tomato-mozzarella fans rank high in both categories. Surprise your guests with this presentation of the traditional Italian Ensalada Caprese. It's simple, yet elegant and unique at the same time.

4 round vine-ripe tomatoes

1 round ball (8 ounces) fresh mozzarella

8 to 10 teaspoons extra virgin olive oil

White balsamic vinegar, optional

**Kosher salt and freshly ground pepper
to taste**

4 fresh basil leaves

Cut a thin slice off the bottom of each tomato so it sits flat. Place one tomato upside down on a cutting board. Make five slits in the tomato, being careful not to cut all the way through. Repeat with remaining tomatoes. Cut mozzarella into thin round slices; cut each round in half. Insert a half circle of cheese between the slits in the tomatoes.

Spoon about 2 teaspoons of oil across each tomato fan. Add a splash of balsamic vinegar if desired. Sprinkle with salt and pepper. Top with a basil leaf. Serve immediately.

MARIE'S SUGGESTED OCCASIONS:
* STARTER SALAD BEFORE A FORMAL DINNER PARTY
* TAPAS-STYLE PARTY
* LIGHT SUMMERTIME SALAD

SWEET AND SIMPLE MIXED GREEN SALAD

SERVES 6

About a year ago, I invited my good friends Allison and Wendy to be guest hosts on an episode of my cooking show. Because they are both fantastic hosts, we decided to focus on how to host a wedding or baby shower. (My guy friends enjoy acting confused when I refer to it as "The Shower Show." Real funny, guys.) Anyway, Allison offered to make a salad that even her husband loves, but she was worried that it might be too easy. Is there such a thing? We made the salad on the show—wow, was I impressed! The textures, colors and flavors create a fabulous combination.

2 bags (5 ounces *each*) spring mix
  salad greens

¾ cup crumbled feta cheese

1 Granny Smith apple, diced

¾ cup dried sweetened cranberries

¾ cup coarsely chopped pecans

½ red onion, thinly sliced, optional

½ to ¾ cup sweet vinaigrette

In a large bowl, combine the greens, feta cheese, apple, cranberries, pecans and onion if desired. Add vinaigrette and toss to coat. Serve immediately.

MARIE'S SUGGESTED OCCASIONS:
* WEDDING OR BABY SHOWER
* CASUAL DINNER PARTY
* SIDE SALAD WITH BASIC GRILLED CHICKEN OR SALMON

CAESAR SALAD FROM THE HEART

SERVES 4 TO 6

This recipe calls for hearts of romaine. Romaine lettuce is the one with an elongated head and dark green leaves. The center leaves, which are used in this salad, are crisp, light in color and seriously succulent when drizzled with Caesar dressing, Parmesan and pepper. My favorite thing about this recipe is there's no chopping involved! For you, that is. Serve this salad with a knife and fork, as your guests will need to do the chopping themselves.

3 large hearts of romaine

½ cup of your favorite Caesar or low-fat Caesar salad dressing

½ cup freshly grated Parmesan cheese

Freshly ground pepper, optional

Pull off and discard the outer leaves of lettuce, which are often wilted and broken. Make a stack of the fresh inner leaves, about 24-30 total. Trim the white stem (no more than ½ inch) off each leaf. Wash leaves and pat dry.

Place four to five leaves on each plate. Drizzle with dressing and sprinkle with Parmesan cheese. Grind pepper over all if desired. Serve immediately with a knife and fork.

MARIE'S SUGGESTED OCCASIONS:
* STARTER SALAD FOR A CASUAL ITALIAN-STYLE DINNER
* EASY AND HEALTHY MIDDAY SNACK
* SIDE SALAD FOR AN EVERYDAY PASTA DINNER

YELLOW TOMATO SOUP TOPPED WITH CRABMEAT

SERVES 6

At a cooking demo I did for a corporate event, I decided to begin with a fabulous Yellow Tomato Gazpacho topped with Crème Fraîche and Crabmeat. It was all going smoothly until I finished the soup and ladled some into a bowl for presentation. A voice from the audience asked, "Can we eat that?" Somewhat startled, I replied, "Well, oh, actually, you see, this is a gazpacho, so it should actually be served cold...and...oh, why not?!" Thank goodness, the audience enjoyed it, but as you can see, I now no longer call this a gazpacho; it's just soup. So serve it at whatever temperature you wish.

7 to 8 tablespoons extra virgin olive oil, *divided*

3 to 4 large yellow tomatoes, quartered

4 shallots, peeled

2 cloves garlic, peeled

1 yellow bell pepper, seeded and cut into large chunks

1 to 2 Serrano peppers, chopped

1/2 cup dry white wine

Juice of 1 lemon

2 cups cubed good-quality white bread

1 teaspoon salt

1 teaspoon sugar

1/2 teaspoon saffron

1 cup water

Freshly ground pepper and additional salt to taste

GARNISH:

1/2 pound fresh lump crabmeat

Juice of 1/2 lemon

2 to 3 tablespoons crème fraîche

1 teaspoon minced fresh mint

1 teaspoon minced fresh cilantro

Kosher salt to taste

In a large pot, warm 4 tablespoons oil. Add tomatoes, shallots, garlic and peppers; sauté for 4 minutes. Add wine, lemon juice, bread, salt and sugar. Bring to a boil. Add saffron; boil for 5 minutes. Add water; cook for 8 more minutes or until peppers are soft.

Transfer to a blender or food processor. While processor is running, let steam escape through the top; this will reduce the liquid and thicken the soup. Add 3-4 tablespoons oil; continue blending until smooth. Strain through a fine mesh strainer. Taste, and adjust salt and pepper. Stir thoroughly after seasoning. Just before serving, make the garnish. In a medium bowl, gently mix the crab, lemon juice, crème fraîche, mint and cilantro until combined. Taste, and add salt if needed. (Crabmeat varies in its level of saltiness, so don't add salt until after you taste it.)

Serve immediately in individual bowls for a warm tomato soup, or refrigerate if you prefer a cold gazpacho. In either case, top each serving with a heaping spoonful of crab garnish.

MARIE'S SUGGESTED OCCASIONS:
* STARTER SOUP BEFORE A FORMAL DINNER PARTY
* WARM WINTERTIME LIGHT LUNCH OR DINNER
* SERVE COLD AT SUNDAY BRUNCH
* SERVE COLD AT AN ELEGANT SUMMERTIME LUNCH

REFRESHING SUMMER GAZPACHO

SERVES 6

Do you ever feel your body craving certain vitamins? Sometimes I don't realize it until I start to eat a certain food, and then I notice that I must be deprived. This happened to me at a restaurant in Austin at my best friend's wedding-party brunch. Most people ordered eggs or omelets, but since it was mid-July, I opted for a bowl of chilled gazpacho. As soon as I swallowed the first spoonful, I could literally feel the vitamins and antioxidants replenishing my body. (The bachelorette party was the weekend before.) So if you're ever in need of a quick vitamin kick, try this cool, refreshing soup.

1 cucumber, peeled and cut into large chunks

1 large red bell pepper, seeded and cut into chunks

2 cups canned tomato *or* mixed-vegetable juice

1 tablespoon red wine vinegar

1 can (14 1/2 ounces) diced tomatoes in juice

1 carton (12 1/2 ounces) refrigerated salsa

1/2 cup coarsely chopped cilantro, optional

1 teaspoon sugar

Kosher salt and freshly ground pepper to taste

1/2 slightly firm avocado, cut into small chunks

1 lime, cut into wedges

In a food processor, mince cucumber and red pepper. Add the tomato juice, vinegar, tomatoes, salsa, cilantro if desired and sugar. Blend again until soup reaches desired texture. Season with salt and pepper. Transfer to a large bowl. Cover and chill for 2 hours.

Serve in individual bowls, topped with avocado chunks and a wedge of lime.

MARIE'S SUGGESTED OCCASIONS:

* QUICK AND HEALTHY SUMMER OR SPRINGTIME LUNCH
* AFTERNOON PICNIC IN THE PARK OR BY THE POOL
* STARTER SOUP BEFORE A CASUAL SUMMERTIME DINNER PARTY

ICEBERG WEDGE WITH BLUE CHEESE AND TOMATOES

SERVES 4

I always see this type of salad on the menu at fancy steakhouses. The irony of it is you can make this simple salad with just two ingredients plus a splash of blue cheese dressing. Fortunately for the iceberg wedge, it happens to go well with tomatoes and blue cheese—two flavors that also go very well with a 20-ounce bone-in rib-eye!

1 large head iceberg lettuce

3 Roma tomatoes

DRESSING:

6 ounces good-quality blue cheese, crumbled

1 cup light mayonnaise

1 cup heavy cream

2 tablespoons white wine vinegar

1 teaspoon kosher salt

Freshly ground pepper to taste

GARNISH:

2 ounces blue cheese, crumbled

Freshly ground pepper, optional

Cut the lettuce into four wedges; chop the tomatoes into bite-size pieces. In a bowl, whisk the dressing ingredients. Place each lettuce wedge on a large serving platter or separate plates. Spoon dressing over wedges; sprinkle with tomatoes and blue cheese crumbles. Grind pepper over all if desired. Serve immediately with a knife and fork.

MARIE'S SUGGESTED OCCASIONS:
* STARTER SALAD BEFORE A FORMAL DINNER PARTY
* SIMPLE MIDDAY SNACK
* LIGHT LUNCH WITH A SOUP OR SANDWICH

WINTER SPINACH SALAD

SERVES 4 TO 6

I tend to shy away from salads in the winter because they typically don't satisfy my craving for something warm. This salad—with hearty spinach, rich Gorgonzola, toasted nuts and juicy winter pears—is an exception. For purposes of comparison, it's nothing like my iceberg wedge recipe (previous page). Enjoy this salad as a starter before a separate full meal, or take a larger portion and make it your lunch!

2 bags (9 ounces *each*) baby spinach

1/2 cup walnut pieces, toasted

1 pear, diced

4 ounces Gorgonzola cheese, crumbled

1/4 cup extra virgin olive oil

2 tablespoons red wine vinegar

Kosher salt and freshly ground pepper
    to taste

In a large salad bowl, combine the spinach, walnuts, pear and cheese. In a small bowl, whisk oil and vinegar. Season with salt and pepper; whisk again to thoroughly combine. Pour over salad and toss gently to combine. Let stand at room temperature for 5-10 minutes before serving.

HELPFUL HINT: To toast nuts, place them in a dry skillet over medium heat. Stir frequently and watch them carefully to make sure they don't burn. When you begin to smell the nuts' fragrance, about 3-5 minutes, they are done. Remove from the heat immediately and set aside in a small bowl until ready to use.

MARIE'S SUGGESTED OCCASIONS:
* STARTER SALAD BEFORE A FORMAL DINNER PARTY
* WARM WINTERTIME LIGHT LUNCH OR DINNER
* SIDE SALAD FOR A HOLIDAY DINNER

SPEEDY ROCKET SALAD

SERVES 4 TO 6

My good friend Jan, whom I've mentioned more than once in this book, taught me this recipe as she was making it up before a dinner party. She had a huge bundle of fresh arugula from her garden, a bag of cherry tomatoes and some goat cheese. Just three ingredients? "Too simple," I thought. "We need toasted nuts or a diced apple...or maybe homemade croutons." Turns out, I was wrong.

After Jan dressed the peppery greens, sweet tomatoes and soft goat cheese with a tart vinaigrette, the contrasting flavors melded together into a salad I couldn't put down and have made several times since that night. If you can't find arugula (or dislike its assertive flavor), substitute mixed field greens, baby spinach or butter lettuce— they'll work just as well.

12 ounces fresh arugula

8 to 12 cherry tomatoes, halved

4 ounces plain goat cheese

1/4 cup extra virgin olive oil

2 tablespoons white *or*
 red balsamic vinegar

Kosher salt and freshly ground pepper
 to taste

Place arugula and tomatoes in a large salad bowl. Using your fingers, pinch off small pieces of goat cheese and drop into the bowl. In a small bowl, whisk oil and vinegar. Season with salt and pepper; whisk again. Taste, and adjust salt and pepper if needed.

About 10 minutes before serving, pour dressing over salad and toss gently to combine. Let stand at room temperature. During this time, the dressing will soften the arugula and allow the flavors to blend. Serve individual portions, equally allocating tomatoes and cheese if possible.

MARIE'S SUGGESTED OCCASIONS:
* STARTER SALAD BEFORE A CASUAL DINNER PARTY
* SIMPLE LIGHT LUNCH WITH A SOUP OR SANDWICH
* LUNCHTIME WEDDING SHOWER
* POTLUCK DINNER PARTY

SAVE-THE-daysides

"So for dinner, we'll have salmon and...um..." This is what I call SIDE-DISH BRAIN FREEZE.

Why are side dishes so difficult to select? There are three main reasons. First, no one wants to be boring. Steamed broccoli = out. Boiled carrots = out.

Second, if a main course has a unique flavor, matching side dishes requires real effort. Take Seared Salmon and Mango Salsa...with Creamed Spinach? No thanks. How about with Maple-Bacon Butternut Squash? No way!

Third, we all have our issues. "I had a salad for lunch"..."I don't eat carbs"..."I'm lactose-intolerant."

In this chapter, here is what I'll do for you: Regarding problem number one, no boring recipes. As for problem number two, I will provide you with suggested main courses to serve with each side dish. And, as for all of your other issues, it's like those TV psychiatrists say, "This isn't really about the food, is it?" Spare me the drama, please, and go fix yourself a peanut butter sandwich.

ROASTED RED POTATOES WITH PARMESAN AND PARSLEY

SERVES 4 TO 6

About once a month, my family and another family (Jan and David and their children) get together for dinner. David always brings very fine wine, and Jan brings a dish or two, plus a lot of great advice. She has that intuitive ability to take any dish from okay to outstanding, regardless of what's in the fridge.

Case in point: I was making these roasted red potatoes, doused in olive oil, and seasoned with salt and pepper. "We need some color on there!" Jan said with enthusiasm. She was exactly right. Within seconds, fresh Parmesan and bright green parsley adorned this dish. Thanks, Jan!

20 small red potatoes, quartered

¼ cup extra virgin olive oil

Kosher salt and freshly ground pepper to taste

1 to 2 tablespoons roughly chopped parsley

¼ cup grated Parmesan cheese

Preheat oven to 450°. Line a baking sheet with foil and brush with some olive oil to prevent sticking, or use nonstick foil.

In a large bowl, toss potatoes with oil until evenly coated. Add salt and pepper, and toss again. Arrange potatoes in a single layer on the prepared baking sheet. Bake for 20-25 minutes, turning once.

Using a spatula, gently slide potatoes into a serving dish. Add about half of the parsley and Parmesan; toss gently. Finish by sprinkling with remaining parsley and Parmesan, and additional salt and pepper. Serve immediately.

GOES WELL WITH:
* MARINATED FLANK STEAK
  (RECIPE ON PAGE 121)
* EFFORTLESS BEEF TENDERLOIN
  (RECIPE ON PAGE 112)
* HOT 'N' CRUNCHY TILAPIA
  (RECIPE ON PAGE 122)

MARIE'S SUGGESTED OCCASIONS:
* CASUAL DINNER PARTY
* FORMAL DINNER PARTY
* POTLUCK COMPANY PICNIC
* EASY WEEKNIGHT DINNER

Q&A with marie

QUESTION:
I've heard cilantro called "Chinese parsley." Will that work here?

ANSWER:
Some may disagree with me on this one, but my instinctive response is no. Cilantro has a wonderful flavor, but it is a very fragrant herb, so be aware of what other flavors you plan to serve with it. In addition, some people dislike the flavor of cilantro, so you might check with your guests before tossing it on these potatoes. Having said that, there is a first time for everything. If you try it, do let me know how it turns out!

PRESTO PESTO COUSCOUS

SERVES 4

Couscous is a lifesaving side dish. So when your foie gras fails you (recipe not available in this cookbook), grab a box of couscous for a far easier but equally elegant side dish. And if you're out of pesto, you're not out of luck. Couscous, which has a naturally nutty flavor, is fabulous when seasoned with a little salt and pepper, or with almost any assortment of sweet or savory flavors. I've made it with sun-dried tomatoes and basil...soft slices of Brie...lemon, sautéed onion and parsley...and even almonds and apricots!

1¹/₃ **cups whole-wheat couscous**

1 **tablespoon extra virgin olive oil**

2 **cups reduced-sodium chicken broth**

3 **tablespoons homemade** *or* **store-bought basil pesto**

¹/₄ **teaspoon salt**

¹/₄ **teaspoon pepper**

Pour couscous into a medium bowl. Add oil and stir to coat. In a medium saucepan, bring broth to a boil; stir in the pesto, salt and pepper. Pour over couscous. Cover and let stand for 15 minutes. Fluff with a fork before serving.

GOES WELL WITH:
* PAN-SEARED SIRLOIN STEAK (RECIPE ON PAGE 109)
* LEMON-DIJON SALMON (RECIPE ON PAGE 117)
* BAKED SEA BASS WITH VEGGIES AND PESTO (RECIPE ON PAGE 110)
* GRILLED TUNA OR OTHER FIRM FISH

MARIE'S SUGGESTED OCCASIONS:
* FORMAL DINNER PARTY
* CASUAL DINNER PARTY
* OUTDOOR BARBECUE
* EASY WEEKNIGHT MEAL

Q&A with marie

QUESTION:
What is pesto, and would it be possible to make my own?

ANSWER:
Pesto is a traditional uncooked Italian sauce, typically made of fresh basil, garlic, olive oil, Parmesan cheese and pine nuts. Pesto is a great way to add flavor to pasta, as well as grilled or pan-seared red meat, poultry or fish. And yes, you can certainly make your own! Just purée all of the ingredients in a food processor until thick and thoroughly combined.

PINTO BEANS WITH A KICK

SERVES 6

I love these beans because, even though the recipe calls for canned beans, you end up with a side dish that bursts with flavor and ends with a bite. The jalapeños add a gentle but memorable kick. And the garnish of fresh cilantro and crunchy bacon will leave you craving more. At least that's what my dad said. When I made this recipe for him for the first time, I said, "Dad! You've got to try a bite of these beans!" He took a bite. And another. Then he looked at me with a smile and asked, "Do I have to stop?"

2 cans (15 ounces *each*) pinto beans

1 jalapeño, thinly sliced

4 slices bacon, optional

3 tablespoons roughly chopped
   cilantro, optional

GOES WELL WITH:
* EVERYTHING EGG-WHITE OMELET
  (RECIPE ON PAGE 18)
* SPICY SPINACH AND MUSHROOM
  QUESADILLA (RECIPE ON PAGE 42)
* ENCHILADAS VERDES
  (RECIPE ON PAGE 118)
* BEEF, CHICKEN OR VEGGIE FAJITAS
* BARBECUED OR SMOKED MEATS

Place beans with liquid in a medium saucepan; add jalapeño. Heat over medium heat until warm. Meanwhile, if bacon garnish is desired, cook the bacon; chop into small pieces. Pour beans into a bowl, for family-style serving, or into individual ramekins. Garnish with bacon pieces and cilantro if desired.

MARIE'S SUGGESTED OCCASIONS:
* EASY WEEKNIGHT DINNER
* HEARTY BREAKFAST WITH AN OMELET
* FIESTA-STYLE COUPLES' SHOWER
* QUICK AND EASY LUNCH

MAPLE-BACON BUTTERNUT SQUASH

SERVES 4 TO 6

Butternut squash is a wonderful side for fall or winter meals. My mom taught me a very simple way to prepare it—just mash it up with some butter and warm cream. I enjoy it that way, but I wanted to add a little flair to the otherwise ordinary dish.

So I thought about what flavors might complement the rich buttery flavor of the squash. Maple was an obvious choice. And then maple syrup made me think of bacon, because I love to dip breakfast bacon in the syrup left over from pancakes. Sure enough, the maple, bacon and butternut squash combination is a winner! So easy, too.

1 large butternut squash

8 slices bacon

6 tablespoons fat-free milk

2 tablespoons unsalted butter

5 to 7 tablespoons pure maple syrup (depending on desired sweetness)

Pinch of kosher salt

Cut squash in half; remove seeds and strings. Place cut side down on a large microwave-safe plate. Microwave on high for 8-15 minutes or until soft. Cool for about 5 minutes. Meanwhile, cook the bacon; cool slightly and chop into small pieces.

Scoop squash into a large bowl; add milk and butter. Mash until smooth. Add syrup, salt and bacon crumbles; stir to combine. Reheat if needed before serving.

MARIE'S SUGGESTED OCCASIONS:
* POTLUCK HOLIDAY DINNER
* WARM WINTER AFTERNOON SNACK
* FORMAL DINNER PARTY
* DISH TO BRING WHEN YOU MEET THE PARENTS

GOES WELL WITH:
* EFFORTLESS BEEF TENDERLOIN
  (RECIPE ON PAGE 112)
* PAN-SEARED SIRLOIN STEAK
  (RECIPE ON PAGE 109)
* ROASTED TURKEY OR HAM
* BASIC GRILLED CHICKEN OR PORK

Q&A with marie

QUESTION:
I don't know much about winter squash. Which one is butternut?

ANSWER:
Butternut squash is a large cylindrical squash. You can recognize one by its long pear shape (sometimes up to 12 inches long) and bright yellow-orange shell. The shell is hard—so be careful when you're cutting it! When selecting a butternut squash, choose one that is heavy (2 or 3 pounds) and has a hard, deep-colored shell that is free of moldy spots. Unlike summer squash, you need not store winter squash in the refrigerator. Just keep it in a cool dark place, and it will stay good for several weeks or up to a month.

LIGHTENED-UP CREAMED SPINACH

SERVES 4

Creamed spinach is one of those ultimate comfort foods that go great with almost any meat. I've served it with steak, chicken, fish, ham and turkey. The one problem with creamed spinach is that it's often very high in fat. So, I modified my favorite recipe and came up with this equally yummy (and vitamin-packed) version. A great way to served creamed spinach is in individual ramekins with a nice garnish of freshly grated Parmesan cheese!

1 pound baby spinach (about 4 cups)

1 tablespoon unsalted butter

1/2 cup minced white onion

2 teaspoons all-purpose flour

1/4 teaspoon salt

1/8 teaspoon freshly grated nutmeg

1/2 cup 2% *or* fat-free milk

1/2 cup cubed reduced-fat cream cheese

1/4 cup grated Parmesan cheese

Place spinach in a saucepan with a small amount of water; cook for 7 minutes. Drain in a colander and squeeze out excess water; set aside.

In a large saucepan, melt butter (don't let it brown). Add onion and sauté for 2 minutes. Add flour, salt and nutmeg; stir well. Cook for about 30 seconds. Add milk and cream cheese; cook until thickened. Add spinach; cook for 1-2 more minutes. Serve immediately with Parmesan cheese on top.

GOES WELL WITH:
* BASIC BAKED BEEF TENDERLOIN (RECIPE ON PAGE 112)
* PAN-SEARED SIRLOIN STEAK (RECIPE ON PAGE 109)
* LEMON-DIJON SALMON (RECIPE ON PAGE 117)
* BASIC GRILLED MEAT, POULTRY OR FISH

MARIE'S SUGGESTED OCCASIONS:
* HOLIDAY DINNER WITH HAM OR TURKEY
* FORMAL DINNER PARTY
* IMPRESS-THE-BOSS DINNER
* COZY WINTER-VACATION COMFORT FOOD
* FIRST-DATE SIDE DISH

SUCCULENT MINI PORTOBELLOS

SERVES 4

If I want something hearty but am not really in the mood for meat, mushrooms can often satisfy my cravings. Maybe it's their meaty flavor, or relatively high content of protein, potassium, niacin and selenium that makes them taste so rich, even though they are relatively low in calories and fat. I love this recipe because it is super-easy, yet ultra-elegant.

3 tablespoons extra virgin olive oil

12 mini portobello mushrooms

Kosher salt and freshly ground pepper

3 tablespoons unsalted butter, melted

2 tablespoons roughly chopped parsley

In a large skillet over medium heat, heat oil; swirl to coat the bottom of the pan with oil. Slice the stem off each mushroom where it meets the cap. Place mushroom caps in pan; cook for 10 minutes or until lightly browned, turning once.

Transfer caps to a serving platter. Season lightly with salt and pepper. Combine butter and parsley; spoon over mushroom caps. Serve immediately.

GOES WELL WITH:
* PAN-SEARED SIRLOIN STEAK (RECIPE ON PAGE 109)
* MARINATED FLANK STEAK (RECIPE ON PAGE 121)
* PORK TENDERLOIN WITH DIJON-HERB CRUST (RECIPE ON PAGE 125)
* OTHER VEGGIE SIDES FOR A VEGGIE PLATTER

MARIE'S SUGGESTED OCCASIONS:
* FORMAL DINNER PARTY
* CASUAL DINNER PARTY
* EASY AND HEARTY WEEKNIGHT MEAL
* HOLIDAY DINNER

SIMPLE SWEET POTATOES

SERVES 4

When I think of sweet potatoes, I usually think of a sugar-laden, marshmallow-topped casserole dripping with butter. Despite its popularity, this dish does a disservice to one of the healthiest vegetables around. For one thing, the sugar in the casserole masks the naturally good flavor of sweet potatoes. And for another, the marshmallows and butter undermine the substantial health benefits sweet potatoes have to offer.

If you are used to the marshmallow casserole, it may take you a while to adjust to a plain baked sweet potato, but I encourage you to try it. Sweet potatoes are extremely high in vitamins A and C, manganese, copper, fiber, potassium and iron. And, unlike white potatoes, sweet potatoes have a stabilizing effect on blood sugar, which means they can fit into a low-sugar diet.

4 small sweet potatoes

2 tablespoons extra virgin olive oil

Light sour cream *or* butter, brown sugar and chopped pecans

Preheat oven to 400°. Scrub sweet potatoes. Microwave two at a time on high for 6 minutes per pair (this will substantially reduce cooking time). Line a baking sheet with foil. Spread oil over foil and on skins of potatoes (careful—they might be hot!). Bake for 15-20 minutes or until tender.

With a fork, create a dotted X on top of each potato. Press in at the ends of potato to push the flesh up. Serve immediately with a dollop of sour cream. For a sweeter flavor, serve with a dot of butter, teaspoon of brown sugar and sprinkle of chopped pecans.

GOES WELL WITH:

* PAN-SEARED SIRLOIN STEAK
  (RECIPE ON PAGE 109)
* EFFORTLESS BEEF TENDERLOIN
  (RECIPE ON PAGE 112)
* ROASTED TURKEY
* GRILLED CHICKEN
* OTHER VEGGIE SIDES TO
  MAKE A VEGGIE PLATE

MARIE'S SUGGESTED OCCASIONS:

* CASUAL DINNER PARTY
* WATCH-YOUR-CARBS WEEKNIGHT MEAL
* HOLIDAY DINNER WITH TURKEY OR HAM
* QUICK AND HEALTHY AFTERNOON SNACK

Q&A with marie

QUESTION:
Why are sweet potatoes considered a low-carb food while white potatoes are not?

ANSWER:
I'm not a nutritionist or dietitian, but from what I have read and heard, sweet potatoes are lower on the "glycemic index" than white potatoes. Basically, this means that sweet potatoes (somewhat ironically, given their name) do not cause as rapid a rise in your blood sugar levels as some other "high-GI" foods.

"Low-GI" foods may help you control your blood sugar levels, increase healthy cholesterol and decrease your appetite. Keep in mind, if you add brown sugar, as I have suggested in this recipe, you may be defeating the benefits of eating this low-GI food. If your blood sugar level is a concern, consider trying low-fat sour cream or simply a sprinkle of cinnamon instead.

LESS-IS-MORE BROILED ASPARAGUS

SERVES 4 TO 6

One of my best friends and I often joke about her aunt's famous Thanksgiving asparagus casserole. You might know the one—canned asparagus, mushroom soup, cheese and crushed crackers? Although I might have enjoyed that sort of creamy casserole when I was a kid, I'm thankful now that the recipe never made its way into our family's tradition. We have always enjoyed asparagus in long, thin apple-green stalks, cooked just until tender and seasoned lightly. If your palate has not yet adjusted to the pleasantly plain, top with grated cheese or a splash of balsamic vinegar.

2 pounds fresh asparagus

2 tablespoons extra virgin olive oil

Kosher salt and freshly ground pepper to taste

2 tablespoons balsamic vinegar, optional

2 to 3 tablespoons grated Parmesan cheese, optional

GOES WELL WITH:
* SALMON WITH MANGO SALSA
  (RECIPE ON PAGE 106)
* LEMON-DIJON SALMON
  (RECIPE ON PAGE 117)
* HOT 'N' CRUNCHY TILAPIA
  (RECIPE ON PAGE 122)
* MARINATED FLANK STEAK
  (RECIPE ON PAGE 121)

Adjust oven rack to uppermost position. Set oven to broil.

Break off tough ends of asparagus. Place in a large bowl; toss with oil, salt and pepper. Place in a single layer on a foil-lined baking sheet. Broil for 4 minutes. Remove from oven and turn asparagus. Broil for 4-5 minutes more or until asparagus is tender and lightly browned.

If you want to add more flavor to this dish, after arranging the asparagus on a serving platter, sprinkle with balsamic vinegar and/or Parmesan cheese.

MARIE'S SUGGESTED OCCASIONS:
* TEATIME WEDDING OR BABY SHOWER
* FORMAL DINNER PARTY
* EASY AND HEALTHY WEEKNIGHT MEAL
* DINNER DOUBLE DATE
* IMPRESS-THE-PARENTS DINNER

GREEN BEANS WITH TOASTED PINE NUTS

SERVES 4

For some reason, the idea that pinecones have nuts in them has always been hard for me to believe. I suppose it's because the pinecone—in appearance and form—is quite different than the shell of a pecan or peanut. As it turns out, you can't just crack open a pinecone to find the nut. The process is much more involved, requiring heating and specialized labor.

As a result, pine nuts tend to be more expensive than most nuts, but it's worth it, and you don't need many. To preserve these precious nuts, store them in the freezer or fridge; otherwise their high fat content will cause them to spoil.

1 pound fresh green beans

1/4 cup pine nuts

2 tablespoons extra virgin olive oil

Kosher salt to taste

Bring a pot of water to boil. (Always do this first!) Trim off stems of green beans; add to the pot. Cook over high heat for 5-6 minutes or just until tender (test one for desired tenderness). In a warm dry skillet or toaster oven, toast the pine nuts until lightly browned and fragrant (watch them—they will burn!).

Drain the beans well. Spread on a platter and let them dry for about 1 minute. Drizzle with oil and season with salt. Sprinkle toasted pine nuts on top. Serve immediately.

GOES WELL WITH:
* PORK TENDERLOIN WITH
  DIJON-HERB CRUST (RECIPE ON PAGE 125)
* MARINATED FLANK STEAK
  (RECIPE ON PAGE 121)
* PAN-SEARED SIRLOIN STEAK
  (RECIPE ON PAGE 109)
* BASIC GRILLED BEEF, CHICKEN OR FISH

MARIE'S SUGGESTED OCCASIONS:
* FORMAL DINNER PARTY
* HOLIDAY DINNER
* MEET-THE-PARENTS DINNER
* DINNER DOUBLE DATE

TOTALLY COOL TATER SKINS

SERVES 4

Baked potato skins are a delicious side dish, especially for kids, and they also make a great appetizer. Plus, they are easy to make and require minimal ingredients. Just be sure to plan ahead so you have time to bake the potatoes.

This version of the recipe is "full fat," but I've provided some easy substitutes in case you want to lighten it up. You could also decrease the amount of butter, or use olive oil instead. In any case, kids (and the kid in all of us) are sure to enjoy these.

4 medium russet potatoes

2 tablespoons butter, cut into 16 small pieces

4 slices bacon

1 cup (4 ounces) shredded cheddar cheese *or* reduced-fat cheddar cheese

½ cup regular *or* light sour cream

2 green onions, finely chopped, optional

Preheat oven to 425°. Scrub potatoes and pierce with a fork. Bake for 1 hour or until tender. When cool enough to handle, cut each potato in half lengthwise. Scoop out the potato pulp, leaving about a ¼-inch shell around the skin.

Place potato skins on a foil-lined baking sheet; place two pieces of butter inside each. Bake for 8 minutes or until crispy. Meanwhile, cook the bacon; chop into small pieces.

Sprinkle cheese over potato skins. Bake until cheese melts. Remove from the oven. Sprinkle with bacon. Top with a dollop of sour cream and sprinkle with onions if desired. Serve immediately.

GOES WELL WITH:
* EFFORTLESS BEEF TENDERLOIN (RECIPE ON PAGE 112)
* BEEF OR TURKEY BURGERS
* GRILLED BEEF OR CHICKEN
* ON A BUFFET OF OTHER SIMPLE SIDES

MARIE'S SUGGESTED OCCASIONS:
* CASUAL DINNER PARTY
* DINNER DOUBLE DATE, WITH KIDS
* WEEKEND COOKOUT
* GAME-WATCHING PARTY

SUMMERTIME TOMATO **SALAD**

SERVES 4

On a hot summer's day in Texas, there is nothing better than this cool and refreshing salad. The juicy tomatoes—combined with sweet basil, a tart vinaigrette and salty feta cheese—are flavorful and satisfying. It couldn't be easier to make or more functional, either. Serve it as a simple side dish. Or add a bed of field greens for a light lunch. If company is coming, spoon the salad over a marinated flank steak for a fabulous dinner!

4 cups cherry tomatoes, quartered

1 cup (4 ounces) crumbled traditional feta cheese

8 fresh basil leaves, minced

¼ cup extra virgin olive oil

2 tablespoons white balsamic vinegar

Kosher salt and freshly ground pepper to taste

Place tomatoes in a large bowl. Add feta cheese and basil. In a small bowl, whisk the oil, vinegar, salt and pepper. Pour over tomato mixture; toss gently, just until combined. Taste, and adjust salt and pepper if needed. Serve immediately.

MARIE'S SUGGESTED OCCASIONS:
* EASY WEEKNIGHT SIDE DISH
* LIGHT SUMMER LUNCH BY THE POOL
* VITAMIN-PACKED MIDDAY SNACK
* GARDEN PARTY WITH THE GIRLS

GOES WELL WITH:
* MARINATED FLANK STEAK
  (RECIPE ON PAGE 121)
* PAN-SEARED SIRLOIN STEAK
  (RECIPE ON PAGE 109)
* BASIC GRILLED CHICKEN
* PAN-SEARED SUSHI-GRADE TUNA

Q&A with marie

QUESTION:
I heard that only Greece can produce "real" feta cheese. Can this be correct?

ANSWER:
Sure is! In 2002, the European Union decided that only cheese made in Greece can be sold under the name "feta." It may sound unusual, but there are other foods that are bound to a location—think Kentucky Bourbon, Italian Parma ham or French Champagne. As you might imagine, several European countries were not happy with the decision, so it may be overturned in the future. In any case, I have not noticed any changes in America. It's always easy to find a variety of feta cheeses in my regular grocery store.

WILTED SPINACH WITH GARLIC AND SHALLOTS

SERVES 4

Wilted, in cooking terms, means limp, but not dehydrated or overcooked. In this recipe, you want the spinach to retain a little body, so when you serve it, it doesn't slide across the plate. Spinach is one vegetable you need to be careful with, because it cooks quickly. If you happen to overcook it, try serving the dish in individual ramekins. This will keep the spinach in place and your presentation pristine!

2 tablespoons extra virgin olive oil

2 cloves garlic, minced

1 shallot, diced

1 pound baby spinach (about 4 cups)

**Kosher salt and freshly ground pepper
to taste**

In a large skillet over medium heat, heat oil. Add garlic and shallot; sauté for 2-3 minutes. (Be careful not to brown or burn the garlic because it will taste bitter.) Add half of the spinach. Using tongs, turn spinach in warm oil until the leaves wilt. Add the rest of the spinach and repeat the process. Season with salt and pepper. Transfer to a serving platter. Serve immediately.

MARIE'S SUGGESTED OCCASIONS:
* ELEGANT SIDE DISH FOR A FORMAL DINNER PARTY
* EASY SIDE DISH FOR A WEEKNIGHT MEAL
* SUNDAY BRUNCH WITH AN OMELET
* HOLIDAY DINNER WITH HAM OR TURKEY

GOES WELL WITH:
* EFFORTLESS BEEF TENDERLOIN
  (RECIPE ON PAGE 112)
* MARINATED FLANK STEAK
  (RECIPE ON PAGE 121)
* PAN-SEARED SIRLOIN STEAK
  (RECIPE ON PAGE 109)
* LEMON-DIJON SALMON
  (RECIPE ON PAGE 117)
* TWO OTHER SIDE DISHES FOR A
  VEGGIE PLATE

Q&A with marie

QUESTION:
What is a shallot and where can I find one?

ANSWER:
The shallot is a member of the onion family, but it looks more like garlic than onions. Like garlic, it has a "head" composed of multiple "cloves." Each clove is covered with a thin, papery skin. I like shallots because their flavor is much milder than most onions and garlic. So you can add one to a dish without worrying about your after-dinner breath!

Their color is usually a light brown, similar to a yellow onion. You can typically find them in your regular grocery store, and certainly at a specialty grocery store, near the onions and garlic. When choosing shallots, look for heads that are plump and firm, not wrinkled, bruised or sprouting. Finally, if you are in a pinch, you can always substitute a yellow or white onion, or skip it altogether!

JIMBO'S MARINATED BROCCOLI SALAD

SERVES 6

My dad gets the credit for this recipe. He has been making it for as long as I can remember. We all love it, although I usually avoid the red onions, my Uncle David can't eat cucumbers and my brother Chris leaves out the olives. The fact that this is possible is actually one of the nice things about this salad. Because each ingredient is served whole or in large pieces, it's easy for selective eaters to dodge whatever they don't like without causing a scene.

3 large stalks broccoli

12 cherry tomatoes

12 to 15 pitted kalamata olives

1 cucumber, peeled and thinly sliced

1/2 red onion, thinly sliced, optional

1 jar (6 to 6 1/2 ounces) marinated quartered artichoke hearts, drained

1/4 cup extra virgin olive oil

2 to 3 tablespoons white balsamic vinegar

Kosher salt and freshly ground pepper to taste

Cut broccoli florets off the stems. Place in a steamer basket or in a saucepan with a small amount of water; steam just until slightly tender but still a little crunchy. Cool completely.

In a large bowl, combine the broccoli, tomatoes, olives, cucumber, onion if desired and artichokes. In small bowl, whisk the oil, vinegar, salt and pepper. Taste, and adjust salt and pepper as needed. Pour over vegetables and toss to coat. Marinate for 10 minutes or longer.

GOES WELL WITH:
* MARINATED FLANK STEAK (RECIPE ON PAGE 121)
* PAN-SEARED SIRLOIN STEAK (RECIPE ON PAGE 109)
* LEMON-DIJON SALMON (RECIPE ON PAGE 117)
* BASIC GRILLED CHICKEN OR FISH

MARIE'S SUGGESTED OCCASIONS:
* EASY WEEKNIGHT MEAL
* WEDDING OR BABY SHOWER BRUNCH
* LEFTOVERS FOR LUNCH
* CASUAL DINNER PARTY

OVEN-ROASTED VEGGIES WITH THYME AND ROSEMARY

SERVES 4 TO 6

The ability to buy an assortment of fresh herbs at my regular grocery store is a fairly recent development. It's a new option that has changed and, I believe, improved much of my cooking. Fresh basil is far different from the dried kind in a jar, as are fresh thyme, rosemary and dill. What a pleasure it is to be able to use vibrant, fresh ingredients. This dish depends on them.

1 medium zucchini, sliced

1 medium yellow summer squash, sliced

1 cup broccoli florets

3 medium carrots, peeled, halved and sliced into sticks

3 to 4 tablespoons extra virgin olive oil

1½ teaspoons minced fresh thyme

1 teaspoon minced fresh rosemary

Kosher salt and freshly ground pepper to taste

8 to 10 large flakes Parmesan cheese, optional

Preheat oven to 450°. In a large bowl, combine the zucchini, yellow squash, broccoli and carrots. Add oil, herbs, salt and pepper; toss to coat. Spread vegetables in a single layer in a large shallow baking pan.

Bake for 15-20 minutes, stirring occasionally. (The zucchini and yellow squash will cook faster than the carrots and broccoli, so you may need to remove them earlier.) Top with Parmesan cheese if desired.

GOES WELL WITH:
* MARINATED FLANK STEAK (RECIPE ON PAGE 121)
* PAN-SEARED SIRLOIN STEAK (RECIPE ON PAGE 109)
* TURKEY AND SPINACH WHOLE-WHEAT WRAP (RECIPE ON PAGE 47)
* BASIC GRILLED BEEF OR CHICKEN

MARIE'S SUGGESTED OCCASIONS:
* CASUAL DINNER PARTY
* POTLUCK DINNER WITH FRIENDS
* EASY WEEKNIGHT MEAL
* LIGHT AND HEALTHY LUNCH

THE main event

For me, *every* dinner is a special occasion. No matter who I'm with or where I am, dinner is a time when the stresses of the day are over. There is nothing left to do but enjoy some excellent food—ideally with family or friends—and chat about the day, current events or nothing in particular.

I grew up with three phenomenally funny brothers. As a result, there was never a moment of silence at the dinner table. Like clockwork, once all six of us were within hearing range, Jim (the oldest brother) would tell a story—fascinating or funny are his two main genres. Chris (our middle brother, and highly trained improvisational comedian) would fire back with a *hilarious* comment, causing Matt (the youngest of us all) to burst into laughter. And then Mom, Dad and I would immediately follow suit.

I have a feeling that laughing at dinner between bites is not "doctor-recommended." But I like to laugh—it's good for the soul—and thanks to my brothers, I'll continue to do so. Sorry, doc, it's just my nature.

SALMON WITH MANGO SALSA

SERVES 4

When I was growing up, my family loved to eat fresh grilled fish with mango salsa. Dad would grill the fish—usually salmon, halibut or tilapia—and I would make the salsa. If the weather was nice, we'd sit outside at our large wood dining table on the front porch.

I'll never forget one Easter when we ate this for lunch outside. My grandmother was there, and so was my sister-in-law's family. Just as everyone was finishing their food, my brothers and I snuck inside and gathered up our homemade confetti eggs. Then we were back outside in an all-out war. Confetti was everywhere, and everyone was laughing. It was a perfect afternoon. To me, little is better than good food and a great time with people you love.

2 mangoes, peeled, seeded and diced*

1/4 cup diced red onion

1 to 2 jalapeños, diced (seeded if desired)

1/2 red bell pepper, diced

Juice of 1 lime

1/4 cup chopped fresh cilantro *or* mint

Kosher salt and freshly ground pepper to taste

3 to 4 tablespoons extra virgin olive oil, *divided*

4 salmon fillets (6 ounces *each*)

Lemon and lime wedges and cilantro sprigs for garnish

* Mangoes should be ripe (with red and yellow skin), but not too soft. Choose mangoes that are slightly firm; otherwise, they will be difficult to dice.

For salsa, in a medium bowl, combine the mangoes, onion, peppers, lime juice, cilantro and salt. Set aside until ready to serve.

Heat a large skillet over medium heat; add 2-3 tablespoons oil. Drizzle the salmon with remaining oil; season with salt and pepper. Place salmon in the skillet, skin side up. Increase heat to medium-high; cook for 3-4 minutes. Gently flip each fillet; cook for 3-4 minutes or until fish flakes easily with a fork.

Transfer salmon to individual plates; serve immediately with mango salsa.

VARIATION: If you like to grill, cook the salmon on an outdoor or indoor grill. Or if you have a grill pan to use on the stove, that will work well, too.

MARIE'S SUGGESTED OCCASIONS:
* FORMAL DINNER PARTY
* SPRINGTIME HOLIDAY DINNER
* IMPRESS-THE-IN-LAWS DINNER
* DOUBLE-DATE DINNER

PAN-SEARED SIRLOIN STEAK

SERVES 4

Need an elegant main course for a dinner party, or just a simple, healthy weeknight meal? This pan-seared sirloin steak serves both purposes! Sirloin steak is one of the leaner cuts of meat, in case you are watching fat and calories. Cheaper than some cuts of meat, it still tastes fantastic when cooked medium and served with sautéed mushrooms and onions.

The best thing about this recipe is you can cook it indoors. So, if it's not good grilling weather, you don't have a grill or you don't know how to use one, this recipe is for you.

4 to 7 tablespoons extra virgin olive oil, *divided*

2 premium choice sirloin steaks (about 1 pound *each***)**

Sea salt and freshly ground pepper

8 to 10 white button mushrooms, sliced

1 white onion, peeled and sliced into individual rounds

In a large sauté pan over medium heat, heat 2-3 tablespoons oil. Season both sides of steaks with salt and pepper. Place in the pan; cook for 6 minutes. Flip steaks; cook for 6 more minutes. (Cook 1-2 minutes longer on each side if you prefer your steak medium-well or well-done.) Using a spatula, remove steaks to a serving platter. Let the steaks rest for at least 5 minutes.

Meanwhile, heat 1-2 tablespoons oil in a medium sauté pan over medium-high heat. Add mushrooms; season with salt and pepper. Sauté until mushrooms are soft and brown. Transfer to a serving bowl. In the same pan, heat 1-2 tablespoons oil over medium-high heat. Add onion rounds; season with salt and pepper. Sauté until onions are soft and translucent. Add to serving bowl with the mushrooms.

Cut each steak in half; season again with salt and pepper. Serve immediately with sautéed mushrooms and onions.

HELPFUL HINT: Cooking meat indoors often generates quite a bit of smoke, so plan to use your vent or open a window.

MARIE'S SUGGESTED OCCASIONS:
* FORMAL DINNER PARTY
* IMPRESS-YOUR-BOSS DINNER
* HEARTY WEEKEND DINNER

BAKED SEA BASS WITH VEGGIES AND PESTO

SERVES 2

And now presenting...the perfect date dinner! It's elegant, tasty and impossible to mess up. Plus, there are no super-strong flavors that could stifle your post-dinner conversation. And, the meal is light enough so that your date will still enjoy a special dessert...or whatever else you have planned. If you can't afford sea bass, or you're not yet sure if your date is (ahem) "worth it," you can substitute tilapia, halibut or salmon.

2 to 4 tablespoons extra virgin olive oil, *divided*

2 fresh sea bass fillets
(about 8 ounces *each*)

Kosher salt and freshly ground pepper to taste

¼ cup homemade *or* store-bought basil pesto

1 carrot, grated

½ zucchini, grated

2 tablespoons dry white wine

Preheat oven to 450°. Place two 12-inch squares of foil on the countertop; brush each with ½ tablespoon oil. Place one sea bass fillet in the center of each square. Season with salt and pepper. Spread pesto in even portions over fillets. Top with grated carrot and zucchini. Sprinkle with additional salt and pepper.

Form the foil into a cup shape around each fillet. Drizzle wine and desired amount of remaining oil over fish, pesto and veggies. Fold edges of foil together to make a sealed package. Place on a foil-lined baking sheet.

Bake for 10-12 minutes or until fish is done. Being careful to avoid hot steam, open sealed packages; transfer the sea bass with vegetable topping to individual plates. Pour remaining flavorful juices over the top.

MARIE'S SUGGESTED OCCASIONS:
* ROMANTIC DINNER FOR YOUR DATE
* EASY WEEKNIGHT DINNER FOR TWO
* FORMAL DINNER PARTY
  (ADJUST TO ACCOMMODATE NUMBER OF GUESTS)

PORK CHOPS WITH CRANBERRY-POMEGRANATE SAUCE

SERVES 6

I stayed away from pork chops after I left home for college. With good reason, I suppose. The way I remember pork chops is this: Battered, pan-fried and overcooked (sorry, Mom!). Now that I know more about pork, I've come to realize what a wonderful and versatile other-white-meat it is.

I love to order it at our famous Texas barbecue joints, but at home, this recipe is my favorite for bone-in chops. A sweet sauce with salty Gorgonzola cheese and toasted nuts adds a powerful punch to this pork plate.

6 bone-in pork chops
(about 6 ounces *each*)

1 teaspoon kosher salt

1 teaspoon freshly ground pepper

2 tablespoons extra virgin olive oil

1 can (16 ounces) whole-berry
cranberry sauce

1/3 cup pomegranate juice

1/3 cup low-sodium chicken broth

1/2 teaspoon fresh lemon juice

4 ounces Gorgonzola cheese, crumbled

1/2 cup chopped walnuts *or* pecans,
toasted

Fresh parsley sprigs, optional

Season pork chops on both sides with salt and pepper. Heat 1 tablespoon oil in a large skillet over medium-high heat. Add three pork chops; cook for 4-5 minutes on each side or until browned. Remove and keep warm. Repeat with remaining pork chops and oil.

While chops are cooking, begin the sauce. In a medium saucepan, combine cranberry sauce, pomegranate juice, broth and lemon juice. Bring to a boil, then reduce heat to low. Simmer for 10-15 minutes or until sauce is reduced to desired consistency.

Transfer pork chops to a serving platter; drizzle evenly with sauce. Sprinkle with cheese and nuts. Garnish with parsley if desired.

MARIE'S SUGGESTED OCCASIONS:

* FORMAL DINNER PARTY
* WINTERTIME HOLIDAY DINNER
* IMPRESS-YOUR-BOSS DINNER
* DOUBLE-DATE DINNER

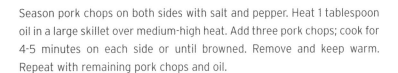

Q&A with marie

QUESTION:
What is the difference between flat-leaf and curly parsley?

ANSWER:
Curly-leaf parsley is the more popular and available of the two. Italian flat-leaf parsley has a slightly stronger flavor. Both are high in vitamins A and C. When buying parsley, look for bright green leaves and no signs of wilting.

EFFORTLESS BEEF TENDERLOIN

SERVES 6

The first time I made beef tenderloin, I was completely spoiled on the quality of beef and the instruction. Nolan Ryan's Guaranteed Tender Meats company was kind enough to provide a whopping 5-pound, top-of-the-line, whole beef tenderloin. In addition, Reese Ryan—Nolan Ryan's youngest son—taught me how to cook it.

The most valuable lesson I learned from Reese is: "Great beef tastes great, so it doesn't need a lot of season-ing." Thus, the short recipe below. Without Reese's wisdom and the kindness of his father's company, I never would have known that this delicacy requires so little effort!

1 whole beef tenderloin (about 3 pounds)

1/4 cup Worcestershire sauce

3 tablespoons store-bought chicken fajita seasoning

3 tablespoons seasoned salt

3 tablespoons freshly ground pepper

Preheat oven to 450°. Place the tenderloin in a deep baking dish. Cover the meat evenly with Worcestershire sauce, fajita seasoning, seasoned salt and pepper. Place on middle rack of hot oven. Bake for 40 minutes for medium-rare. (If you are using a meat thermometer, press it into the thickest part of the meat; it should read 140° for medium-rare and 155° for medium.)

Remove from the oven and let rest for 15 minutes before cutting. Note that the temperature will increase about 5° as the meat rests. When ready to serve, slice meat against the grain.

MARIE'S SUGGESTED OCCASIONS:
* FORMAL DINNER PARTY
* WINTER HOLIDAY FEAST
* DINNER TO IMPRESS

CAPELLINI WITH NO-TIME-TO-COOK TOMATO SAUCE

SERVES 6

I adore this dish. When I'm in a time crunch, the "no-cook" sauce makes my life easier, and that's something I always appreciate. But what I really love are the ingredients—fresh tomatoes, basil, parsley, garlic and mozzarella. Each bite is like a trip to Italy!

I like to use capellini (aka "angel hair") because it cooks quickly, but feel free to use another pasta. Try a whole-wheat version if you are looking to add whole grains and fiber to your diet.

6 to 10 tablespoons extra virgin olive oil, *divided*

4 cups cherry tomatoes, quartered

1 tablespoon minced garlic

4 tablespoons minced fresh basil

2 tablespoons minced fresh parsley

1 round ball (8 ounces) fresh mozzarella cheese, cut into bite-size pieces

Kosher salt and freshly ground pepper to taste

1 pound capellini

1 cup grated Parmesan cheese, optional

6 to 8 sprigs fresh basil

Begin boiling a large pot of water over high heat. Add two large pinches of table salt and 1-2 tablespoons oil. (Oil will keep pasta from sticking together.)

Place the tomatoes in a large bowl; stir in the garlic, basil, parsley, mozzarella, 4-6 tablespoons oil, salt and pepper. Set aside.

When the water reaches a rolling boil, add capellini. Cook for 5-7 minutes or until al dente. (The pasta should offer a slight resistance when bitten into. It should not be soft or mushy.) Immediately drain hot water and pour pasta into a large serving dish. Drizzle with 1-2 tablespoons oil and toss gently. This, too, will keep pasta from sticking.

Pour tomato mixture over pasta. Add additional salt and pepper if necessary. Toss gently to combine. Serve immediately with Parmesan cheese if desired. Garnish with basil sprigs.

MARIE'S SUGGESTED OCCASIONS:
* EASY WEEKNIGHT MEAL
* LAST-MINUTE DINNER FOR YOUR DATE
* CASUAL DINNER PARTY

HEARTY-BUT-HEALTHY CHILI

SERVES 4 TO 6

My good friend Laura is an excellent cook. Aside from a little guidance from her mother, she is self-taught, just like me. So we enjoy laughing about our "learning experiences." There was the time she and her husband mistakenly added 4 heads of garlic instead of 4 cloves to their burritos. Then there was the time I used 1 cup of lemon juice instead of 1 tablespoon in my apple pie. Her mistake resulted in some highly potent garlic breath. Mine? Last place in my home-economics pie contest.

Laura and I also enjoy exchanging recipes. When I taught her how to make biscotti, we were so occupied with each others' latest gossip that we forgot the sugar! So far, we have both made this healthy variation of chili, which she passed on to me, without error.

1½ **pounds lean ground beef**

1 **package taco seasoning**

1½ **cups water,** *divided*

2 **cans (15 ounces** *each***) pinto** *or* **black beans with liquid**

2 **cans (14½ ounces** *each***) diced tomatoes with juice**

4 **cups fresh** *or* **frozen corn**

2 **tablespoons ranch salad dressing**

½ **tablespoon dried red pepper flakes, optional**

TOPPINGS:

Shredded cheddar cheese

Chopped fresh cilantro

Sliced fresh jalapeños

In a large pot, brown the ground beef over medium-high heat, about 8-10 minutes. Add taco seasoning and 1 cup water; stir to combine. Add the beans, tomatoes, corn, ranch dressing, red pepper flakes if desired and remaining water. Cook over low heat for 10 minutes to allow flavors to combine.

Top individual servings with cheese, cilantro and jalapeños. Serve with warm bread or tortilla chips.

VARIATIONS: Use one can each of pinto and black beans. Substitute two 14-ounce cans of corn for fresh or frozen.

MARIE'S SUGGESTED OCCASIONS:
* GAME-WATCHING PARTY
* WARM WEEKNIGHT DINNER
* CASUAL WINTER-HOLIDAY DINNER PARTY

STUFFED CHICKEN ITALIANA

SERVES 1 (MULTIPLY FOR MORE!)

I've noticed that people tend to shy away from stuffed meats because they assume they require too much work. This recipe isn't difficult at all—the stuffing can be made in minutes, and after that, it's just like cooking a plain chicken breast.

This dish reminds me of the lasagna my mom use to make when we were growing up. It was filled with spinach, ricotta and Parmesan cheese, then topped with shredded mozzarella. The difference, of course, is that you get a substantial serving of protein instead of carbs. Perfect!

1 cup baby spinach

1 heaping tablespoon low-fat ricotta cheese

1 heaping tablespoon grated Parmesan cheese

Kosher salt and freshly ground pepper to taste

1 boneless skinless chicken breast

2 tablespoons extra virgin olive oil

1 tablespoon shredded mozzarella cheese

1 tablespoon diced prosciutto

¼ cup marinara sauce, warmed

Fresh basil leaves, minced

In a microwave-safe bowl, microwave the spinach for 1 minute. Stir in the ricotta and Parmesan cheeses. Season with salt and pepper.

Using a sharp knife, slice the chicken breast in half horizontally, creating a pocket. Spoon spinach mixture into the pocket. Season both sides of chicken with salt and pepper.

In a sauté pan, heat 1 tablespoon oil over medium heat. Sauté chicken for 8-10 minutes on each side. Set oven to broil and line a baking sheet with foil. When chicken is cooked, place on the baking sheet. Sprinkle mozzarella on top and place in the oven. Broil just until mozzarella is melted (about 2 minutes).

While chicken is broiling, toss the prosciutto pieces into the hot pan that you cooked the chicken in. Cook until browned, about 2 minutes. Spoon marinara sauce onto a serving plate. Place stuffed chicken breast over sauce. Top with prosciutto and minced basil.

MARIE'S SUGGESTED OCCASIONS:
* EASY WEEKNIGHT MEAL FOR ONE
* CASUAL DINNER PARTY (MULTIPLY ACCORDING TO NUMBER OF GUESTS)

LEMON-DIJON **SALMON**

SERVES 4

Need a quick, easy and healthy main course for lunch or dinner? This is the recipe for you. Salmon is high in omega-3 fatty acids, B vitamins, selenium and magnesium, and it's low in saturated fat. For those of you on low-carb diets, or even for those of you who aren't, salmon is a great source of protein. Aside from the health benefits, salmon is a delicious fish that is relatively inexpensive, easy to cook and goes great with all kinds of side dishes.

4 salmon fillets (6 ounces *each*), with skin on

5 tablespoons extra virgin olive oil

2 tablespoons Dijon mustard

1 tablespoon lemon juice

Kosher salt and freshly ground pepper to taste

Finely chopped fresh dill

Preheat oven to 425°. Place salmon fillets, skin side down, on a foil-lined baking sheet. In a small bowl, mix the oil, mustard, lemon juice, salt and pepper. Spread evenly over each fillet.

Bake for 8-10 minutes or until fish flakes easily with a fork. Remove from the oven and cool for 3-5 minutes. Transfer salmon to a serving platter or individual plates. Sprinkle with fresh dill and serve.

MARIE'S SUGGESTED OCCASIONS:
* CASUAL DINNER PARTY
* EASY WEEKNIGHT DINNER
* DOUBLE-DATE DINNER

ENCHILADAS VERDES

SERVES 4 TO 6

My late grandmother Maria Garza grew up in Tampico, Mexico. She taught my mother, who then taught me, about authentic Mexican cooking. These green enchiladas are made the way my grandmother used to make them—by dipping the tortilla first in sauce and second in hot oil, and then filling it with chicken, cheese or chopped hard-boiled eggs.

10 tomatillos, peeled

1 jalapeño, stem removed

2 to 3 teaspoons kosher salt *or* **to taste**

1 cup extra virgin olive oil, *divided*

12 to 14 corn tortillas

2 chicken breasts, cooked and shredded

5 hard-boiled eggs, chopped

2 cups (8 ounces) shredded cheddar cheese

1 cup crumbled queso fresco

GARNISHES:

Sour cream *or* Crema Mexicana

Roughly chopped fresh cilantro

Lime wedges

Diced tomatoes

Finely shredded iceberg lettuce

Diced white onion

In a large pot of water, cook tomatillos and jalapeño over medium-high heat for 15 minutes or until tomatillos are very soft and light yellow. Transfer to a food processor or blender. Add 2 teaspoons salt. Blend until liquefied. Taste, and adjust salt if needed.

Heat 2 tablespoons oil in a medium saucepan. Add tomatillo sauce. Cook over medium-high heat, stirring frequently, until the sauce starts to bubble. Remove from the heat.

In a small saucepan, heat 2-3 tablespoons oil over medium heat. When oil is hot, dip one tortilla at a time into the tomatillo sauce and then into the saucepan of hot oil. (Be careful—the hot oil may pop!) Let the tortilla cook for about 30 seconds in the oil. Using a spatula or tongs, turn the tortilla and let it cook again on the other side for about 30 seconds.

Remove the tortilla from the oil and lay flat on a plate (the tortilla should be soft). Place shredded chicken, chopped egg or cheddar cheese in the center. Roll tortilla so the ends are folded under and touching the plate. Repeat the process with the remaining tortillas, adding more oil to the pan as needed.

Top each enchilada with remaining tomatillo sauce from the saucepan; sprinkle with queso fresco. Serve immediately with desired garnishes.

MARIE'S SUGGESTED OCCASIONS:
* CASUAL DINNER PARTY
* FIESTA-THEMED COUPLES' SHOWER
* EASY WEEKNIGHT MEAL

MARINATED FLANK STEAK

SERVES 6 TO 8

Not too long ago, I used to be wary of cooking red meat. I worried that I would overcook it or undercook it, and I had no idea how to flavor or garnish it. So, I did exactly what I should not have done: I decided to cook a marinated flank steak—six of them, actually—to serve as one of many appetizers at an art party I was hosting. Over 100 people were invited.

The marinade was based partly on sheer instinct ("Hmm...I bet teriyaki and soy sauce would be good") and partly on my dad's advice. ("Put some red wine and garlic in there.") It worked! Now, this is my go-to meat dish anytime I have to cook for a crowd. It's delicious on its own and with the tomato-blue cheese topping.

2 flank steaks (1½ pounds *each*)

¼ cup teriyaki marinade

¼ cup reduced-sodium soy sauce

¼ cup red wine

¼ cup extra virgin olive oil

3 cloves garlic, minced

Freshly ground pepper to taste

**OPTIONAL TOMATO-
BLUE CHEESE TOPPING:**

1 bag (12 ounces) vine-ripe cherry
   tomatoes, quartered

¼ cup extra virgin olive oil

2 tablespoons white balsamic vinegar

4 ounces blue cheese, crumbled

4 to 6 fresh basil leaves, minced

Kosher salt to taste

OPTIONAL CONDIMENTS:

Dijon mustard

Horseradish sauce

Steak sauce

Place one flank steak (lying flat) in a large ovenproof dish with 2-inch sides. In a small bowl, mix the teriyaki marinade, soy sauce, wine, oil, garlic and pepper. Spread half of the mixture over steak. Top with the second flank steak and remaining mixture. Marinate for 30-60 minutes at room temperature.

Set oven to broil. Place one flank steak on a foil-lined baking sheet. Broil on top rack for 6 minutes. Remove from the oven and flip steak. Broil second side for 6 minutes. Do the same with the second steak. Let steaks rest for about 15 minutes before cutting.

If topping is desired, make it while the steaks are resting. In a medium bowl, toss the tomatoes with oil and vinegar. Add blue cheese, basil and salt; toss again.

Using a sharp knife, cut steaks against the grain. Serve immediately with the tomato-blue cheese topping and condiments of your choice.

PARTY TIP: If you prefer to serve this as a party appetizer, omit the topping. Arrange sliced steak on a large serving platter. Fill a basket or tray of dinner rolls, sliced three-fourths of the way through the middle. Place small labeled bowls of Dijon mustard, horseradish sauce and steak sauce next to the rolls.

MARIE'S SUGGESTED OCCASIONS:
* CASUAL DINNER PARTY
* SERVED IN SMALL ROLLS AT A COCKTAIL PARTY
* BIG-TIME GAME-WATCHING PARTY

HOT 'N' CRUNCHY TILAPIA

SERVES 6

Hot 'n' Crunchy Trout is a fairly famous dish in Austin. I tried to make it once, and I had to go to three different grocery stores before I could find fresh trout! After that experience, I didn't make it again. That is, until I realized– hey–tilapia might work!

Tilapia is a fabulous fish that should be available at any basic grocery store. It is also relatively cheap, which is always a good thing–especially if you are cooking for a crowd. Finally, tilapia has a mild flavor and flaky texture that doesn't distract from the fabulous crunchy, nutty, spicy and slightly sweet crust it gets in this treatment.

½ **cup finely ground almonds**

½ **cup finely ground pecans**

4 cups cornflakes, crushed into coarse, non-uniform crumbs

2 tablespoons sugar

2 to 4 tablespoons dried red pepper flakes

2 tablespoons kosher salt

2 cups fat-free milk

3 large eggs

6 fresh tilapia fillets (4 to 6 ounces *each*)

8 to 10 tablespoons extra virgin olive oil, *divided*

Lemon wedges

Rémoulade *or* tartar sauce

In a large rectangular container, use your hands to combine the almonds, pecans, cornflakes, sugar, pepper flakes and salt until well mixed. In another large rectangular container, whisk milk and eggs to make an egg wash.

Dip one fillet into egg wash and then into crumb mixture; press crumb mixture onto the fillet. Set aside on a foil-lined baking sheet. Repeat the process with remaining fillets.

In a large heavy sauté pan, heat 3-4 tablespoons oil over medium-high heat for about 3 minutes. Toss a cornflake in the oil; if it sizzles, the oil is hot enough to use. Gently lay a fillet in hot oil. If crumb mixture falls off the top, press more onto the fish. Sauté for 4-5 minutes on each side. Crust should be a golden, crunchy brown. Avoid turning fillet more than once so the crust stays intact.

Turn oven to 180°. When you finish sautéing the fillet, place on a clean foil-lined baking sheet; place in warm oven until all of the fish is ready to be served. Cook the remaining fillets, adding more oil to the pan as needed. Garnish with lemon wedges; serve with rémoulade or tartar sauce.

MARIE'S SUGGESTED OCCASIONS:
* CASUAL DINNER PARTY
* EASY WEEKNIGHT OR WEEKEND MEAL
* DINNER FOR YOUR DATE

CALDO DE MARISCO (SEAFOOD SOUP)

SERVES 4

Seafood is my favorite type of food, and Mexican ingredients are my favorite flavors. So it's no surprise that I absolutely love this soup! Be forewarned: You may have to hunt around a bit for the proper chiles, but—at least in my opinion—it's definitely worth it.

3 large potatoes, peeled and chopped

3 carrots, peeled and chopped

3 ribs celery, chopped

9 dried chile guajillos

4 dried chile arboles

1 clove garlic, peeled

1 to 2 tablespoons extra virgin olive oil

1 pound medium shrimp, peeled and deveined

½ white onion, minced

1 cup roughly chopped fresh cilantro

1 pound halibut, deboned and cut into medium-size chunks

Kosher salt and freshly ground pepper to taste

Rustic bread *or* fresh tortillas, warmed

Fill a large pot half full with water. Add potatoes, carrots and celery. Cook over medium heat until soft, about 15 minutes. Remove from the heat. Pour vegetables into a colander; set aside.

On a flat skillet over medium heat, toast guajillos and arboles until lightly browned, turning so they brown evenly on each side. Once browned, add chiles to a pot of water and cook over medium heat (this will soften the chiles). Once softened, remove chiles from the pot, but save the chile water.

Remove and discard seeds and pith from chiles. Wash chiles with water. Place in a food processor or blender. Add garlic and about ½ cup of the chile water; blend until smooth. In a medium skillet, heat oil over medium heat. Add chile mixture. (Be careful—the hot oil may pop!) Heat for 5-10 minutes or until thickened.

Fill a stockpot half full with water; bring to a boil over high heat. Add shrimp and reduce heat to medium-high; cook for 5-7 minutes or until shrimp are pink and opaque. Add vegetables and chile mixture; cook for 5 more minutes.

Add onion and cilantro; stir to combine. Then add chunks of fish; cook for about 15 minutes. Season with salt and pepper. Serve with bread or tortillas.

MARIE'S SUGGESTED OCCASIONS:
* HEARTY WEEKEND MEAL
* POTLUCK DINNER
* CASUAL DINNER PARTY

PORK TENDERLOIN WITH DIJON-HERB CRUST

SERVES 4

Pork tenderloin is a mild, lean, versatile meat that lends itself to a variety of cooking methods. You can slice and pound it into cutlets, dice it into cubes, toss it on the grill or oven-roast it, like I opted to do in this recipe.

Oven-roasting a whole tenderloin requires minimal prep time, as does this easy, flavorful crust. Notice that you don't need to marinate the meat. Just coat the tenderloin with the Dijon sauce, press on the crust and pop it in the oven all at once. This leaves time to prepare side dishes and dessert, enjoy a glass of wine with your guests, or catch your favorite television show.

1 pork tenderloin (1½ pounds)

Kosher salt and freshly ground pepper

1 shallot, peeled

1 large egg

2 tablespoons Dijon mustard

Juice of 1 lemon

¼ cup capers, drained

1 cup fresh bread crumbs

1 tablespoon minced fresh thyme

1 tablespoon minced fresh rosemary

¼ cup finely grated Romano cheese

Preheat oven to 350°. Season pork tenderloin with salt and pepper on all sides. In a food processor, purée the shallot, egg, mustard, lemon juice and capers. In a small bowl, toss the bread crumbs, herbs and Romano cheese.

On a foil-lined baking sheet, spread about a fourth of the bread crumb mixture in a line the length of the tenderloin. Pour about a fourth of the Dijon sauce over the crumbs. Set the tenderloin on top of the sauce; press down so the sauce and crumbs stick to the underside of the meat. Pour the rest of the sauce over the top and sides of the tenderloin. Gently press remaining crumb mixture on the top and sides so the crust sticks.

Bake for 40-45 minutes or until crust is lightly browned and a meat thermometer reads 155°. Remove from the oven and let rest for 10 minutes (it will continue to cook as it rests). Slice into thin rounds (don't worry if some of the crust falls off). Serve each person three to four slices.

HELPFUL HINT: To make fresh bread crumbs, process three to four slices of good-quality white bread in a food processor until you have small, uniform crumbs.

MARIE'S SUGGESTED OCCASIONS:
* CASUAL DINNER PARTY
* EASY WEEKEND MEAL
* POTLUCK DINNER
* WINTERTIME HOLIDAY FEAST

YOU-DESERVE-IT desserts

Dessert. It's the last, and often most pleasurable, experience of any occasion.

The key, I think, is not always the dessert itself, but rather how well it fits the event. Although you can find most fruits year-round these days, it would seem strange to serve my Peach 'n' Blueberry Cobbler on a cold day in the winter after a holiday dinner. Or, ugh, imagine offering my Oh-You-Shouldn't-Have Chocolate-Covered Strawberries to your boss and her husband? Awkward!

Point being: Pairing dessert with a meal, guest or occasion is just as important as designing the rest of the menu. For this reason, you simply *must* have a variety of recipes for desserts that you can whip up with confidence.

In this chapter, I provide you with fruity desserts, chocolate surprises, one towering cake, a pie for every season, festive cookies, coconut cupcakes and more. Armed with these recipes, maybe you'll find yourself taking charge of dessert at the next dinner party—without having to spend a bundle at the bakery!

Now that I think about it, maybe you should focus on these recipes before the others. Ernestine Ulmer would. As she once wisely said: "Life is uncertain. Eat dessert first." Sounds good to me!

SIMPLY SUPERB STRAWBERRY SHORTCAKES

SERVES 8

My mom often made strawberry shortcake for us when we were kids. It was my favorite dessert, especially in the summer. Instead of cooking the strawberries, I merely marinate them in sugar. This process softens the berries and brings out the juices, leaving you with the vibrant red filling and a sweet sauce to pour over the rich buttery cakes. Add a spoonful of lightly sweetened whipped cream for an extra indulgence.

1 3/4 cups all-purpose flour

1/4 cup plus 6 tablespoons sugar, *divided*

3 teaspoons baking powder

1/2 teaspoon salt

1/2 cup cold unsalted butter, cut into eight slices

1 large egg

1/3 cup plus 1/4 cup heavy whipping cream, *divided*

4 cups fresh strawberries

TOPPING:

1 pint heavy whipping cream

2 to 3 tablespoons sugar

2 teaspoons vanilla extract

Preheat oven to 425°. Place the flour, 1/4 cup sugar, baking powder and salt in a food processor; add butter. Pulse until the mixture looks like cornmeal (do not overmix). In a small bowl, whisk egg and 1/3 cup cream. Pour into the food processor; pulse until dough holds together (dough will be soft and slightly sticky).

Using a spoon and your hands as needed, form a small biscuit about 3 inches in diameter and 3/4 inch thick. Place on a foil-lined baking sheet. Form seven more biscuits and place on baking sheet, about 1 inch apart. Brush remaining cream across the top of each biscuit. Sprinkle with 2 tablespoons sugar. Bake for 12-15 minutes.

While biscuits are baking, wash, hull and slice the strawberries into a large bowl. Add the remaining sugar and toss to coat. Cover with plastic wrap. Marinate at room temperature for 30 minutes.

For topping, in a small mixing bowl, whip the pint of cream. When cream is almost whipped, add sugar and vanilla; continue whipping until firm. Refrigerate until ready to serve.

Remove biscuits from oven. Cool for 10 minutes. Slice biscuits horizontally in half. Spoon strawberries and juice over the bottom halves; place top halves over the berries. Add a dollop of whipped cream.

MARIE'S SUGGESTED OCCASIONS:
* CASUAL DINNER PARTY
* MEET-THE-PARENTS DINNER
* SPRING OR SUMMERTIME HOLIDAY LUNCH
* WEDDING OR BABY SHOWER (MAKE MINI SHORTCAKES)
* SWEET TEATIME SNACK WITH FRIENDS

IT'S-EASIER-THAN-YOU-THINK PIE CRUST

MAKES 1 CRUST

I often hear people talk about how they are afraid to make a pie crust from scratch. As long as you follow two key rules, there's nothing to fear. First: Don't overmix the dough. Second: Use cold butter and ice water. Both are intended to keep the butter from combining too much with the flour, which will keep your crust flaky and light.

One additional note: Don't expect perfection! No two pie crusts are ever alike, and just when you think your crust is the ultimate failure, it may turn out to be your best one yet. It's happened to me many times. Happy baking!

1¼ **cups all-purpose flour**

1 **teaspoon sugar**

⅛ **teaspoon salt**

½ **cup unsalted butter (very cold!),**
  cut into eight slices

About 4 tablespoons ice-cold water

I use a food processor to make my pie crusts because it's easy. If you don't have one, use beaters or a pastry cutter to mix the ingredients.

Place the flour, sugar and salt in a food processor; pulse a few times, just to combine. Add the butter; pulse several times until butter and flour begin to combine. Stop when the mixture has the texture of cornmeal. Then begin adding water, 1 tablespoon at a time, and pulsing between each spoonful, until the dough is just moist enough to hold together in a ball, but still looks like cornmeal.

Spread a large piece of plastic wrap on the counter (approximately 1-2 feet long). Gently dump the dough (it will still be a little crumbly) onto plastic wrap. Pull together the plastic wrap and mold it around the dough so the dough forms a ball inside the wrap. Place in the refrigerator for 30 minutes. (This is a good time to work on the pie filling.)

When you are ready to roll out the crust, remove dough from the refrigerator, unwrap and let sit at room temperature for about 5 minutes.

Flatten the ball of dough slightly so it will be easier to roll out.

Toss some flour on your countertop, pastry cloth or rubber mat.

Place the flattened dough in the center. Using a rolling pin, roll out the dough into a circular shape that has about the same thickness all the way around. Continue rolling and turning until the circle is evenly rolled out.

The other way to roll out your dough is to simply roll the pin from the center out toward each side until you have an even round circle. This may take practice.

Once the circle of dough is large enough to fit your pie plate, gently place it on top of the plate. You'll want the edges to hang over the plate edge slightly.

Gently press the dough into the bottom of the plate. Using your hands, tuck any dough that overhangs the plate into an even edge.

Use your hands to even the edge if needed.

Finally, crimp the edges with your fingers
for a decorative scalloped shape.

If you are making a filling that needs to be
cooked (such as pecan or apple),
pour the filling directly into the unbaked pie crust.

In addition, if you are making a two-crust pie
(such as apple), you will need to make a second crust to place on
top of the filling. Then seal the two crusts around the edges. Create
a scalloped edge if desired. Finally, make four even slits on top of
the crust to let the steam escape as it bakes. If you plan to make a
filling that doesn't require cooking in the oven (such as Key lime),
you will need to prick the bottom and sides of the crust with a fork
to prevent bubbles from forming in the crust as it bakes.

Bake the pricked crust at 425° for 12-15 minutes or until golden brown. (If using
an ovenproof glass plate, cut the time to 9-12 minutes.) Cool thoroughly, at least
30 minutes, before adding a cold filling.

MARIE'S SUGGESTED OCCASIONS:
* ANYTIME YOU NEED A PIE CRUST...

THESE FABULOUS BROWNIES

MAKES 2 DOZEN SQUARE BROWNIES OR 1¹/₂ DOZEN CUPCAKES

Of all partially premade desserts, boxed brownies aren't so bad, right? They're easy, too: Just add an egg, some oil and water. And that's exactly what led me to wonder—What's in that box? I decided I didn't really want to know and instead, I came up with my own brownie recipe.

These Fabulous Brownies are everything you could want—super-rich chocolate flavor with moist cake-like texture—without the things you don't, like unnecessary preservatives or a chemical aftertaste. Also, because brownies are often difficult to cut into neat, even squares, I like making individual brownies using a cupcake pan.

When I'm feeling creative, I stick a tall sprig of fresh mint in the center of each cupcake brownie, creating what looks like a potted plant. They're just perfect for a springtime party when everything is beginning to bloom!

8 ounces unsweetened chocolate

¹/₂ pound unsalted butter, softened

2¹/₂ cups sugar

¹/₂ cup packed brown sugar

2 teaspoons vanilla extract

5 large eggs

1¹/₂ cups all-purpose flour

¹/₄ teaspoon salt

¹/₂ cup chopped walnuts, optional

OPTIONAL FROSTING:

4 ounces cream cheese, softened

¹/₄ cup unsalted butter, melted

¹/₄ cup good-quality unsweetened
   powdered chocolate

1 cup confectioners' sugar

Preheat oven to 375°. Grease a 13-inch x 9-inch x 2-inch baking pan or two 12-cup muffin tins with soft butter or nonstick cooking spray (or line muffin tins with paper or foil liners).

In a medium saucepan over low heat, melt chocolate and butter. (Be careful not to burn the chocolate; if you do burn it, start over.) In a large mixing bowl, beat sugars, vanilla and eggs (adding eggs one at a time) for 6-8 minutes. Add flour and salt; beat just to combine. Add melted chocolate mixture; beat again, just to combine.

Pour batter into the prepared pan. Bake for 20-25 minutes (for cupcakes) or 35-40 minutes (for rectangular pan) or until a toothpick inserted into center comes out clean. Cool for 20 minutes if you will be frosting them, or 10 minutes if serving unfrosted and warm.

If frosting is desired, in a small mixing bowl, beat cream cheese until smooth. In a separate bowl, stir the butter and chocolate until smooth. Add to cream cheese; beat again. Add confectioners' sugar; beat until smooth. If brownies were baked in the rectangular pan, cut them into squares first and then frost each one individually. This method will improve the presentation of the frosted brownies.

MARIE'S SUGGESTED OCCASIONS:

* DESSERT-THEMED COCKTAIL PARTY
* GIFT FOR NEW NEIGHBORS OR FRIENDS
* CASUAL DINNER PARTY
* SPRING OR SUMMERTIME PARTY

NUNN FAMILY APPLE PIE

SERVES 8

My great-grandmother Ruby Nunn always enjoyed her apple pie with a slice of sharp cheddar cheese. As a child, I remember how classy she seemed, compared to me with my slice and a messy melting scoop of vanilla ice cream. This recipe is named after her. In her honor, I will always give my guests a choice of sides. But it's always ice cream for me!

8 medium Granny Smith apples

1 tablespoon fresh lemon juice

²/₃ cup packed light brown sugar

1 tablespoon ground cinnamon

1 teaspoon ground nutmeg

2 pie crusts (see It's-Easier-Than-You-Think Pie Crust recipe on page 130)

¹/₄ cup unsalted butter, cut into eight slices

Preheat oven to 375°. Peel and slice apples (slices should be thin, but need not be uniform). If you have a food processor, use the slicing blade to speed up the process.

Place apple slices in a large bowl. Add lemon juice, brown sugar, cinnamon and nutmeg; using your hands, toss until all slices are fairly evenly coated.

Place one pie crust in a 9-inch pie plate. Add half of the apple mixture. Place four slices of butter, spaced evenly, on top of the apples. Add remaining apple mixture, arranging the slices so they form a small mound. Top with remaining butter.

Place second pie crust over filling. Seal the edges of both crusts by pressing the crusts together, and then tucking them under to form an even edge.

Use your hands to form a decorative scalloped edge if desired. With a sharp paring knife, make four 1-inch to 2-inch slits in the top pastry. The slits should form a cross shape, but without meeting in the center.

Cover edges of pie crust with a pie shield or ring of foil (to keep the crust from overbrowning). Bake for 30 minutes. Remove foil. Bake for 15-20 more minutes or until apples are tender when a toothpick is inserted through one of the slits. Cool for 1-2 hours before serving.

MARIE'S SUGGESTED OCCASIONS:
* WINTER HOLIDAY DESSERT
* FORMAL DINNER PARTY
* DESSERT-THEMED COCKTAIL PARTY
* BIRTHDAY CELEBRATION FOR PIE LOVERS

MARIE'S FAMOUS BISCOTTI

MAKES ABOUT 2 DOZEN

If there's any dish I am known for, it's these biscotti. I have made literally thousands over the past several years—the bulk of them around the holidays. I start baking in mid-December and continue until the day before Christmas. When they are decorated, packaged and ready, my younger brothers and I drive around the city delivering our goods. Our friends respond with: "They're here!" or something equally cheerful. For me, traditions like these are what the season of giving is about.

$1/4$ cup canola oil

$3/4$ cup sugar

3 teaspoons vanilla extract

1 teaspoon almond extract

2 large eggs

$1^3/4$ cups all-purpose flour

1 teaspoon baking powder

$1/4$ teaspoon salt

$1^1/2$ cups chopped pecans

Preheat oven to 300°. Line a baking sheet with parchment paper or foil.

In a large mixing bowl, mix oil, sugar, extracts and eggs. In a separate bowl, mix flour, baking powder and salt. Add to wet ingredients and mix until combined. Mix in pecans.

Using wet hands (dough will be sticky!), separate dough into two piles on the prepared baking sheet, about 2 inches apart. Using wet hands, spread each pile into a rectangle (about 4 inches wide, 12 inches long and 1 inch tall). Bake for 30-35 minutes or until light brown. Remove from oven. Cool for 5 minutes.

Reduce heat to 200°. Transfer one rectangle to a cutting board. Using a large sharp knife, cut the rectangle on the diagonal into $3/4$-inch slices. Lay biscotti on their sides on the baking sheet. Repeat with the other rectangle.

Bake biscotti for about 20 minutes or until hard. Remove from the pan to cool on a wire rack.

VARIATION: Coat half of each biscotti with melted chocolate or melted Wilton's Candy Melts. While coating is warm, decorate with Wilton's sugar crystals or seasonal sprinkles on the top and sides.

MARIE'S SUGGESTED OCCASIONS:
* HOLIDAY GIFTS FOR YOUR CLOSE FRIENDS
* HOUSEWARMING GIFT FOR NEW NEIGHBORS
* SERVE WITH COFFEE FOR A SNACK OR LIGHT DESSERT
* WEDDING OR BABY SHOWER
* DESSERT-THEMED COCKTAIL PARTY

PEACH 'N' BLUEBERRY COBBLER

SERVES 8

When peach season comes around, my mom always requests this cobbler. I always agree (if I'm in a hurry, sometimes on the condition that she peel the peaches). Compared to some other desserts, this is one of the easiest around. All you need are one saucepan, two bowls and one baking dish, plus a baking sheet to ensure a clean oven. If you use a fork to mix the dough, you don't even need to dirty your beaters. Now that's my kind of recipe!

2 cups sliced peeled fresh peaches

2 cups fresh *or* frozen blueberries

¼ cup sugar

¼ cup packed light brown sugar

1 tablespoon cornstarch

½ cup water

1 tablespoon lemon juice

DOUGH:

2 cups all-purpose flour

1 cup sugar

3 teaspoons baking powder

1 teaspoon salt

1 cup fat-free milk

½ cup unsalted butter, softened

TOPPING:

2 tablespoons light brown sugar

1 teaspoon ground cinnamon

1 teaspoon ground nutmeg

Preheat oven to 375°. Place peaches and blueberries in a deep baking dish or individual ramekins. In a small saucepan, combine sugars, cornstarch, water and lemon juice. Cook over medium heat, stirring constantly, until thick. Pour over fruit and stir gently to coat.

In a large bowl, combine flour, sugar, baking powder and salt. Add milk and butter. Mix with a fork or beaters until fairly smooth (a few lumps of butter are okay). Spoon dough over fruit mixture. In a small bowl, mix the brown sugar, cinnamon and nutmeg. Sprinkle evenly over dough.

Place baking dish or ramekins on a foil-lined baking sheet (in case juice spills over). Slide baking sheet into the oven. Bake until top is golden brown, about 30-35 minutes for ramekins and 40-45 minutes for a large dish.

MARIE'S SUGGESTED OCCASIONS:
* CASUAL DINNER PARTY
* SUMMERTIME LUNCH OR DINNER
* WEDDING OR BABY SHOWER
* HOUSEWARMING GIFT

SOPAPILLAS WITH ICE CREAM AND HONEY

MAKES 16 SOPAPILLAS

Soh-pi-PEE-yuhs are a Spanish dessert, similar to the American doughnut, but not as sweet, or the French beignet. In fact, if you covered a cooked sopapilla with powdered sugar instead of cinnamon and granulated sugar, you could call it a beignet.

My favorite memory of this dessert is the time my brother Chris had about 20 of his friends from Northwestern University (near Chicago) come to our house (in Austin) over the holidays. We made them a full fajita buffet, with rice, beans and guacamole. For the finale, I made sopapillas. One of Chris' best friends, Matt, ate at least eight of them! For a chef, there is no higher compliment.

2 3/4 cups all-purpose flour

3 teaspoons baking powder

3 teaspoons sugar

1/4 teaspoon salt

1 large egg

2 to 3 tablespoons unsalted butter, softened

1 cup fat-free milk, room temperature

4 cups canola oil, *divided*

TOPPING:

2 cups sugar

2 to 3 tablespoons ground cinnamon, optional

1/2 gallon vanilla ice cream

1 small jar of honey

In a large bowl, mix together the first seven ingredients. Knead dough on a floured surface for 5 minutes (dough will be sticky; if needed, sprinkle flour on your hands and the dough to minimize sticking). After kneading, set the dough in the bowl and cover with a dish towel. Let rest for 15-30 minutes.

When you are ready to cook the sopapillas, put about 3 cups of oil in a medium pot. Heat to 360-370°. If you don't have a thermometer, use a piece of the dough to test the oil—if the dough sinks, then quickly rises and floats in the oil, it's hot enough.

Pinch off a small portion of the dough and shape into a ball (about the size of a golf ball). Using a tortilla press or your hands, flatten the ball into a pancake-like shape. Drop into the hot oil. The sopapilla should float in the oil as it cooks. If it falls to the bottom, the oil is not hot enough. If it browns too quickly or burns, the oil is too hot. Make adjustments to the oil temperature as necessary.

Using tongs, flip the sopapilla so it cooks on both sides. Using tongs or a slotted spoon, remove sopapilla from pot when both sides are lightly browned. Combine sugar and cinnamon if desired; sprinkle over sopapillas while still warm.

Repeat the process to cook the remaining sopapillas, adding more oil as needed. Serve sopapillas with ice cream and a squeeze of honey.

MARIE'S SUGGESTED OCCASIONS:
* FIESTA-THEMED PARTY
* CASUAL FAJITA DINNER PARTY
* SWEET BREAKFAST SERVED WITH COFFEE INSTEAD OF ICE CREAM

FIVE-MINUTE FRUIT, CHEESE AND NUT PLATE

SERVES AS MANY AS YOU WISH

If you have the correct ingredients, this elegant display can easily be thrown together in about 5 minutes. And fortunately, the "correct" ingredients can consist of a long list of things. Basically, as long as you have some variety of cheese, crackers, fruit and nuts, you're set. I try to always keep these basic items on hand in case of surprise guests.

Oh, if you happen to be out of fruit or nuts—not to worry! Just call it a cheese plate and no one will ever know the difference. Finally, although I opted to put this recipe in the dessert chapter, this platter works well as an appetizer, too.

CHEESES (choose 3 to 4 types):
Brie
Cheddar (sharp)
Colby-Jack
Cream cheese
  (topped with jam *or* chutney)
Feta
Goat cheese (seasoned *or* plain)
Gouda (smoked)
Mozzarella (fresh)
Parmesan *or* Romano
Queso fresco
Roquefort *or* blue cheese
Swiss

FRUITS (choose 2 to 3 types):
Apricots (dried)
Blackberries
Blueberries
Grapes (seedless)
Pears (sliced)
Strawberries

NUTS (choose 3 to 4 types, salted, seasoned *or* plain):
Almonds (whole)
Cashews (halved *or* whole)
Hazelnuts (whole)

Macadamia nuts (whole)
Pecans (halved)
Pistachios (in shell)
Walnuts (halved)

CRACKERS (choose 3 to 4 types):
Baguette (thinly sliced)
Baked pita chips
Round buttery crackers
Sesame crackers
Small snack toast
Table water crackers (also known as water biscuits)
Whole-grain wheat crackers

Set out selected cheeses, fruits, nuts and crackers on a large serving platter, a clean cutting board, or a marble or slate cheese board. Arrange various ingredients so that colors, textures, sizes and shapes are interspersed to create a presentation that is pleasing to the eye.

Be sure to label the cheeses so your guests know what they're about to sample. Either write the names on small cards (such as place cards) or, if you're using a slate cheese board, you could write the cheese names right on the board with chalk.

If you have plenty of time to prepare the platter, your goal should be to select cheeses that come from a variety of sources or regions. For example, Roquefort is an ewe's milk cheese from the South of France. Parmesan (or Parmigiano-Reggiano) is a cow's milk cheese, originally from Italy. Fresh mozzarella, which comes from the milk of a water buffalo, is also an Italian cheese. Queso fresco is derived from cow's milk and is commonly known as a Hispanic cheese. Gouda, also a cow's milk cheese, is Dutch in origin and delightful when smoked. If you get confused, check the package or ask for help. Some specialty grocery stores have cheese separated according to type of milk and/or region.

If you don't have time to put a lot of thought into your platter, just aim for some variation based on color and texture. As a general rule, cheese should be served in wedges or blocks with several separate knives. Cheddar, Swiss and Colby-Jack may be served in thin slices. Fresh mozzarella, because it is difficult to cut, may be served in small squares, or you can purchase it in small plain or marinated balls. Each guest should have a small plate and napkin (especially if you are serving blueberries or blackberries!).

MARIE'S SUGGESTED OCCASIONS:

* WINE AND CHEESE PARTY
* APPETIZER OR DESSERT FOR A FORMAL DINNER PARTY
* QUICK SNACK FOR SURPRISE GUESTS
* EASY PLATTER FOR A TEATIME WEDDING SHOWER
* HOUSEWARMING PARTY
* POPULAR-TV-SHOW-WATCHING PARTY

ITALIAN CREAM CAKE CUPCAKES

MAKES 2 DOZEN

My youngest brother, Matt, loves cupcakes, especially on his birthday. These are one of his favorites. I love them, too, and not only because they're easy to make. I love the texture of the pecans and coconut against the soft cake and creamy icing. I love the slight bitterness that the buttermilk adds to offset the sugar and sweetened coconut. The buttermilk also helps keep the cake—as any cake should be—moist and memorable. I hope you enjoy these cupcakes as much as Matt does.

1/2 pound unsalted butter, softened

2 cups sugar

1 teaspoon vanilla extract

2 cups all-purpose flour

1 teaspoon baking soda

1 cup buttermilk

6 large eggs

1 cup chopped pecans

2 cups sweetened shredded coconut

ICING:

1 package (8 ounces) cream cheese, softened

1/4 cup unsalted butter, softened

2 cups confectioners' sugar

2 teaspoons vanilla extract

Sweetened shredded coconut, optional

Preheat oven to 350°. Line two 12-cup muffin tins with paper or foil liners.

In a large mixing bowl, beat butter and sugar until fluffy. Stir in vanilla. Combine the flour and baking soda; add to butter mixture, alternating with buttermilk and beating in between. Beat in eggs. Fold in pecans and coconut.

Fill lined muffin cups about three-fourths full. Bake for 25-30 minutes or until golden brown. Cool completely before icing.

In a small mixing bowl, beat icing ingredients until creamy. Add a small drop or two of food coloring if you want to add color to the icing. Spread a generous amount over each cupcake. Sprinkle with coconut if desired.

MARIE'S SUGGESTED OCCASIONS:
* KIDS' PARTIES (LET THEM HELP DECORATE!)
* WEDDING OR BABY SHOWER
* SWEET TREAT FOR AN AFTERNOON LADIES' GET-TOGETHER

GARZA FAMILY
MEXICAN WEDDING COOKIES

MAKES 3 TO 4 DOZEN

These are my mom's favorite cookies. She loves their rich buttery flavor, nutty texture and light sugary coating. I love them for the same reasons, and also because their white color makes them stand out among other traditional cookies, such as chocolate chip or peanut butter.

These cookies are often made in two different shapes—small round balls, as I recommend here, or crescent shapes. If you choose the latter, you can call them cuernitos, which means "little crescents" in Spanish.

½ **pound unsalted butter, softened**

2 **cups confectioners' sugar,** *divided*

3 **teaspoons Mexican vanilla extract***

1 **teaspoon almond extract**

2 **cups all-purpose flour,** *divided*

¼ **teaspoon salt**

1 **cup finely chopped pecans**

* If you can't find Mexican vanilla, feel free to use regular vanilla extract.

Preheat oven to 350°. In a large mixing bowl, beat butter, 1 cup confectioners' sugar and extracts until creamy. Add 1 cup flour and salt; beat just until mixed. Using your hands, mix in the pecans and remaining flour (dough will be sticky and a bit tough).

Form dough into small balls. Place on foil-lined baking sheets about 1 inch apart. Bake for 15-20 minutes. While cookies are still warm, roll in remaining confectioners' sugar. Cool on a wire rack.

MARIE'S SUGGESTED OCCASIONS:

* FIESTA-THEMED PARTY
* SMALL COOKIES FOR A CROWD
* DESSERT-THEMED COCKTAIL PARTY
* GIFTS FOR NEW NEIGHBORS OR FRIENDS

MY MOM'S LUSCIOUS "KEY" LIME PIE

SERVES 6 TO 8

The first thing my mom taught me to make was a pie crust, and then this pie. When she made the crust, Mom used the tines of a fork to combine the flour, salt, sugar and butter. Later, we upgraded to beaters. Now, I use a food processor for all of my crusts. What hasn't changed—and I'm certain never will—is the luscious lime filling and creamy bittersweet topping.

Key limes are smaller, rounder and more yellow than regular green limes. They can sometimes be difficult to find (outside of Florida, that is). As a result, I've used regular limes in this recipe often, so feel free to do the same.

1 pie crust (see It's-Easier-Than-You-Think Pie Crust recipe on page 130)

1 cup sugar

3 tablespoons cornstarch

1 cup heavy whipping cream

1/3 cup fresh lime juice

1 tablespoon grated lime peel

1/4 cup unsalted butter, cubed

1 cup (8 ounces) sour cream

TOPPING:

1 cup heavy whipping cream

1/4 cup sugar

2 teaspoons vanilla extract

3/4 cup sour cream

Preheat oven to 425°. Make pie crust according to recipe instructions. Using the tines of a fork, prick the bottom and sides of the crust so it doesn't bubble when baking. Bake crust for 12-15 minutes or until golden brown. (If using an ovenproof glass pan, cut the time to 9-12 minutes.)

In a saucepan, combine the sugar and cornstarch. Stir in cream, lime juice, lime peel and butter. Bring to a boil over medium-high heat, whisking constantly. Reduce heat and simmer for 10 minutes. Cool to room temperature. Fold in sour cream. Spread into baked crust.

For topping, in a small mixing bowl, beat whipping cream for 2 minutes on high. Add sugar and vanilla; beat again until firm. Fold in sour cream. Spread over filling. Refrigerate for 4 hours before serving.

MARIE'S SUGGESTED OCCASIONS:
* FORMAL DINNER PARTY
* SPRING OR SUMMER BIRTHDAY
* IMPRESS-YOUR-BOSS OR DATE DINNER
* HOUSEWARMING GIFT FOR NEW NEIGHBORS OR FRIENDS

SOMETHING-TO-CELEBRATE CARROT CAKE

SERVES 10

I first made this cake for my dad's 45th birthday. My dad loves cake, and I wanted to make him something he would remember. As they say, "Be careful what you wish for." Now, it's understood that I will make this cake for him every year. I don't mind, of course, but I've learned to enlist the help of my mom or brothers.

Although I consider all of my desserts to be easy (or at least relatively easy), this one takes the most time, effort and equipment. Even so, when you finish, not only will you have burned enough calories to enjoy a slice, you will be fantastically proud. And you should be! Not everyone has the confidence to make a tiered carrot cake with cream cheese icing.

2 cups sugar

4 large eggs

1 cup canola oil

4 cups grated carrots

2 cups all-purpose flour

2 teaspoons baking soda

1 tablespoon ground cinnamon

1/2 teaspoon salt

1/2 teaspoon ground nutmeg

CREAM CHEESE ICING:

1/4 cup unsalted butter, softened

1 package (8 ounces) cream cheese, softened

2 teaspoons vanilla extract

1 box (16 ounces) confectioners' sugar

Preheat oven to 350°. Grease three 9-inch cake pans with soft butter or non-stick cooking spray.

In a large mixing bowl, beat the sugar and eggs for 2 minutes. Add oil and carrots; beat to combine. Combine the dry ingredients; add to carrot mixture and beat to combine. Pour evenly into prepared pans. Bake for 25-30 minutes. Place on wire racks and cool completely.

For icing, in a medium bowl, beat butter, cream cheese and vanilla until creamy. Add confectioners' sugar, about 1 cup at a time, beating after you add each cup. Icing is finished when all ingredients are thoroughly combined and creamy.

When you are ready to ice the cake, gently remove one cake layer from its pan and place it on a serving platter. Gently spread icing across the top until you have a fairly thin, even layer. Remove the second cake layer from its pan and gently set on top of the iced layer. Ice the top of the second layer. Remove the third cake layer from its pan and place on top of the iced second layer. Spread icing around the sides of all three layers until evenly coated. Finally, spread remaining icing neatly over the top of the cake. Refrigerate for at least 15 minutes before serving.

MARIE'S SUGGESTED OCCASIONS:
* SPECIAL BIRTHDAY PARTIES
* FANCY WEDDING SHOWER
* FORMAL DINNER PARTY
* DINNER TO IMPRESS THE IN-LAWS

A BERRY MERRY PARFAIT

SERVES 4

Fairly recently, fresh berries have become famous in the health community. They're full of antioxidants, fiber and vitamins, and they taste great, too. Of course, the creamy topping in this parfait isn't so healthy. If you want to enjoy both, but happen to be feeling a little pudgy around the edges, use a little less creamy filling in your parfait, or serve a smaller portion.

1 cup heavy whipping cream

¼ cup sugar

2 teaspoons vanilla extract

¾ cup sour cream

1 cup fresh strawberries, hulled and quartered

1 cup fresh blueberries

1 cup fresh blackberries

1 cup fresh raspberries

1 ounce dark chocolate, finely grated

4 fresh Bing cherries

In a small mixing bowl, beat whipping cream until thick. Add sugar, vanilla and sour cream; beat just until combined. Refrigerate if you don't plan to serve this dessert immediately.

Place a spoonful of the cream mixture into a parfait glass, sundae glass or other small glass bowl. Sprinkle two to four of each type of berry on top of the cream. Add another spoonful of cream and then more berries. Continue the process until you reach the top of the glass. Top with grated chocolate and a cherry.

HELPFUL HINT: A fun way to serve these parfaits is in stemless wine glasses such as Riedel O's, like we did for the photo.

MARIE'S SUGGESTED OCCASIONS:
* AFTER A WEEKNIGHT MEAL OR CASUAL DINNER PARTY
* ANY SUMMERTIME OCCASION
* MIDDAY SWEET SNACK

DOUBLE-SHOT-OF-BOURBON PECAN PIE

SERVES 6 TO 8

Without this pie, and my friend Allison, I'm not sure I would have a cooking show today. In November 2004, Allison learned that she and her husband, Eric, would be hosting Thanksgiving dinner for their family and in-laws. She was nervous, and understandably so.

Although she is a fantastic hostess, she had never made a pie from scratch. So we decided I would come over to her house on a Saturday afternoon and we would make pies. In less than an hour, we made this pie and a pumpkin pie, each with a homemade crust. After the lesson, she was convinced (as was I, again) that making pies and pie crusts is "easier than you think." This motto became the theme of my show. Many thanks, Ali!

3 large eggs

1 cup packed dark brown sugar

1 cup light corn syrup

2 tablespoons unsalted butter, melted

3 teaspoons vanilla extract

2 tablespoons bourbon

1 3/4 cups coarsely chopped pecans

1 pie crust (see It's-Easier-Than-You-Think Pie Crust recipe on page 130)

Preheat oven to 350°. In a large bowl, beat eggs lightly. Add brown sugar, corn syrup, butter, vanilla and bourbon; stir until well blended. Add pecans and stir until combined. Pour into pie crust.

Cover edges of pie crust with a pie shield or ring of foil (to keep the crust from overbrowning). Bake for 25 minutes. Remove foil. Bake for 30 more minutes. Cool before serving.

MARIE'S SUGGESTED OCCASIONS:

* FORMAL DINNER PARTY
* DESSERT-THEMED COCKTAIL PARTY
* WEDDING SHOWER GIFT, IN PIE PAN REQUESTED BY COUPLE
* HOLIDAY TREAT FOR COLLEAGUES AT WORK

OH-YOU-SHOULDN'T-HAVE CHOCOLATE-COVERED STRAWBERRIES

MAKES ABOUT 1 DOZEN

Nothing says romance like chocolate-covered strawberries. Maybe it's because the vibrant red fruit resembles a heart. Or maybe it's the sultry chocolate coating that gently cracks against your teeth and then melts across your tongue. Whatever the case, I think you'll be surprised how easy these are to make. Around Valentine's Day, you can often find extra-large strawberries with long stems. I recommend these if you can find and afford them—their size and large green tops make an excellent presentation. Otherwise, regular strawberries will work fine.

One last note: If you have leftover chocolate, throw some mixed nuts right into the bowl of warm chocolate and toss until coated. Spread the mixture onto a sheet of waxed paper and let cool. (Refrigerate if needed.) You'll end up with a tasty chocolate-nut brittle. My family enjoyed the brittle as much as the berries!

1 pint medium to large fresh
  strawberries

2 teaspoons canola oil

3 ounces semisweet baking
  chocolate

Wash the strawberries and dry them well. Line a baking sheet with waxed paper.

Add 2 inches of water to the bottom of a double boiler; place over medium heat. Place the chocolate and oil in the top of the double boiler. As the chocolate melts, whisk with the oil. When the chocolate is almost melted, remove the pot from the heat and continue to whisk until smooth.

Dip each strawberry, one at a time, into the warm chocolate and place on the prepared baking sheet. Reheat the chocolate as necessary if it starts to cool and thicken. Refrigerate the berries for 20-30 minutes. Carefully remove from the waxed paper and serve immediately.

HELPFUL HINT: Using a double boiler keeps the chocolate away from touching direct heat, which could cause it to burn. If you don't have a double boiler, you can make your own. Put about 2 inches of water in a small pot, then set a heatproof glass bowl so it rests on top of the pot without touching the water underneath. You may need to try a few different bowls to determine which one fits.

MARIE'S SUGGESTED OCCASIONS:
* VALENTINE'S DAY FOR YOUR SWEETIE
* ANNIVERSARY SURPRISE
* DESSERT-THEMED COCKTAIL PARTY
* WEDDING OR BABY SHOWER
* EASY DESSERT FOR SURPRISE GUESTS

recipe index

mydeepestgratitude

TO SHAWN, for following up on a random phone call about aprons; for putting your time, heart and soul into this book and related projects; for working on too many early mornings and late nights; for your confidence, persistence, patience, encouragement, good judgment, generosity and friendship.

TO GEORGE, for letting me be a small part of your remarkable life; for reminding me to always have fun; for teaching me—through actions rather than words—about balancing life, business and family, with family always at the forefront.

TO RUE, for your invaluable guidance and expertise; for being willing to sail a little faster with this book than you normally might; for meeting, trusting and supporting everyone on the team; for your sweet nature and kindness—I could not have hoped for a better person to manage the publishing of this book.

TO KRIS, for editing this book with skill, speed, confidence and composure; for the time and effort you put forth to meet our deadlines; and for treating this project as if it were your own—I appreciate and admire the attention to detail you put into your work.

TO ELLEN AND TUTU, for translating my ideas, hopes and dreams into art and design with jaw-dropping perfection; for the solid time and effort you both put into this book; for being wonderful to work with throughout this exciting process.

TO EMANUEL, for responding to a unique production request three years ago, and for putting in several hundreds of hours of filming and editing since then; for your encouragement, friendship and prayers; and for teaching me what it means to dedicate your life to the service of others.

TO JOHN, for playing at the Continental Club one Thursday night in June; for supporting me through all of my projects and especially while I worked on this book; for a regular supply of flowers; for teaching me what it means to have faith; and for your humor, generosity, friendship, compassion and love.

TO MY OLDER BROTHER, JIM, for filming my first cooking show, which planted the seed for the second; for your wisdom, advice and friendship throughout our lives; for I.T. support on a moment's notice; for your fabulous photography in this book; and for always being there for me, no matter what.

TO MY SISTER-IN-LAW, LAURA, for contributing your class, organization, patience, wisdom and unsurpassed design-sense during the photo shoot for this book; for being part of my family and, most important, my brother's dream-come-true.

TO MY YOUNGER BROTHER CHRIS, for being my first live audience on *Kids' Cooking!* many years ago; for pursuing your passion and reminding me to do the same; for enjoying my food and always making a point to tell me that you did; for sharing your kind and generous soul with everyone around you.

TO MY YOUNGEST BROTHER, MATT, for your charm, confidence and good humor; for eating my food and always wanting seconds; for reminding me that sleeping in, having fun, and spending time with family and friends is what life is all about.

TO MY PARENTS, for encouraging me through all of my various endeavors; for being there for me no matter what the circumstances; for teaching me about truth, integrity, hard work, unconditional love and the importance of family; for a fabulous kitchen that inspires me to cook and entertain whenever I can; and for encouraging all of your children to pursue what they love.

TO PUBLIC ACCESS TELEVISION MANAGERS, employees and viewers, for supporting my cooking show to an extent I never imagined; for your patience with my homemade syndication system; and for letting me be a part of your lives.

"Spread love everywhere you go.
Let no one ever come to you
without leaving happier."

~Mother Teresa of Calcutta

What Did They Give You for Your Soul?

At the top of the ladder
With the world at your feet
Did you pay for your sainthood
With what you took from the street?

Now you're a neon messiah
In your black limousine
But how many bracelets
Hide a rip at the seam?

Well you've paid with your flesh
But when the truth is told
At the end of the line
What did they give you for your soul?

Rings on your fingers
And bars on your door
Did you get what you wanted?
Will you die wanting more?

It's a trip to the moon here
The Fourth of July
A one-way ticket to the highest of highs.

Now your face looks like a stranger
And you knew this town could change you
But somehow you stayed.
It seems your glass is never empty
And those regrets are flowing plenty
For what you've betrayed...

Yes, you've paid with your flesh
But when the truth is told
At the end of the line
What did they give you for your soul?

- Mark Côté

Introduction

Growing up was not an easy time for me. Like many of the actors in this book, I came from a dysfunctional family. My mother and father got divorced when I was very young. My mother never stayed in one place for very long and therefore neither did I.

After high school, my mother sent me to the American College in Paris for a year and there I discovered my love for photography and film. I loved to escape into the world of movies, experiencing different eras, love stories and cultures.

Later, I moved to New York City and there I went through my going-out period. I went to parties for Madonna and Sade. In those days, Chazz Palminteri and Dolph Lundgren worked as bouncers at clubs like the Limelight. Since NYC is one of the film capitals of the world, actors are very prominent in the club scene. I found it easy to relate to them as they often came from backgrounds similar to mine.

In a way life was fun but in another way it was very superficial and contingent on "image." I started getting lost in the image I had created for myself. I really didn't care about politics or what went on in the wider world, because I didn't honestly feel I could do anything to affect change. I thought I was my own person, yet I was lost within myself. I had lost the child in me who had dreams, who wanted to love and needed love in return.

Moving to Los Angeles to work on my book, *The New Breed: Actors Coming of Age*, was the beginning of my journey back home to myself. I chose actors to be in that book who I felt were honest in their intentions toward acting, who weren't in it for the fame and fortune but because it fulfilled their inner souls. I am very grateful for their candor and for the time they spent with me, uncontrolled by publicists and managers. These actors took a chance and went after their dreams at the risk of failure. Their integrity has rewarded them with success and the very fame and fortune some were afraid to have.

While in Los Angeles, I continued to be social, only now I was going to premieres and screenings. I also continued to photograph actors. Eventually I got over any starstruck feelings I had and I tired of these events. Still I met and photographed David Duchovny before "The X-Files," Sandra Bullock before *Speed* and Jared Leto before he got "My So-Called Life." Amazingly, more than half the actors and actresses I interviewed and photographed between 1987 and 1993 went on to become megastars.

So how did I get to all these people? How did I know? I think it's a combination of fate, intuition and unconscious manifestation.

These interviews serve to remind us that despite the fact that these actors and actresses have been immortalized on celluloid and are constantly written and talked about, they are people just like you and me with their own unique personalities, strengths and insecurities. I read a quote recently from Johnny Depp. He said, "Why should I be considered any different from Joe the garbage man or the guy selling doughnuts down the street? Why can't I be as human and emotional as anybody?"

My husband, Fredrik, and I worked together closely on this book and we had a lot of fun doing it. I hope that you will find pleasure and gain insight into these actors' lives and into the world of Hollywood.

I support all of you in following your dreams and remember, persistence and determination can take you anywhere you want to go.

Karen Hardy Bystedt

Photo by Kelly Garrison

Keanu Reeves

River's Edge, *a film about apathy among America's youth, had a powerful affect on me. One of the film's stars, Keanu Reeves, stood out. His character, Matt, was young and greasy, as Keanu describes him, yet he was also beautiful and hopeful. I contacted Keanu through his manager, Keith Addis.*

Keanu greeted me outside his two-bedroom apartment in Los Angeles, which he shared with a roommate. The apartment had the feel of a college dorm, with clothes strewn about, and empty glasses and a bottle of red wine on the table.

I photographed him outside in a nearby lot, where he parked his 1969 Amazon black Volvo with 007 Ontario plates. A year later, he crashed it, and I'd see him around town riding on a Norton motorcycle.

When we finished, Keanu played me his favorite record and started wailing to the Butthole Surfers. Francois, my make-up artist, winced, but the music seemed to touch Keanu to the core.

I saw Keanu recently at San Diego's Belly Up Tavern, where he was playing bass with his band Dogstar. Girls screamed and threw their panties on stage at the anticipation of Keanu. After the show, Keanu, sporting his short Speed *haircut, greeted me with a kiss. In the light of his tremendous fame, it's amazing how modest and humble he still is. It seems stardom has quieted Keanu. When I first met him in 1987, he was a boisterous urchin.*

I grew up mostly with my mother in Toronto. There was a time when we didn't have any money. All of the bags in our cupboards were yellow and black, 'cause that's what generic food brands are in Toronto. Somehow we ate and maintained a lifestyle that was OK.

I went to four different high schools. When I got out of grade eight, I picked the school that was the best academically, even though I wasn't a very good student. I was the only one from my school who went there. Bang, it was a whole new world. The agony and ecstasy that was grade nine. One day, in grade 10, I was playing basketball and a friend asked me to go along with her to an audition at the Performing Arts High School.

I auditioned also and got in. I was happy and then I got kicked out. I guess I was a little crazy then because it was grade 11 and it was acting and it was weird. I got kicked out because I was a little too rambunctious and shot my mouth off and was not generally the most well-oiled machine part in the school. I wasn't really a loner. All through high school, I was always in plays and on the basketball team and in the chess club. My last year, I went to what they call Free School and held a part-time job making pasta.

Deciding to become an actor really didn't happen until I was 17 or 18. I started taking classes at night, mostly out of respect for acting. I was taking classes and playing hockey a lot and I started crashing some auditions with friends from the Performing Arts High School. I got some jobs, then I got an agent, and it all sort of fell together. I started doing community theater and commercials. I did a Coke commercial and this killer Kellogg's commercial.

My first big part was in a play in Toronto called *Wolf Boy*. I played Bernie, a suicidal jock who goes into an insane asylum.

I moved to L.A. two years ago. I was in Toronto and had come to a point where I had done most of what I could do there. The theater community and I weren't really ready for each other. I was 19 and full of energy and I would go to auditions and they'd be, "Great, great, maybe next year." I was tired of playing the best friend, thug number one and the tall guy. I'd gotten an audition for a movie-of-the-week for Disney called *Young Again*, where I was reading for best friend number one, but the director liked me and had me read for the lead. In L.A., I met Hildy Gottlieb at ICM (International Creative Management). She told me, "When you get your act together..." Eventually, I got the job and a green card so I was legal. I got in my dumpy 1969 Volvo and drove out here with $3,000. I stayed at my stepfather's and proceeded to go into the darkness that is L.A.

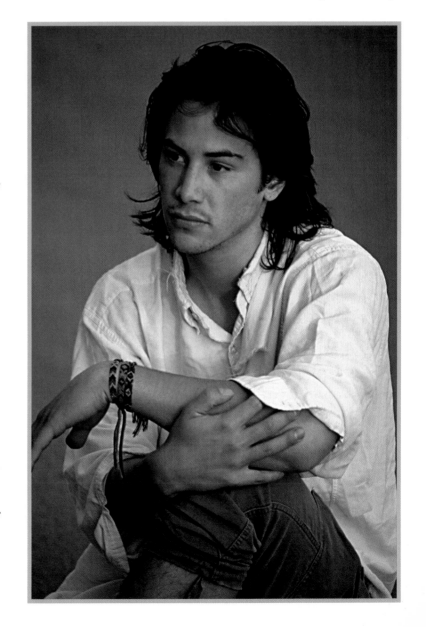

Then I did *River's Edge* and a film called *The Night Before*. It seems to me in Hollywood you have to do a quirky comedy to lose your cinematic virginity. I've done a couple of them.

I just finished a film called *Bill & Ted's Excellent Adventure*. Lots of time traveling, mind bending and twisting. It's cool because there's no swearing and hardly any violence. There is some dark innuendo in it. I hope it's funny. We changed it a lot and I think for the better too.

That was an experience of having fun and working and trying to do it and hopefully succeeding. Stephen Herek was great with us and the other actor, Alex Winter, was inspiring. I got to play a guy who's like a child of nature. He's almost an idiot savant, except he's not that smart. But he's pure and good. He's a good soul.

I jumped into this thing (acting) without an ultimate goal. It was something I wanted to do, and it's just been recently that I've realized that if I don't have goals, people are going to fuck with me and I really hate that. Now my goal is to do good work. I figure in the scheme of being in Hollywood now, with my life as it is, I would like to play a very neurotic, crazy, mean, evil character. I'd like to play someone who's just fucking ugly. Oh, in general, to get better at the bass. I picked it up a year and a half ago.

Most scripts I read are bad. Hollywood's a strange place. It's a very specific market. A lot of what you're going to see is quasi-literal entertainment. It's hard to bring new ideas when they're out to make money. Wow, man, what do I look for in a script? I totally want to be enlightened, dude; interesting stories, interesting people, characters, development, ideas being proposed, clash, conflict, hate, love, work, death, success, fame, failure, redemption, death, hell, sin, good food, bad food, smells, nice colors and big tits.

What roles am I looking for? Someone really evil, dark and ugly. Most of the characters I've played so far have been very good people. They all have a certain innocence and naivete and I think I'd like to sort of exploit other stuff. Hopefully soon, I will be a major asshole coming to a theater near you. Body, spirit, balls and toe jam.

What kind of preparation do I do? It's so abstract. Acting is such a weird fucking thing, man. For every role and every beat it's just so different. All I can say is that I try to give and I try to learn.

Do I do preparation? No, I treat it lightly. I just basically look over what I have to do the day before and if I don't have time, like if I have to vacuum or something, I do that instead. Me? Of course. How can you not?

I would only do a nude scene if it was a good nude scene. I won't do superfluous nudity. If you're asking whether or not I'm embarrassed about my body? Sometimes (laughs). I would take my clothes off in front of the camera if I was comfortable with it.

I'm 23 and I've been studying since I was 16. My studying has been very nomadic and has been of a fairly wide range. I went out to Pennsylvania for a summer. There was this house in Rose Valley. All the actors lived in the house. The theater was just a quarter mile down the road. You just hung lights, did box office and studied five hours a day. That was intense. So yeah, studying is important.

My manager and agent all serendipitously came together. I thank the gods. One thing that's cool about being in Hollywood and doing movies is that somehow if you happen to be in a film that makes a lot of money, you get power. I don't want too much power, man. I don't want to be like Eddie Murphy, being so far out there that it is no longer feasible to be an actor. But I would like to have enough things so that people would be curious. I'd like to have my say and not be screaming at the walls.

I guess I'm successful in that I'm getting a chance to do what I want to do. What sacrifices have I made to do that? I don't know if they're sacrifices because I've gotten to do what I wanted. Privacy. Yeah, man, obviously, because it's a public domain.

You're in a movie and people see it. That's not a major thing for me. I haven't experienced fame yet. My sacrifices are still pretty much in my small world. I'm not really out there yet. Life hasn't really been affected by that.

How does my image differ from who I am? I'd like to say that I'm not all that naive, but I am. And I'd like to say that I'm not all that innocent, but I am. In terms of misconceptions about me, probably that I'm clean or that I'm short.

What do I like best about acting? I almost said, "CHICKS AND SEX AND FUCKING AND MONEY," but that hasn't happened yet. The best thing about being an actor is acting. I mean, what else is there?

I've been recognized on the street about 12 times. I feel like a young pubic hair. I keep getting checked out and played with sometimes. The heaviest thing actually happened to me two days ago. I met this kid, who's about 17, who looks just like Matt (Keanu's character in *River's Edge*), and he said, "Whoa man, you're my idol," and he gave me all this free food and shit at the restaurant he worked at. That was cool.

Who would I like to play on screen? The young part of me would like to play Rimbaud. Imagine, someone who's writing sonnets in Latin at 17, telling his teachers that they're full of shit. By 20, he's totally disillusioned and he leads a life of debauchery and dies in the gutter. That sort of appeals to my artistic cool deep side. There are others. Rimbaud just came out of the top of my head.

Movie remake? Anything I say is obviously a snapshot and in this snapshot I would say *The Ruling Class*.

Oh, man, if I have to talk about spirituality, man, I have to get more wine. In the gutter is man's essence, in the essence is the gutter of man. Well, I don't involve myself in any organized religion. I checked it out when I was 11. Since then I haven't needed it. I totally don't want to bum anybody out. Here we go, God! My own God? Do I believe in my own God? Well, I seem to pay petty respect, whenever I talk about my success, I talk about retribution for my success, that you must pay for it. I guess in some sort of deep-rooted way I feel I haven't. I don't agree with that. Maybe I'm paying tribute to irony. It's the sort of thing that can make you bitter. But, yeah, I guess I believe in God. No, I don't believe in God. I don't know. Those are things that are still in turmoil.

My biggest fear is that my underwear will have a stain on it if I'm ever with a woman that I've never slept with before. That's a major fear.

I'd rather laugh than be in a corner crying. But you know everything is a flash, man. All I can say is that I'm 23 and there's a poem by Walt Whitman that goes, "In my youth I thought long long thoughts." I am sort of a sensory hound. I've been a sensory hound ever since I can remember.

I used to live my life out of a basket. I would make money from a commercial and I'd put it all in a basket. I'd go to the bank and say, "I'd like to cash this check for $4,000." They'd go, "Wouldn't you like to open a checking or a savings account?" I'd say, "No man, just give me my money." For the next year I'd live my life out of the basket. But things got complicated. And when things get complicated I bail. Even when I was poor, I had accountants do my taxes. I have no idea and no interest in paying attention to that (money matters). I live very simply and that is something I want to do. I'm basically a pretty rudimentary fellow.

Which actress would I most like to play opposite? Oh, I don't know, man. Who would I like to fuck the most? Meryl Streep, because even if I wasn't good, she would fake it the best. No, I haven't slept with most of my leading women. I'm practically a celibate monk.

This is what I think is happening with actors in Hollywood. A lot of people I've worked with have a sense of darkness and sticking to their guns with their point of view

of acting. I think that there are a lot of heavy actors who are going to surprise people. They are sincere and generally well-bred and smart about what they are doing. We are getting more theatrical in our acting styles in the sense that we are taking more risks. John Cusack is an example of someone who we haven't seen pull the bag out of the hat yet. He's sometimes cute, he's annoying, he's a jock. He is representative of someone who isn't doing it because of the market but who will probably end up doing something where we'll go, "Whoa, hey!" We hope so, because I'd like to spend six bucks and feel it was worth it. When I go to see *Beverly Hills Cop II* in Times Square at midnight and people are getting stoned and talking to the screen, I don't think they are satisfied.

How do I fit in? I guess I'm just doing what I'm doing, trying at least. I'm trying to pursue what I'm curious about, trying to survive and hopefully not be fucked up the ass by irony and the gods.

Keanu Reeves, September 1987

Johnny Depp

In 1987, Johnny Depp was already a teen idol through his starring role on the television series "21 Jump Street." He was living in a modest one-bedroom apartment in an art-deco building on Whitley Avenue in Hollywood. I would run into him several times late at night when he'd be hanging out with Nicolas Cage and other friends at Canter's, a popular after-club eatery.

I recently photographed Johnny again. His hair had grown but his angelic face remained much the same. Stardom had not inherently changed him; he was still soft-spoken and sweet. I did notice, though, a newfound inner strength and self-assurance.

Johnny wanted to go beyond doing traditional leading-man roles and he has.

$\mathcal{I}$ grew up in many different houses. One in Miramar, Florida, sticks out in particular. We lived at 68th Avenue and Court, on the corner of a busy street. The house was a three-bedroom built in the sixties. It constantly smelled of my mom's cooking: soup, beans and ham. I remember my brother and sister fighting. I had a poodle named Pepi. I shared a bedroom with my brother, who is 10 years older than me. He listened to a lot of Van Morrison and Bob Dylan.

We moved constantly. My mom just liked to move for some reason. By the time I was 15, we had lived in about 20 houses. It was hard. Depending on how far we'd move, you'd have to make new friends. Fortunately, I didn't have to change schools often. But we never stayed in one neighborhood for long. At the drop of a hat, we'd go.

My mom was a waitress; she'd been a waitress since she was 14. My father was the Director of Public Works in Miramar. They divorced when I was about 16.

To this day, I hate it when I have to move from location to location. I get very angry, as a result of having to move so much as a kid. I live in Hollywood now, but I'm in Vancouver shooting "21 Jump Street" about nine months of the year.

I was very mischievous as a boy. I loved tape recording people when they didn't know. One time a friend and I dug a really deep tunnel in my backyard. We covered it with boards and leaves. I was attempting to dig a tunnel into my room. I liked to push it and see how far I could go. If you knew me during high school, I think you'd describe me as "the kid with long hair who was always playing guitar." I wasn't big on participating in school activities. I used to bring my guitar to school and I'd skip most classes to sneak into guitar class.

The teacher would give me a practice room to play in. That's pretty much what I spent my high school years doing.

You know, I never made the decision to become an actor. At least not in the beginning. I got into it off-the-cuff. I moved from Florida to Los Angeles with a band I was playing with called The Kids. A friend of mine introduced me to Nicolas Cage and we started hanging out. Nick thought that I should try acting and see what would happen. At the time, I wasn't making much money. I played a few clubs with the band here and there, but I still had a lot of time. So, I decided to give it a shot. Nick set up a meeting for me with his agent and she sent me to read for a movie. They gave me a script to study. Two days later, I read for it and they gave me the role. That was *Nightmare on Elm Street*.

Doing *Nightmare on Elm Street* was a trial-by-fire sort of thing. I'd never acted before. I'd never done school plays; nothing. The fact that it was totally new to me was a tremendous challenge. I'd never done anything like this, hitting marks and saying lines and thinking about why my character was doing what he was doing. It was totally the opposite of being in a rock 'n' roll band. In a band, you are four people, all working together to write great songs or to get a record deal. In acting, I found it was just me. It all depended on me and my own choices. I didn't have to answer to anyone about what I wanted to do. The band wasn't doing well, so I turned my energies toward acting.

As you become more well known as an actor, more people get involved in you, directly and indirectly. You've got the "Suits" or "Bigwigs," as I call them, the "yeses" and the "nos." Sometimes, they want you to do things that maybe you don't believe in or feel like doing, like promos. I tend to follow my instincts and say, "No, I'm not going to do that." It causes trouble, here and there. But I think the main thing is to be honest, rely on your instincts and do what you feel is right and not necessarily rely on what other people think.

Television is a little frustrating for me. There's no time for preparation. In features, you have loads of time to do the work. And the work is the most important thing of all. I think that in the beginning of an acting career, everybody wants to achieve notoriety or stardom. In the beginning, that was very glamorous to me.

You want to be famous because you want to be good at what you do and you want to be recognized for it, right? Now, being famous isn't as important to me. My goal is to keep learning because I'm nowhere near where I want to be. Like I said about the fame thing: if that becomes the motivation behind everything, even if you achieve it, you're going to get stuck there and you're not going to go any further.

I don't believe in the whole "leading-man thing and that's all he's ever going to do." I mean I'd like to shave my eyebrow or my hair off, or do anything. I want to hopefully, with some of the roles that I do later on, make people see things in a different light, so that they won't just go with the flow and feel they have to be or act a certain way, just because the President says, "That's the way it is." I'd like to do as many different roles as I can.

I try to read as much as I can. *On The Road* by Jack Kerouac is one of my favorite books. There are a lot of books I've read that I'd like to film. I love the concept of *The Metamorphosis* by Franz Kafka. I'd like to become a giant cockroach. I love Van Gogh. I've always been interested in people who had mental torment, weirdos. I think everybody is pretty whacked out in their own way. I deal with my anxiety by smoking a lot of cigarettes and listening to very loud music. I like Bach, the Georgia Satellites, Led Zeppelin and Tom Waits. I like Tom Waits a lot.

When I was a kid, I did drugs when I freaked out. I mean, I was in a rock 'n' roll band in Florida, the cocaine capital of the world. Drugs are really prominent in the club scene, especially there. They were hurting me physically and mentally. Drugs were dragging me down. They were killing me. I quit. Now, I just smoke like a fiend.

I would never do a role that glamorized self-abuse or racism. Racism freaks me out. The black and white thing. The term "nigger" is still used constantly. Why is somebody who's black a "nigger"? It doesn't register. Living in Florida, there's

tons of rednecks out there. I mean, these guys want to hear "Sweet Home Alabama" 24 hours a day. Racism freaks me out a lot.

The homeless are pretty important to me. There are a lot of people out there who have no food, no home and no money. A lot of them are there by choice but some can't help it. I wish some of the people with the big bucks, instead of buying a Rolls-Royce or another Mercedes, would give a little scratch to the people who are hurting. I don't know about sacrifices. I think once you make a choice to be an actor, there's always a balance between good and bad. You've got to go through hell to get to heaven. In every good there is evil; in every evil there is good. Through everything bad that's happened to me, I've learned from it, which is OK.

People usually think that if you're an actor and you're 24 and you look a certain way that you're an asshole. So they treat you like an asshole at first. Then they realize that you're a human being and a nice guy.

As far as actors go, I like Marlon Brando, Jack Nicholson and Walter Matthau. I respect Nick (Cage) a lot. He's trying to go for something really different and he's in a great position to do that. He's very intense and he's got really innovative ideas. I think he's going to do a lot.

Why would a director choose me? I can only say that hopefully, there's something underneath my look or image that maybe hasn't come out yet, that he thinks he could bring out. I want to try to do things differently. I want to experiment. I want to express different things at some point. It's just the beginning. I'm not even born yet. I'm still trying. I'm still pushing. I hope I never stop pushing. I don't ever want to get to a place where I feel satisfied. I think if I do that, it will all be over.

Johnny Depp, December 1987

David Duchovny

In the summer of 1992, I met David Duchovny at a beach party in Malibu given by a mutual friend, publicist Jimmy Dobson. Jimmy told me that David was a really talented actor and he lent me a tape of David's movie, Julia Has Two Lovers. I found David's performance both magnetic and refreshingly original.

Several weeks later, I ran into David at a premiere for Brad Pitt's movie Johnny Suede and later at a private screening of Kalifornia, which co-starred David and Brad. The only people in attendance were David, Brad, their agents, the director, Dominic Sena, Jimmy Dobson and me.

We met for our interview at his older brother Danny's house in Malibu. David decided to put on one of Danny's wetsuits for the shoot. We walked down to the beach to take the photographs. Afterward, when we sat down on the deck to talk, David pointed out the pelicans diving into the crashing waves.

David Duchovny, through his role as FBI agent Fox Mulder in "The X-Files," has become a worldwide phenomenon.

$\mathcal{I}$ am from the Lower East Side of New York City. We lived on 11th Street and Second Avenue. It's a cross between a Ukrainian and a Puerto Rican neighborhood. Growing up, I went to both private and public schools, so I had a street education and a preppy education at the same time, although as I went into higher education I became more preppy. I went to the Collegiate High School for boys, which is a really fancy school in the middle of Manhattan. Everybody had tons of money. I was the Lower East Side contingent on a scholarship. A lot was made of being smart in my family because both my parents were lower middle class. They put a lot of emphasis on getting ahead through education and it was very important to my mother that I get a college degree and for me to be a good student, which I was. If you learn how to be a good student you run the risk of not finding out what it is you truly want to do because you're good at a lot of different things or you're good at getting by the system that people have set up. From ages five to 20, I'd always list that I wanted to be a lawyer or a doctor on all those tests they give you. What I really wanted to be was a basketball player. I played a lot of basketball but my hands never grew. I'm only six feet tall and I can't jump very well but I'm a good shooter. My father always used to joke with me because he knew that I wanted to be a pro ball player. He'd always tell me I had small hands.

I'd come out in the morning when I was eight or nine years old and tell him if you watch my hands closely you'll see that they're growing. Of course it was all in my mind. So basketball was no good and second to basketball would have been pro baseball. All I ever wanted to do was play ball. I don't know why but that's the way I felt.

I went to Princeton College, which is about as preppy as you can get. I guess I had a hell of a lot of discipline and a lot of fear and those combined made me a really good student. I could study eight or nine hours a day and still be on the basketball team and get my A's. But nothing penetrated me. I was just afraid to fail. I really didn't know what I wanted or what moved me beyond basketball or sex. Those were two things that were very black and white to me, where I could feel in the moment. I had a high school girlfriend and then I met a girl in college who I stayed with for five years. I'm not saying that my experience with sex was any more mystical than anybody else's. I'm just saying that it was an area where I felt alive.

I was kind of drifting along, which might seem like a weird thing to say because I was seemingly doing so well. I was talented in a bleak way and I was just scared shitless that I wasn't going to be the best at what I was doing. But I didn't know what I wanted to do. I just wanted to be the best. That's kind of sick when I think about it. I guess I wanted to be loved and I thought the only way to be loved was to be the perfect person or some kind of golden boy.

After college, I took a year off and bartended in New York City. I applied for scholarships thinking that if I continued to be a student I could somehow put off defining myself. Many great thinkers have the point of view that one is an eternal student. Emerson said, "Each man is my master in something and from that I endeavor to learn from him." Zen tells you to have a beginner's mind and that's true. But there's also something about being subservient and not having the confidence to say, "All right, I control my world here and I'm going to do something as a master rather than a student."

But I continued to be a student. I knew how to work well within that system. I got a scholarship at Yale, and they actually paid me money to go there. They paid graduates who were interested in becoming professors with the hope that they would teach at Yale. So now I feel guilty because I took their money and I'm not a professor. I have an ABD, which means "All But Dissertation." My mother still hopes that I will one day finish my Ph.D. but I don't think so.

Yale is famous for its drama school. There was a bunch of actors running around. I thought they were more fun to hang around with than my peers. I started writing a play, and in order to learn more about writing I decided to take an acting class. In

acting, I felt like I was playing ball again. Acting brought me to the surface. I felt the education I had was cerebral and academic and that I hadn't educated a part of me that gets angry or that cries or that plays a lot. I really hadn't educated my heart. I had a brain the size of a house and a heart the size of a pea so I had to even that out a little. I didn't wake up one morning and say, "Well David, you've become awful cerebral. You're a very dry, cold person. Why don't you see what your emotions are like underneath all this vocabulary?" But I think people are instinctually drawn to people and areas that can teach them something. At the time you don't know why. But then ten years later you go, "Oh, that's why I was with that terrible woman." It was to learn this lesson which I didn't learn till now. There's nothing wasted. I think the better part of me was drawn to a discipline where I could feel rather than think.

I mean, I didn't set out to become an actor. I set out to act. And that was so much fun. The idea of actually making a living at it was so frightening because so many other things are contingent on it. It's the most frightening thing to try and make a living at because you put all your shit in other people's hands. It was hard at first because I had been so embraced by academia and all of a sudden I was getting rejected from Foot Locker commercials.

Before I thought of being an actor professionally I had no fear because I was a teacher and a writer already and I thought, *Well why not try this?* I auditioned for anything: commercials, soaps, TV, movies. My first acting job was a Lowenbrau commercial. I was petrified. If you can suck on a commercial without any copy, I sucked. I remember I was so tight that the cameraman and director put tape over their noses to make me laugh. That even made me tighter 'cause I thought, *My God, I'm so bad that they're treating me like an infant.* I was on screen for a few seconds and they actually paid me money. But I remember going home and thinking, *You stink, you'll never do this, you're too uptight.*

After that I did a movie called *New Year's Day* by Henry Jaglom. That was the first time I'd ever spoken on camera. I didn't even audition. The star of the movie was a woman named Maggie Jacobson, an ex-girlfriend of mine. They wanted someone to play a bad ex-boyfriend. Henry likes to advertise that his movies take off from real life. So it was tiresome for people to think that I was as scummy as I was in the movie. That was my first movie job and I thought I was going to be a star and get all the roles I wanted after that, but I found you have to work for it. I did *New Year's Day* over Christmas vacation. Then I went back to school and finished up that year, but I knew it was over.

I came out to L.A. because I wasn't getting anywhere in New York. That initial fearlessness that I had because I hadn't committed to life left me immediately. All of a sudden the auditions became important. I had to learn how to be professional.

I first moved to West L.A. and then I got a rent-controlled sublet in Santa Monica. I wrote a lot of poetry. I went through a period of rejections, getting close on things but not getting them, having no money, leeching off friends and losing lovers because they thought I was a no-good bum. That was in 1988. Eventually I got better and things turned around. I did a movie called *Julia Has Two Lovers*. We did it in a week and it cost $25,000

to make. I never thought anything would come of it. When we got worldwide distribution it gave me more confidence that maybe I could do this. Then I got a little part in *Don't Tell Mom the Babysitter's Dead*, which allowed me to pay my bills for a little while. It was just a matter of keeping my head above water until I could start moving. *The Rapture* and a part in "Twin Peaks" followed.

It has been a steady incline, which I'm happy with. I feel a little more confident that I know what I'm doing now. During my first few jobs I felt, *let me get through this experience without embarrassing myself. Let me not fail.* As I got more comfortable, my goals changed to: *Let me do something interesting, let me create something of import, let me do something positive rather than avoid something negative.*

When you die, you don't want to say about yourself, "Well, I maintained a certain level of adequacy over a shocking amount of years." Then of course the danger is, when you aspire you can also fall. What are my dreams now? I think everybody has something to express in their lives. I want to find the thing that I'm great at.

I live on the beach in Santa Monica. I am a morning person. A normal day when I'm not working is getting up at around 7 a.m. I read for a while. I'll write or I'll do a crossword puzzle. I sound like an old man. Then I'll do something physical for a couple of hours. I'll play basketball or I'll swim or run. I just have to do that for my sanity. In the afternoons I'll read or write poetry or I'll go to an acting class. I cook well enough for me, but I wouldn't subject anyone else to what I make. In the evenings I go to movies and plays in town or I visit my friends. I do yoga. I got my ears pierced at this wild place in West Hollywood called the Gauntlet. I decided to go for two holes instead of one.

I think it is possible to value yourself enough to say, "Myself is unique. There's never been anybody like me. Therefore, it is my duty on this earth to manifest that self in that unique way." I'm not infallible and I think you can live your life developing yourself, while spiritually you also realize that yourself is the biggest piece of shit. It's a joke, it's a cartoon, it's a creation, it doesn't exist. But the fact that it's a cartoon doesn't make it any less lovable or any less beautiful. In fact it gives it a kind of sadness. Where do I see myself 10 years from now? I don't know. Ten years ago, I never would have imagined myself sitting here now.

David Duchovny, September 1992

Laurence Fishburne

*W*hile at a trendy club on Sunset Boulevard, actress/model
Lisa Marie—Vampira in Tim Burton's Ed Wood—introduced
me to Laurence Fishburne. We sat next to him at the bar and
Laurence and I struck up a conversation. He told me he was
an actor.

I had been looking for a talented African-American actor
to include in my book The New Breed. When Lisa Marie
later told me that Laurence was incredibly talented and that
he had co-starred in Francis Ford Coppola's Apocalypse Now
when he was 16, I knew I had found who I'd been looking for.

Since I photographed him in 1987, acting opportunities have
opened up for African-American actors.

I can only add that Laurence Fishburne is a charming,
humble, down-to-earth guy and that he has a lovely smile.
His success is well-deserved.

$\mathcal{I}$ grew up at 19 Fiske Place in Brooklyn, New York. To get to my apartment you had to climb up three flights of cold, dark gray marble steps. I remember having to walk up those steps in front of my mother sometimes when I was bad at school. It would be like the longest walk in the world.

We lived in apartment 3C. Our bedrooms faced the street, and at three in the afternoon, you could always hear the kids outside playing stickball, roller hockey, tag or whatever. My house was always filled with the incredible aromas of African-American cuisine: fried chicken, chitlins, greens, grits, biscuits, bacon and occasionally lasagna. I had an Italian friend whose house I would go to for dinner a lot and I grew up very fond of lasagna, so my mother would make it once in a while.

My parents separated when I was three and got divorced when I was ten. I was an only child. I saw my dad at least once a month on a Sunday and we would go to the movies. When I came back to the neighborhood at 6 p.m., I'd act out the movie I'd seen for all the kids on the block. Most of them came from large families, so they couldn't afford to go to the movies. That was my first experience with acting.

I've been acting professionally since I was ten, but I didn't start to take it seriously until I was 16 or 17. Up until that point, acting was something I enjoyed and was good at. It was also a way for me to survive. I'm not a very physical person and growing up where I grew up, there was ample opportunity to get into physical confrontations. Instead of saying, "Well, I'm just gonna kick your ass," I'd use my acting prowess and fuck them up mentally.

The experience that changed the way I looked at acting was working on *Apocalypse Now* with Francis Ford Coppola. I began to look at acting as an art form. Francis looks at film as something that hasn't even begun to be tapped the way it ought to be. The film business, i.e., Hollywood, hasn't utilized the medium to its fullest potential and has robbed cats like me and other young actors of the possibility of doing wonderful things with a new art form.

There is also a peculiar problem I have to deal with every day of my life. The problem is called racism. Regardless of all the wonderful work I have done and will do, the fact remains that I am an African American. I'm a black person. There are hundreds of scripts that go to white actors that I will never see. The majority of stuff I get sent on says "BLACK," which is why I don't get submitted piles of scripts. There are just not that many of them. I don't have the flexibility to look at certain kinds of roles. If I'm available to go out and do a role, what I try and do is make sure my vibe is a vibe that any young black American or black man on the planet can relate to in a certain way. After all, that's what I represent on the screen. Racism is a bitch. It exists and I just have to do the best I can.

When I got back from *Apocalypse Now*, I was 17. Everyone said, "Larry, you'll work all the time." If I had been a white boy, I'd be making more than Charlie Sheen, based on talent alone. That really fucked me up for a while, but I go with it. At least I'm working.

When a cat sits down to write a screenplay, he's concerned with his story and his primary characters. The rest of it is not as well thought out. For a white cat to write a story that has black characters in it, there's no telling how much he knows about black people. Once upon a time, I used to shake my head and say, "This is bullshit." I don't expect him to have a clue anymore. How could he have a clue? Since I have all the baggage about that, I just bring my bags.

To make it as a black actor, you have to work hard, stick around and deal with people as people. It can be really frustrating sometimes. I used to deal with my frustrations by getting fucked up a lot. Now I just work through things and try not to let it interfere with my work. It's like that line in *Harvey*, when Jimmy Stewart says, "You can be oh so smart, or oh so pleasant." At work, I try to be oh so pleasant; in life I try to be oh so smart.

Working with Spike Lee on *School Daze*, I got to be pleasant and smart. Spike passed me the ball and said, "Run with it, homeboy." The film is about black people, and there is a difference. Aside from the pigmentation, there are cultural differences among us; language, speech patterns, body language. All black people don't talk the same. This was my first opportunity as an actor to really let loose. There's a possibility that *School Daze* will open up a lot of doors for me, but there's also the possibility that people will say, "That was nice, next." I'm prepared for that. I'm still prepared to play the third character in someone else's movie. It really doesn't matter because I'm about my craft. That's what I take seriously.

Actors I know sit around all the time having discussions about acting and this one and that one. "That cat," we say, "is weak." Why? "Because he's not about the craft. He's about that other starry-eyed shit."

I like it when I meet my brother on the street and that cat says, "My brother, I like what you're doing in the movies." My biggest fear is becoming very successful and recognizable and not knowing how to handle it. That's another reason I've always been into being an actor as opposed to wanting to become a star.

The reason it's impor-
tant that my people recognize me is that people of
African descent in this country and in a lot of countries
around the world get bom-
barded with negative images
of themselves. That goes
back to, Why does the black
man always have to play the
pusher, the pimp and so on?
The reality is that a lot of us
still do that. I fight racism
by trying to be right as rain
and by promoting a positive
self-image. That's what I'm
doing to make a difference
in the movies and that's
what I'm doing to make a
difference in the world.

Laurence Fishburne,
November 1987

Courteney Cox

It was in early 1987 when I first heard the name Courteney Cox. My Norwegian girlfriend, Katrina, was living in a downtown loft in the middle of New York City's Little Italy with her Liverpudlian roommate, Paul, who on a trip to Los Angeles had met and fallen madly in love with a beautiful actress named Courteney Cox.

Later that year, I visited Paul at the downtown clothing mart and met Courteney, who had just landed the role of Alex Keaton's girlfriend on "Family Ties." She was extremely self-assured, one of those women who appears to have everything in their lives under control.

Since I've always believed in following life's leads, I asked Courteney if I could interview her for my book. We met at her house in the hills above Hollywood. I was impressed at her taste and at how amazingly put together and organized her house was for a woman so young.

Courteney would later appear opposite Jim Carrey in Ace Ventura: Pet Detective *and go on to co-star in one of television's mega-hit sitcoms of the '90s, "Friends."*

$\mathcal{M}$y parents got divorced when I was 10, while I was away at camp. Even though they were already separated, the divorce really upset me. When I got home from camp, my brother and I tried to set my parents up on dinner dates. He'd take my father and I'd take my mother, and we'd meet at Wendy's. We tried everything, but nothing worked.

My dad moved from where we lived in Birmingham, Alabama, to Florida, and my mom got only $400 a month from him in alimony and child support. We didn't have a lot of money to buy clothes or to do what we wanted to do. I got very resentful toward my mother and as a result, very independent.

When I was 13, I got my first job after school. I wanted to buy clothes and save money for a car. I called names out of the phone book to raise money for the Retardation Foundation. I was very ambitious. All through high school, I took a full load of classes and worked 40 hours a week.

My mother remarried and my stepfather's nephew is Miles Copeland, who managed the Police and owns I.R.S. Records. Whenever the band would come to Birmingham, Miles would fly down for the show and stay at our house. He would always say to me, "Courteney, you've got to get out of here. You're too ambitious to stay in Birmingham. You're going to have to leave at some point, so why don't you come to New York?" I'd laugh at him and say, it was a nice dream, but get real.

During my senior year in high school, the Police played a show in Birmingham. Two weeks later, Miles invited me to one of their concerts in New York and said he would take me for an interview at the Ford modeling agency. I was very excited, but I wondered how he was going to get me in. I'm only 5 feet 5 inches, and it wasn't like they were excited to meet girls from Alabama who had never done anything aside from ads for a local department store.

Miles had gotten me the interview by bribing an agent with two free Police tickets for that night's sold-out show. When they met me they thought I was too short, but decided

48

to send me out on two interviews anyway. I lucked out. One of the interviews was for *Young Miss* magazine. I booked the job that day, and, when I graduated from high school a few weeks later, I moved to New York.

When I first got there, I slept on different people's floors. I finally saved enough money to be able to afford an apartment and moved to the Upper West Side, where I shared a one-bedroom. Apartments are so expensive in New York and all the money I made went to pay for rent. My best friend lived downstairs. I used to call her and say, "I don't have money but do you want to have dinner?" Then I'd bring down a can of tomato soup, a loaf of bread and a tub of whipped butter. I'd have six slices of bread and butter and a bowl of tomato soup. Once in a while I'd add a can of tuna. That's all I ate for nine months. But I was ambitious and I wanted to succeed.

I hated modeling. I wasn't tall enough or beautiful enough to become a real model. Once I got my first commercial, I quit print. I started taking acting lessons and speech lessons to lose my Southern accent. My real break came when I got the Bruce Springsteen "Dancing in the Dark" video. Brian DePalma cast me over a couple hundred other girls. He wanted someone who could look surprised when Bruce pulled her out of the audience, take after take, and that was me.

After I did that, I was flown out to Los Angeles to screen-test for a pilot, which I didn't get. But I did end up getting the series "Misfits of Science," because by chance someone had walked me over to that set after my screen test. After doing the film *Masters of the Universe*, some guest TV roles and a movie for NBC, I got "Family Ties."

On the show, I play Alex's (Michael J. Fox) girlfriend, Laura. She seems like an easy role to play, but she and I are so completely opposite. Sometimes, I'm amazed at some of the words that come out of her mouth. It's strange. My friends see me on the show and say, "You would never have done that." I explain that it's a role. I'm not playing Courteney Cox. "Family Ties" is going to last one more season, and I'm now looking for dramatic roles. A lot of people put down television, but working in front of 300 people every week has been an incredible learning experience for me.

There are so many levels of success and right now I'm at the bottom. If you're talking about real SUCCESS, my goal right now is to just get through each day and try to keep my eyes open and learn as much as I can. I'm by no means where I want to be yet as an actress. I still have a lot that I want to accomplish.

Courteney Cox, November 1987

Brad Pitt

Bill Danzinger, an assistant agent at Triad Agency, approached me about photographing a new young actor he represented named Brad Pitt. Some of Triad's other agents felt that Brad, with his "pretty boy" looks, would only have a limited appeal, but Bill disagreed. He felt that Brad Pitt had the talent and drive to make it big, very big.

Brad was 20 minutes late for our interview because he had just finished eight loads of laundry at the laundromat. I photographed Brad up on the roof of my Franklin West Towers apartment in Hollywood.

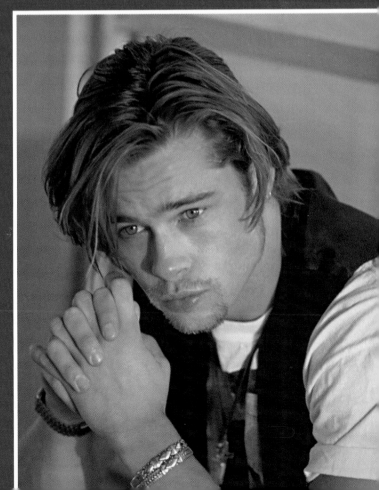

*J*ohn Malkovich is king. He grooves me. I'm from Swingfield, Missouri. I call it Swingfield because it is so exciting. That's sarcasm, in case you didn't catch that. The Springfield Mall, home of the Kickapoo Chiefs. I went to Kickapoo High School. When I first got out here and this is the truth, I'm thinking I'm pretty cool and I meet this girl and she's a California girl, right? Blond to the brain. I told her I was from Missouri and she said, "Is that a state?" So, then I thought, *Oh, so that's the kind of respect Missouri gets out of you.* Yeah, I'm from Missouri, 2.3 kids, dogs in the yard, picket fences. The whole game.

Apple pie intravenously. Basketball. I'm a hoosier, right? It's the best. Growing up there, we don't have anything like the North and South Poles. We don't have acting. We have the local rep theater, but it's like high school productions, if you're lucky. I didn't tell anyone what I wanted to do. I'd always dream about being an actor but I never thought of it realistically 'cause it's just not something you think of there. You're going to be an accountant or an engineer or you're gonna open up a lawn service. That's what there is. And I used to be bummed because I figured I wasn't getting an opportunity, growing up in Missouri. But now that I live here and I see how messed up things are out here, I'm thankful I'm from there. Everything works perfectly, you know. Like the big guy takes care of things, right? So I'm out here at my right time.

My family was the best. It was the only way I could come out here. I was in my junior year at the University of Missouri, majoring in advertising and graphic design, when I packed up and left at the end of 1986. I told my parents I was coming out here to the Art Center in Pasadena. I figured I would just try this (acting) on the side, but things just started clicking.

What were my dreams? I haven't hit them yet. That's all. I haven't hit them yet. I'm getting there. I dreamed of opportunity because I knew things could happen. There's more, I'll be honest. When I was sitting there in my little backyard, playing with my puppy or whatever, eating Twinkies and drinking Kool-aid, I'd dream of fame. It sounds so frickin' cheesy, but there were flicks that moved me, that kind of shaped me as a kid. I remember my dad took me to the drive-in to see *Butch Cassidy and the Sundance Kid* and I remember crying at it. At the end, remember the scene when they get blown away and it freezes on them? Flicks like *Ordinary People* and *Cuckoo's Nest*, they move you and shape you and I want to be a part of that. But also sitting in my yard, in my sandbox, I'd dream of fame and fortune. The lifestyle of the rich and famous is very attractive to someone out there. I'm being perfectly honest, that was part of the attraction at home, to be the number one guy. Then you get out here and you just want to be good. You start to get into it. I didn't know anything. I didn't study acting at home. I got out here and I had so much frickin' stuff to learn.

Yeah. I was always in the movie theaters. I'd go to apethons. They'd show five movies back to back, all the ape movies, *Planet of the Apes*. That was the best.

My coming out here was the classic story but it was such an adventure, it was cool. I had $300 to my name. My car, a dented silver Datsun which I named "Runaround Sue," was loaded up. I had my luggage high up to the back of my head and all the way to the top on the passenger side, so that I couldn't see behind me and just had a little room to shift. My philosophy was, all I need to see is forward. I'm heading west and that's all I need to see. I was such a dork. I just remember driving out and each time I passed a state line, I'd be like, *Yeah*! I was so excited. And then I pulled into town (L.A.) and I had my first meal at McDonald's and it was like, Now what do I do?

I met these eight guys who had this crummy apartment and I crashed there for about half a year. I did all sorts of odd jobs, like dressing up as chickens, being a delivery boy and driving strippers around. I did anything that was flexible, so I could figure out

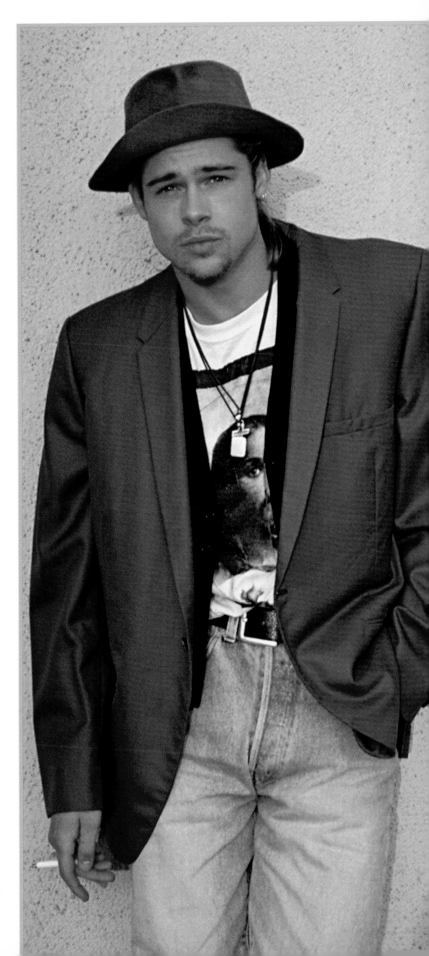

how to get into this frickin' business. I started doing extra work the first week I was here. I wanted to see how things were done. I mean, I didn't even know you had to have a head shot. I just dove in and things started clicking. Yeah, I had to learn, I mean, I wanted to, I didn't have a choice, right?

I got into a good acting class within the first three months, which is amazing. There are so many bullshit ripoffs out here. It pisses me off, 'cause they're messing with people's dreams and making money off them. It makes me mad, because I was one of those people. I was driving strippers around on weekends to make extra money at nights. I'd take them to bachelor parties. I did it for about two months and then I couldn't hang with it. But then on the last night I drove, one of the new strippers told me about this acting class. A famous actor friend of hers, whose name I won't mention, went to this class. So, I figured, if that person's in it, it's good enough for me. I went to it. It was great. Then I got a scene partner. She had an audition with Triad Agency. (Triad has since merged with the William Morris Agency.) She asked me if I'd do the scene we prepared for class in front of all these agents. I said, "Yeah, I guess so, whatever." Boom. I got signed. It was a scene from *Ordinary People*. No, she didn't get signed. The fact was they took a gamble on me because I'd never done anything and I wasn't in the union. But then that's half the battle. Here I am, sitting in all these audition rooms and I'm seeing these people who I've watched on TV or in films my whole life and I'm intimidated as hell. I freak out and I can't do anything for a few months. Nothing comes out 'cause I'm also so intimidated by these casting directors, I just had to kick myself in the butt and say, Let's go, 'cause here it is. Here's your dream, sitting right in your lap. And so I went. Boom. It's been non-stop since then. That was over two years ago. It's been nice. Roy London was my acting coach. I still study with him. He's a brilliant man. You meet very few brilliant men

in the world. (Roy London has since passed away.) He taught me everything about the craft. And I've still got a ways to go. That's what's cool about it, you're always learning. It's a constant change. I love it.

I went home for Christmas and my buddy showed me his new house. He's married and he's building a new deck in the back. And he showed me his new power tools that his parents-in-law got him for Christmas. And he was proud of them. It's cool, though, because I go home and I see my buddy working behind a plumbing counter and he's got his truck and his wife and he's got the woods and the lakes and I tell you what, he's so much happier than most people out here who you admire as your heroes. You grow

up with heroes and you come out here and meet them. I've been kind of disappointed. So now my philosophy is, Keep your heroes, they're important to have, just don't get to know them. It's very sad. Yeah, they're just people. They're just frickin' people.

My first job was a recurring role on "Dallas." I played this little kid whose hormones were running amuck and who was always messing around with Priscilla Presley's daughter. Then they started to throw me in these *Teen Beat* magazines. Man, it was a nightmare. That's such a huge trap, you know. You burn out so hard. I was in there like a month. I just didn't know these things. Then I yanked myself. I said, Yank me, keep me away from them. Yeah, I think it can hurt you. What's the key? The key is longevity. So you've got to stay low, do quality work and cruise and do your own thing. Like do a film and then go off and be a trucker. That's what my dad does. He owns a trucking company. After you see all this crap out here, it makes you want to go out on the road. Be a cowboy. Ride horses. Like Sam Shepard, my man. Sam Shepard is a demigod. I think he plays it the most cool. He stays low. He's got his horses. He's a brilliant writer. He's the man.

I did "Dallas" for half a season and then I moved on. Then I did a "Growing Pains" and then a "21 Jump Street." After that I did a movie that hopefully will never be out called *Cutting Class*. We shot a film in Yugoslavia, *Dark Side of the Sun*, which was cool. I played a kid who has this skin disease, where he can't be exposed to the sun. It's true they have to live their lives in the dark. He decides to live three normal days in the light. He rips off his protective mask, which makes him look like an executioner and he is just this innocent blond-haired boy. We filmed in a thousand-year-old stone city, built by hand. Napoleon Bonaparte's castle lay up on the hill. We did one scene where I was in the water with a dolphin who hung out in the bay. I hopped in and the dolphin started to swim around me and

pretty soon it was like Sea World, only we were out in the ocean. I'd grab his dorfs and he'd pull me down and he'd pull me back up. It was amazing. I can still feel him.

I just finished a pilot for a new series called "The Kids Are Alright" up in Canada. It's so well written. It's the writing, you know. It's always the writing. But the good roles are going to people like Sean Penn because he's in a good position now. So the key is to hop to that level and then the brilliant writing starts coming in. I don't know if this is going to go but I have a good feeling about it. That's what it's about, instincts. Everything is about instincts. But you know what, I'm not worried one bit, because if it doesn't go, there will be something else. Things have been working. (The series wasn't picked up.)

Spirituality. I just know that when you're with God, then credit's

going to go where credit's due. The key is to rely on that and not to worry about things. You do not worry. Everyone worries out here. Worrying is the biggest waste of time because things will work if you have faith. That's the word, that's the only word. If you start thinking you're too cool, you're gonna lose it. That's why it's good just to hang out with your buddies and your family and stay low. STAY LOW.

In between jobs I volunteer as a counselor, a big brother kind of thing for kids at a shelter downtown. Most of them are black and Hispanic. They've grown up in crack houses and are always in trouble. I mean, how do these people even get a chance, starting out that way? But it's amazing to see these people. They're very cool. We have all this free time. In between jobs you do it a lot. If you get a job that takes you away, it kind of hurts. They understand, but it's hard to get in tight with them, where they can really trust you, if they know you're leaving. All they need is love. That's all it is. That's one thing I've come to realize, that if you're in the public eye, which I haven't even touched what it can or will be yet. But you have this responsibility. People are watching you. I know I've been disappointed by people. That's all. No big thing. I'm not preaching or anything. It's more personal too, because it kind of makes me feel better.

We're just bums right now. Frickin' Barney (Brad's roommate) borrows my underwear and it bums me out. He doesn't borrow them, he just takes them. This guy can afford a toothbrush, right? But he doesn't, he uses mine. It really bums me out. I have no grungies left. No boxers, you know. I'm doing the old reversal boxer routine. In fact I just got back from doing laundry. I did eight loads at the Laundromat. Then you just wear them all, till there's nothing left and it's all on your floor in the end. God forbid if we ran out of (toilet) paper. It'll be a week until I finally get off my lazy butt and go get it.

We don't even own a TV anymore. It broke down three months ago. The next day we were going to get one. I never read at home, but since I got out here I've been reading constantly. It's the writing. It moves you and it makes you think. People like David Rabe and David Mamet and Lanford Wilson. I can't believe what a waste of time I've grown up my whole life, hanging out in front of the TV.

Music? That's down the line. We just did a song called "From Saul to Paul Back to Saul." Everybody talks about everything here. We're just talking right now. But it's going to happen because we're going to make it happen. Man, because that's all we want. That's all we want. And call it cocky, but you gotta be.

Brad Pitt, May 1989

Mary Stuart Masterson

It was a freezing cold winter day when Mary Stuart Masterson and I rendezvoused in Washington Square Park in New York's Greenwich Village. The trees were bare and the ground was covered with snow. Even though it was so frigid, Mary Stuart looked quite composed.

She was caught in a moment of frustration because an independent film she wanted to do had been held up. It was important to her to play meaningful roles and not just take any job that was offered. Years later, when I saw her perfect performance as the schizophrenic young woman in Benny and Joon, *it was obvious that Mary Stuart Masterson had become the actress she wanted to be.*

I grew up in a 12-story building with six apartments on each floor in Manhattan. The halls always smelled of burning cabbage and really smelly pot roast or meatloaf. I guess that's partly why I'm a vegetarian.

I used to wake up at 6 a.m. every morning and put on Carly Simon. I'd run around dancing with our wonderful old dog, Friendly. He was my best friend. Often I would play in this place we called "the dirt park" because the ground was dirt there. I used to play war. It was the boys against the girls, but I would

always play on the boys' team. I was more a flirt than a tomboy. I flirted by knowing the boys better, understanding them and joking with them. I knew they appreciated that more than girls flipping their hair and giggling a lot. They couldn't stand that and neither could I.

I went to a private school on the Upper East Side called Dalton. The first day I walked into my English class, Jenny Lumet, who became my best friend, says I was wearing a baby-blue sweatshirt, baby-blue cords and ribbons in my hair. She says I said "surreal" three times in one sentence and she couldn't stand me. I don't remember that, but I do remember trying very hard to fit in. On the senior page of my yearbook, it says, "Mary Stuart Masterson came back after ten years, and she had to hurry back to the theater where she was starring in, directing, choreographing, dancing in and producing a show called *Mary Mary*." I found it offensive, but it did indicate my role in the school. I sort of did everything.

I've wanted to act ever since I can remember but I resisted it for a while because I couldn't stand the idea of nepotism. My father is a director and my mother is an actress. I tried to do everything but act. Dancing was my creative outlet. I think I learned to act through choreographing and improvising in dance. Choreography taught me how to physicalize a thought or an emotion in an abstract way while still maintaining a specific meaning for me. I learned through physical movement to speak to the heart without having to speak to the mind.

Getting a part in *Some Kind of Wonderful* propelled me into acting. But I didn't really consider myself an actress until I did Horton Foote's play *Lily Dale* off-Broadway. It was the first time I made my own decisions of my own volition. You really learn to commit on stage. In film I had held back a little. I really believe in rehearsals now, especially for film. You can't be truly spontaneous until you have the whole structure and arc of the character worked out in your mind. You have to know what you're trying to do in every scene in every moment. If you have all that down and you know your lines then you're totally free to do anything you want. That's a joy.

The biggest problem in Scriptland is that no one has a decent story. Studios are into doing "concepts." They'll say, "Let's do a story about a girl who's in the rodeo." That's OK, but what happens? In the first scene, she's riding in the rodeo. In the next scene she's riding in the rodeo, and so on. Nothing happens, nothing changes. She doesn't learn anything and the audience is not enlightened. What happened to the story? I look for a good story and characters that aren't in any way stereotypical. I look for being able to see under the surface of a character. I look for quirky characters that

try, struggle and overcome obstacles. I'd love to play people from very different lifestyles than mine. I want to play white trash, a journalist, a paralegal and women with brains. No one thinks a woman under 30 can have brains anymore.

I think my role in affecting people is to truthfully play a part, no matter how ugly or sinister it may be. As long as it's truthfully played and not exploitative, then I hope people can make up their own minds. My job is to try and empower them. America is the most apathetic country in the world right now. I think television does that. My choice is not to do movies with stereotypes that have 500 murders an hour or that make Russia look like the bad guy. I went to Russia with a group of actors organized by SANE/FREEZE. The project was called Filmmaker's Exchange. Before I left I was scared, but when I got there I was moved to see people in the Soviet Union wanted peace even more than we did. We made a documentary for high school students around the country. We put together footage from our trip with '50s Red-scare propaganda footage and clips from *Red Dawn* and films like that.

My biggest fear is nuclear holocaust. I'm for a nuclear freeze and I'm really concerned with the environment. I recycle my newspapers and return my bottles. I'm trying to find out how to conserve water and energy and help control pollution. All of our natural resources are dwindling. It's a huge problem and people don't even notice. If we don't kill each other with a bomb, then how are we going to survive on this planet anyway?

Spiritually, what's important to me is staying true to myself and accepting the fact that there was something happening before the Big Bang. Whether you call it God,

Buddha, Allah or you don't call it, there's a force inside all of us and it has to do with nature.

What's the biggest misconception about me? Probably that I take myself extremely seriously and that I have no sense of humor. That's not true. Being in film, everyone thinks they know you. From a fan that's a compliment, because that means you've achieved something. But it pisses me off when people in "the business" say things like, "I know Mary Stuart Masterson and this is her." They think they can predict you and package you into a McDonald's clamshell thing. Hollywood tries so hard to work by formula, but it never works.

I'd love to play Louise Brooks on-screen. I'm fascinated by her. She was a woman with so much power over people, yet you could never tell if she was being manipulated or if she was the one doing the manipulating. It's that power of attraction and repulsion

that attracts me. Now, I think that parts for women are outrageously good, relative to the '60s or '70s. What you have to do is develop roles yourself, otherwise you end up playing sweet and boring or a ballbusting executive.

The interesting thing about my acting peers is that we don't all work together, we come from different backgrounds and we don't all know each other. You can't put us all in one category. There is no hook—we're individuals.

Why should a director choose me? Because I'm willing to try new things and I don't make ordinary choices.

Mary Stuart Masterson, January 1988

Stephen Baldwin

*I*n the fall of 1986, I met Stephen Baldwin coming out of a tanning booth at a salon in the West Village in New York City. I had already heard about Stephen from Chris, an employee of the salon, who was aware that I was searching for actors to photograph. Stephen and I became friends. Coincidentally, at around the same time, I met Billy Baldwin (Stephen's brother) and Julia Roberts at my girlfriend Gianna's place. Billy had just returned from a modeling stint in Milan bearing gifts from Gianna's then-boyfriend. Julia and Gianna shared a manager, but Julia had not yet done Mystic Pizza.

Stephen would come to my place and perform scenes from his auditions for me. When he acted, there was an intensity in his eyes that seemed to set a spark in his being. He was amazingly talented and, in a way, a little lost. Acting seemed to center him. Billy, his manager, Pat Reeves, and I were all thrilled when Stephen got his first job, a Scholastic after-school special about an all-boys school. Soon after, he booked The Beast, co-starring Jason Patric.

After I moved to L.A., Stephen stayed with me a couple of times when he had meetings in the city. (I would accompany him to many social functions at clubs around town where we'd bump into actors such as Sean Penn.) It wasn't long before production companies would put Stephen up at hotels like the Sunset Marquis and the Mondrian in Hollywood.

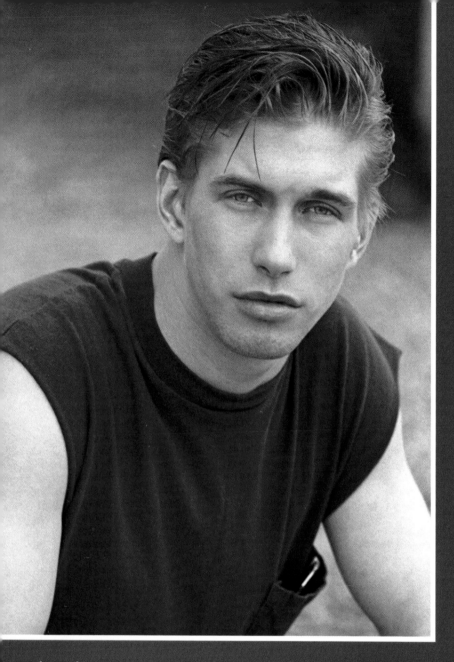

I have three brothers, Alec, Daniel and Billy. I'm the youngest. We grew up in Massapequa, Long Island, outside of New York City. Whenever my brothers would get mad at me, I would run under my mother's skirt for protection. She would always stand up for me. I was her baby. My father was a social studies teacher. He was a great, selfless, compassionate man who dedicated 30 years of his life to teaching and to being there for all his students. I didn't fully appreciate his greatness until after his death. He instilled in my brothers and me a sense of responsibility toward society. (Both Alec and Billy always talked about going into politics.)

As a kid, I was a little terror, but I was also able to charm and I loved to entertain. In high school I was the cutup and a ham, but I knew how to pull the wool over people's eyes and get away with murder. I'd have friends stand guard while I was behind the wall kissing some girl and I'd just generally try to get away with as much insanity as I could.

I started acting in high school and I found the more I pursued it, the more I became interested in it. When I touched on a human emotion and was able to put myself in a situation, it fascinated me. There has been nothing in my life so far that has even come close to that feeling.

I moved into the city and started taking classes at the American Academy of Dramatic Arts. Most of the time I stayed at my brother Billy's place on the Upper East Side. I remember on the first day of class, my teacher asked if anyone was there to study acting to become famous. Eight people raised their hands. Then he asked if anyone was there to study acting because they wanted to become rich. Ten people raised their hands.

Finally he asked if anyone was there to study acting but didn't know why. Me and another guy raised our hands. He said, "You two stay. The rest of you leave until tomorrow—you don't need to be part of this discussion." We spent the morning talking about acting and instinct.

Now I'm looking for projects that are going to freak me out and also attract me on an instinctual level. "The Beast," a film I did last year, made me feel like that. The film deals with the Soviet invasion of Afghanistan and my character—a Russian kid who is in a music class in Stalingrad one day—overnight finds himself in Afghanistan with maybe two weeks to train for combat. I had never even had a passport before going to Israel to shoot that movie. Before I left, I was told I was going to receive military training and at the time it sounded really cool. But when I found myself in the middle of training, I remember thinking, *What the hell am I doing here? I* was scared and frightened. All of a sudden, I felt an intense affinity for my character. The experience made me appreciate acting more than ever. I remember sitting on top of the tanks we were training with at 2 a.m. and looking at the stars. There are a million stars over Israel. I sat there listening to Mozart on my Walkman, trying to put myself into the whole spiritual vibe of the land and in that moment I realized, *Man, there's no way, unless I were reincarnated into a Soviet boy, that I would ever experience something like this if I weren't an actor.* It was really a trip.

Acting is a never-ending struggle for me because of my outrageous pursuit of perfection. It's almost on a psychotic level. When I want a part really badly, I freak out sometimes. When I go into an audition, I can't be so into a script that the director will think I'm a fucking weirdo, so I try to control that. The fire in my eyes, so to speak, will get the point across.

There's a monologue in Edgar Lee Masters' *Spoon River Anthology* which basically states, "Live your life, man." and that's what I try to do in my work and in my life, no matter what the repercussions are. If I feel it's right, I live it.

There are a lot of politics involved in this business and a lot of schmoozing that people feel they have to do in order to get somewhere. I personally would rather just bury my head in the ground. What I've done is surround myself with a manager, Pat Reeves, and an agent, Michael Kingman, who support me, fight to get me auditions and keep me in line when I get too crazy. I'm lucky to have that support in my life.

Stephen Baldwin, April 1987

Sandra Bullock

*S*andra Bullock was my neighbor for three years. I first met her in January 1991 through her house guest John Ryan. She had just moved into a spacious ground-floor, two-bedroom apartment around the corner from me on Sierra Bonita near Melrose Avenue.

I was first struck by Sandra's "old movie star" looks; she reminded me of a cross between a young Katharine Hepburn and Lauren Bacall. She was also quite unfazed by her beauty and seemingly down to earth. As I got to know her, I saw that she was unaffected, ambitious and amazingly confident. There was no doubt in Sandra Bullock's mind that her career would go forward, so neither was there in John's or mine. Yet I had been working on a Japanese campaign for Edwin Jeans and I could not convince the advertising agency to use Sandra because she was still too much of an unknown.

John used to complain when Monster, Sandy's miniature Yorkshire terrier puppy, would shit all over the apartment, because he would have to clean it up.

*S*ometimes I would bring over my dog Oslo, a white boxer puppy, and he would pick up Monster and throw her around. It made us laugh because Monster would always come back for more. Sandy eventually adopted another dog which she named Pony, and they all moved to a house with a yard on Detroit Street.

One day, Sandy and her then-boyfriend, actor Tate Donovan, asked if I knew of any apartments for rent. As it happened, a beautiful apartment in my building was available. Tate soon became my neighbor, and I began to see Sandy more often.

When I mentioned to her that I was studying German, she told me that she spoke the language and that her mother had been a famous German opera star. Sandy and her younger sister had traveled throughout Germany during their childhood. After that, Sandy would occasionally help me with my homework.

Rock climbing was one of Sandy's passions. She and a group of friends would do their climbing at places like Idyllwild, in the high desert. Meanwhile, Sandy was cast in an independent film written by a mutual friend titled *When the Party's Over* for which she got paid $4,000. I took an agent friend, Brian Swardstrom, to the screening, and he agreed that Sandra had something special. Sure that her next film, *Love Potion Number 9*, co-starring Tate, would bring her to another level, Sandy discussed hiring me to do some publicity shots. But the film was not the success she'd hope it would be.

In 1992, Sandy wanted to see how she looked in a short wig and asked me to take some photos. I had always wanted to photograph Sandy in a more glamorous way so I lent her a black sequined dress. She did her own make-up, and, along with Oslo, we proceeded to the roof.

Later, Sandy asked me to photograph her again, this time with Tate. She wore jeans and a white T-shirt, and had swept her hair back in a French twist. We spoke often about my interviewing her, but since we were neighbors and I saw her so often, we just never got around to it. Then Sandy was cast opposite Sylvester Stallone in *Demolition Man* in a role she took over from another actress who was apparently not sexy enough. Fredrik and I

attended a party she had at a Hollywood club to celebrate. *Speed* followed shortly after, and sure enough, Sandra Bullock had arrived. The box-office success of *While You Were Sleeping* propelled her to superstardom, a major feat for any actor, but especially for a woman in today's Hollywood.

John Ryan once told me that he and Tate would joke about how Sandy would never have a bad audition. They would ask her how it went and she would always say, "It was great. It was great." Whatever the audition was for, she always managed to find something positive in it. She would never concentrate on the negative.

Sandy always celebrated her birthday with a big party. She loved to dance, was a great hostess and always made sure that everybody was taken care of and having a good time.

When Sandy was at the threshold of her success, I remember visiting her last rental house on Sierra Bonita. She was scraping the walls of her bathroom when the phone rang and her answering machine began to record the message. It was Robert Duvall, with whom she had worked on *Wrestling Ernest Hemingway*. Upon hearing his voice she picked up the phone. Sandy was now hanging with the big boys. She was on her way.

I didn't see her much after that. She and Tate drifted their separate ways, and she had an unfortunate falling-out with John Ryan. But I'm happy that so many of her dreams came true. Sandy wanted to own a house in the hills, she wanted to be able to afford a Land Rover and she wanted to be a star.

Willem Dafoe

*I*n September of 1987, I arranged to meet Willem Dafoe
at my friend Hannes Schick's photo studio at the corner of
Bowery and Second Avenue in New York City. Willem's
young son, Jack, accompanied him and watched anxiously
as I photographed his father sitting on the street where the
homeless were lined up at a shelter next door for a free
hot meal.

The angles in Willem's face make him a photographer's
dream. I loved his performance in To Live and Die in L.A.
and thought he stood out in the already beautifully cast
Platoon. When I met Willem he was very involved in
the Wooster Group, an avant-garde experimental theater
workshop located in Manhattan's Soho district.

Willem is a true artist whose integrity as an actor has
allowed him to create a space all his own.

$\mathcal{I}$ grew up in Wisconsin. Our house seemed very big to me as a child. It was a classic white brick house. Our property bordered on farmland. I could literally walk outside my front door and be in the middle of a field. My father was a surgeon. We lived in a distinctly middle-class area on the outskirts of town, which was just starting to get built up. My mother would describe me as a sweet kid. I decided to be an actor when I was very young. It was something I enjoyed doing. When you grow up in a large family (I was one of eight kids), you've got to find your identity and turf in that family. I was the cutup. I would get attention by doing gags and fooling around. That kind of naturally led to my writing plays as a child. I loved history. I used to write plays that were historical dramas and incorporate a lot of action into them. I remember my first play. It was called *The Alaskan Gold Rush.*

I started making my living through acting when I was 18 with a group called Theater X. They were based in Milwaukee, Wisconsin, but for the three years I was with them we were very seldom there. We hooked up with a good producer in Europe, so we performed a lot there. It was a great experience being with a company that developed and created its own work. But it was hard work and I made just enough to live on. After a while I got frustrated and since I've always been ambitious I moved to New York intending to become a commercial theater actor.

I looked around, and between what was available to me and what interested me, I could find nothing. So I started going downtown to see performances. I went to a performance called *Rumstick Road* by the Wooster Group. I didn't understand it but the performers were really good and the place felt very important. I started hanging out with them and eventually I became a regular member. I like plays and realism as much as the next guy, but to me what we do is a little more interesting, because it's not an imitation of something. It's more like making something from thin air, or from stuff around you.

How do I prepare for a role? I like it when your personal history runs parallel to your fictional history, and they sort of criss-cross each other and inform each other. Then it all feels like the same thing and it's very exciting. That's why, when I'm making a film, I respond to exotic locations and toys and interesting people. Professions are fun. When I did *To Live and Die in L.A.*, it was fun to learn to counterfeit money. There's nothing esoteric about it. If I know how to counterfeit money, then I am a counterfeiter. If you are working with weapons and you know how to  use them, it's in your body. The most important thing about preparation is getting the stuff in your body. In *Platoon*, the preparation was very important. To learn to move through the jungle with your body. I don't believe I, Willem, can be anyone other than I am, but through my body and in my mind there are infinite possibilities, so it's all about applying my whole history, whoever I am, to a series of actions and out of those actions comes this character. I like big, classic, genre pieces: cops, robbers, heroes, good boys, bad boys and lovers, stuff that's fun to do, characters that have substance and that I'm curious about.

What have I sacrificed for success? I try not to think in those terms. I don't think I've sacrificed anything, and I'm not sure I'm a success. Once you get elevated to a certain level, people start watching you. I'm interested in my life, and I'm crazy enough to want other people to watch me. I like being watched. I like company. I don't have a lot of friends and I don't go out a lot, but I'm social somewhere deeply. I like people to be with me.

The biggest misconception about me is that I'm big. People think I'm really big when they see me in the movies, but I'm only 5 feet 9 inches and I weigh 145 pounds. That is actually quite slight for a man.

Which of my peers do I respect? Put it this way, I've got no shrine in my bathroom for anyone, and when I go out to a place where I know there are going to be celebrity types, I don't think about meeting anyone in particular.

When I was young I wanted to be a great actor. Did I want to be a movie star? I think romantically, I just wanted to be a great actor, and I still do. Now that I'm a little older, it's gotten more sophisticated. I want a good life. I want an exciting life and I want to be able to do great roles.

It's very difficult for me to look at scripts. I'm better at telling what is bad than what is good. A lot of scripts are totally effect-oriented. The tradition, particularly with a commercial movie, is to get way ahead of themselves. They want to see the movie before they get there. They end up too vague and lacking heart. For me to invest my time I look for a script with clarity and heart.

So why am I an actor? For my own pleasure and to create beauty. I hope people will enjoy what I create.

Willem Dafoe, September 1987

Laura Dern

*I*n Smooth Talk, *the film version of Joyce Carol Oates' short story, "Where Are You Going, Where Have You Been?"—which I had read in a literature class at the American College in Paris—Laura Dern's performance as the vulnerable teenage girl who naively becomes victimized by an evil man rang frighteningly true for me.*

I knew then that Laura Dern had that unique quality it took to be a star. I didn't find out until much later that she was the daughter of actors Diane Ladd and Bruce Dern.

In person, she struck me as earthy, feminine, spiritual and a good sport. Laura didn't blink an eye when I asked her to hike up a hill with me so that I could photograph her against the mud cliffs above the Hollywood reservoir.

$\mathcal{J}$ grew up in Los Angeles, in a suburb near Coldwater Canyon. It had a middle-class feel to it. Ours was an all-female house—my mother, my grandmother and me. My room was my place, my solace. I was a creative child, a little confused but always searching.

When I was nine, I decided to become an actress. I had done a little extra work, and after Marty Scorsese complimented me on being able to sustain 20 takes of licking an ice cream cone (in *Alice Doesn't Live Here Anymore*), I was hooked. My parents conveyed to me the hardships of acting, but their understanding of their craft, combined with their passion for it, was so beautiful that it overshadowed the struggle. When I told my mom I wanted to become an actress, she said, "If you want to do it, you're going to have to do it on your own. And you've got to study for at least two years before you start auditioning."

So I went to the Lee Strasberg Institute. When I was 11, I met an agent at the house of a family friend. I told her that my parents wouldn't help me but that I really wanted to be an actress. She told me to come to her office and do a monologue for her. Afterward, she sent me up for this movie called *Foxes*. I lied and told the casting director that I was 14, but could play 17. I screen-tested for the director, who thought I looked too young. But he liked me and gave me two scenes in the movie. That was my first job, and from then on, I dedicated myself to my career.

During high school, I was very busy with acting, school and participating in student government. I was very political and very liberal. One could have a great argument with me. I was kind of independent. I was an actress.

As a teenager, producers and directors and casting directors would tell me, "We don't want you, we want her because she's prettier," or "She looks more right for the part," or "She's a better actress." Insecurities creep in; egos creep in. You can really get trapped into that. Suddenly you find yourself acting because you want attention, to be in the limelight and to be worthy. You want to be accepted. It's easy to get trapped. I had to fight that.

There have been lots of times when somebody has said, "Sure, I'd love to meet Bruce Dern's daughter." That may get me in the door, but it never gets me the part, ever.

Most scripts are the worst. So many people get caught up in what's marketable. How are you going to know what's salable unless you try it? If it's different, how are you going to know if it's going to work or not unless people see it? The studios buy what's been proven, whether it's Sly Stallone or whatever the fad is at the moment. I get sick of seeing trends in scripts. I love seeing people doing things that are different, just simple stories. Just truth.

I look for truth. When I start hearing characters say words that are not believable, then how could I say them? I really care about the state of the world right now, and I look for scripts that will make a difference, even if it's a small one.

I felt the film *Smooth Talk* was important. No one had ever looked at a young girl's sexuality on film like that before. I had to think for a long time whether or not to do *Blue Velvet*. Ultimately, my trust in David Lynch won out. His vision is fantastic. When I first read the script, I really wanted Sandy to have some strength so that the audience could see the light in the darkness.

The more I work, the more excited I get about all the things I can learn. The more you learn about yourself through studying, the more pure you become and the more

pure you can be on screen. To me, learning about yourself and learning about acting is the same thing. Working on sensory things, knowing how to recall textures, being able to go back to how you felt, all make your performance more honest. When making a film, there is so much make-believe around you. It's hard to be honest a lot of the time.

My biggest sacrifice has been college. Sometimes I just want to be a person having fun, going crazy over midterms. I feel guilty about not going to college. I went to UCLA for two days before I got *Smooth Talk* and to USC for two months before I got *Blue Velvet.*

I love to read and paint and go horseback riding and there's no time to do those things right now. Eventually I'll want a family and children, and coordinating that with my career will be a struggle. I also want to be involved with the future of the world. I'm really scared about our future.

What spiritual things are important to me? Learning to come from a place of love. Learning to be satisfied with myself and to feel worthy. And in my acceptance, being able to share that with other people. That's a major battle. I need to become grounded in a sense of myself where it's quiet and at peace.

I would love to star in an on-screen biography of Monet, but I'm not an old man. He just enjoyed the simplicity of life so much. I'd really like to play someone who's constantly discovering life through simplicity.

If I could remake any movie, I'd probably choose *Stage Door.* I'd love to do any of the parts in that film. The beauty of that movie was that actresses like Katharine Hepburn, Ann Miller and Lucille Ball were all in it before they were famous.

I love Katharine Hepburn. She's perfect. During that period, actresses had the opportunity to show different sides to themselves. Today, leading ladies have to do more with fewer films.

My ideal leading man? I got my wish once—Kyle MacLachlan. Kyle reminds me of Cary Grant. I want to work with everybody who's great. I'd also like to work with my parents.

Why should a director choose me? Because I would commit. I could guarantee a hundred percent commitment, whereas some actresses are not ready to do that.

I feel I am the kind of actress who can enjoy acting without falling victim to the business. Politically and socially, the world is now a new place because of everything from AIDS to nuclear arms to teenagers being stars of movies. Maybe my generation of actors can be a more conscious one. That would be really nice and an honor to be a part of.

Christian Slater

In 1986, while I was still living in New York City, an actor friend of mine, Alan Boyce, told me to watch out for this really talented kid named Christian Slater.

After I moved to Hollywood in 1988, I would often see Christian at premieres and clubs. One time we ran into each other and ended up drinking shots of tequila together at Formosa Cafe, a landmark bar and restaurant in Hollywood. We moved on to Mickey and Joey's, an espresso bar co-owned by Mickey Rourke. Amazingly, Mickey himself was behind the bar serving cappuccino.

On a sunny afternoon in April of 1989, I picked up Christian outside his West Los Angeles apartment building. We drove to Venice Beach for the shoot, and started the interview in the car.

On the way we stopped at a Lucky supermarket so Christian could buy some smokes. He took the tape recorder with him.

Yep, going into Lucky. That man who honked at us pissed me off. Here I am now, walking into Lucky to buy a pack of smokes. Do you have any cigarettes here? I just want one pack. Now I'm walking out of Luckys. Karen, where are you? Where did you park? I'm standing outside Lucky. Oh, there you are. See, now I found you.

I grew up in New York City. My mother and father got divorced when I was six. I feel like I was always a step ahead of everybody because I did have a mother and father who were in the business. My father was an actor. My mother is a casting director.

I hated school. There wasn't one subject that interested me. I went to this prep school called Dalton on the Upper East Side. I felt like I was being groomed to be a lawyer. I wasn't into that at all. It wasn't my scene hanging out there. I wasn't into being a preppy kid. I always knew inside that I was going to be an actor.

When I was nine years old, they wanted to hold me back a year, after I had toured with *The Music Man* for nine months. My mother transferred me to the Children's Professional School because they had a correspondence system set up so that I could continue to act and still keep up.

I got *The Music Man* because Michael Kidd, the director, had seen me on a talk show with my mother and he called me in for an audition. I sang "Zip-a-Dee-Doo-Dah" for him and Dick Van Dyke and they liked it. I knew what I wanted to do, but I was terrible at nine. I would wave to my mother in the audience.

Initially, my mother really didn't want me to become an actor because she knows how difficult and competitive "the business" is. She didn't want me to get hurt. I used to kid her by telling her I was going to be a lawyer, just to make her happy.

Since she was working full-time, I had this cool guardian who'd go around with me to auditions. My mother ended up giving me my first television job, five lines on a soap opera. I played a kid who fell off his skateboard and went into a clinic to get patched up.

I started to get plays off-Broadway and then on Broadway. By the time we moved to L.A., I had grasped the professionalism of acting. Now my mother is happy for me. She knows that I'm very serious about acting. She knows that it's what I want to do for the rest of my life.

I'm instinctual, mainly. I go over a script and whatever feels completely natural and comfortable, I go with. It comes naturally, I suppose. Acting classes to me are malarky. Actors are born, not made.

I'm just an actor. Beyond that, I really don't know who I am. I'm 19 and I'm completely confused about that. I guess I'd say that I'm a nice guy who has fun at what he does and is basically playing. I guess that's how work should be.

Acting was always the main thing that got me going. It's really fun for me. When I'm working, I'm most comfortable. I'm at ease with myself. I don't go out at night and I'm on a good schedule.

I need to get a hobby or something because when I don't work, I'm usually out playing, making a fool out of myself and enjoying it. But it's acting that really centers me.

Most of my friends are either in the music business or in the film business. I sing a little. I may cut an album one day. I'm 19 years old and I'm starting to explore women right now. They are a fascinating subject to me. Very intriguing.

I like to be the hero. If I were stranded on a desert island, shipwrecked and alone with a woman, we would… What? No sex? Then I would probably take command

of the situation and build us a boat. And she would fall madly in love with me and we would get married when we got back. I've also fantasized about being James Bond.

I have a secret desire to move to Montana and get a ranch, to get away from major cities. I want to live in a one-street community. I'd probably go out of my mind after a week but it would be so nice to go and just relax somewhere. GET AWAY FROM IT ALL.

Christian Slater, April 1989

Esai Morales

In 1984, when I first photographed Esai Morales in New York City for my book Boy Crazy, *he had recently co-starred in the film* Bad Boys *with Sean Penn. His gritty performance caught my attention. Afterward, we saw each other often at clubs such as Heartbreak, the Milk Bar and Area.*

In 1987, I photographed Esai again, this time outside his house in Hollywood. He had just adopted a pit bull puppy named Paco.

Esai had become very socially conscious. He would always voice his opinions to the press and organize events to raise money for such causes as Amnesty International.

Esai has since starred in La Bamba, Mi Familia *and* Death in Granada *with Edward James Olmos and Andy Garcia.*

My mother would say I was a very good boy when I was sleeping. I was a terror. I never stopped asking questions or taking things apart and trying to put them back together again. My mother was an organizer for the International Ladies' Garment Workers Union. One of my earliest memories is of eavesdropping on her conversations with her coworkers, telling them not to take the abuse of their boyfriends or husbands.

I don't remember my father and mother ever being together. She left him when I was two. Respect was one thing she taught me. It backfired on her during my rebellious teen years, when I wanted as much respect as she did. I didn't understand why, after growing up with "The Brady Bunch," there was a monopoly on respect in my family. It was just the whole "Latin thing."

I grew up in the Bronx and Brooklyn, and was a reluctant loner. I had a lot of time to be introspective. I was a dreamer and a feeler, the Walter Mitty of the South Bronx. The neighborhoods we lived in always started out nice and then depreciated because poor people and uneducated people had nowhere else to go. Some neighborhoods in the South Bronx aren't great. People blame it on the Hispanics and blacks. I think it's a superficial aspect of why the neighborhood has gone downhill. A lot of the city money isn't going into cleaning up the neighborhood. When people see blacks there's a stigma attached. And I try to wonder why. Why is it that way? It's easy to see the history of blacks. They were brought out here as slaves and then they were supposedly freed, but then they are treated as dirty, as more ignorant, as genetically unfit and marginally human, which is such a cruel thing.

Some friends in high school might say, "Ah, Esai was a wise guy." I tried to be the class clown. I had a lateness problem. Once, my mother went to Puerto Rico to check up on some property she owns there. I couldn't be late again or I was going to be kicked out of school. I decided to go to school at 2 a.m. and camp out there. I snuck over the wall in the parking lot and scaled another wall inside the courtyard. I found an open window and got in. I remember being terrified. I thought they had Doberman pinschers or guards with guns who would shoot at me. I fell asleep on the stage on top of the piano, wrapped up in a velvet curtain. Performing Arts High School gives kids like me a structural level. It was a high school made up of marchers

to different drummers. I couldn't have survived a regular high school. I was already suicidal in Performing Arts. I was different. I would say things not everyone wanted to hear, especially girls. I was a pain in the ass because I was a very passionate young man. I wanted to be in love, but I never found anyone to reciprocate or felt anyone was worthy enough to be with me.

I never decided to be an actor. It was something that was inevitable. As a five year old, I wanted to be a scientist, a lawyer, a fireman and president of the United States. I believed I could do all those things well. I was a natural mimic and realized I could go through the motions and be almost anything I wanted to be as an actor.

At one point I thought my ethnicity was a handicap, but then I realized that there are not very many well-represented intellectuals that are Hispanic. I really don't think that being Hispanic should be an issue. Just don't rule me out because I'm Hispanic. Do not *not* consider me just because I'm Hispanic. With the success of a movie like *La Bamba*, America realizes that it may be less prejudiced than it thought it was. Hollywood kind of presumes what America wants and unfortunately, the profit modem gears people (the film industry) to give America what it wants as opposed to what America may need as well. That makes me sad. We are a money-hungry society.

My first acting role was playing Arturo, a hyperactive child in a PBS educational series for teachers. My professional goal was to become a very popular actor, to become the best actor I could be. My goal as an actor today is to make a difference.

I'm not in the place professionally I can or should be. All the great scripts go to Tom Cruise and all-American stars first, and then they might trickle down to me eventually. I get a lot of scripts that have been rejected.

I look for a good story. Why just do *Rambo*? I feel cheated when I see things like that. I feel like a fool. I'm paying my hard-earned money to see a cartoon of people killing each other. We're exercising this hatred inside of us.

I like taking people on a journey, because I'm a director at heart. I look for a journey because for six or seven dollars, I think people should go somewhere. One day I will direct feature films.

My biggest sacrifice for success as an actor has been privacy. You sacrifice the ability to be left alone if you want to be and the ability to know if someone is being completely honest with you. Everybody wants a little bit of stardust. To find someone you can get along with in life is hard enough, but when you're an actor it's even harder.

I don't know the full extent of my image. I know people think I'm this broody, Latin, sexual God, but I'm a person who thinks and feels a lot. I'm just a human being. I don't think we should limit ourselves to being this or that—we are all so much more.

Why should a director choose me? There's an honesty in my work. It's not complete, but it's something I want to develop. I have staying power because of that mission. I won't abandon it.

What kept me going between *Bad Boys* and *La Bamba*? I could have taken a lot of work and been on a TV series, but I don't want to sell soap or cars. Faith had a lot to do with it. Every once in a while I'd scrape bottom. I remember signing an autograph once, and wanting to ask the person for 30 cents to ride the subway. I think those experiences are some of my fondest. They make me realize it's not about the superficial things. Life is not about getting on "Entertainment Tonight" or "Lifestyles of the Rich and Famous." The prize is not the prize itself, but the journey and realizing what it is that will make life worthwhile for you.

Esai Morales, August 1987

Melanie Griffith

Melanie Griffith's wild performance in Jonathan Demme's Something Wild *blew me away. When Kevin Koffler, the writer I hired for* The New Breed, *suggested that I include Melanie in my book I thought it was a great idea.*

Coincidentally, I was privileged to be taken on several tours through Shambala, a wildlife preserve founded and run by Melanie's mother, actress Tippi Hedren, who starred in Alfred Hitchcock's The Birds. *It is a beautiful place where peacocks strut and where lions and tigers, many rescued from defunct circuses and zoos, have generous land in which to roam. I also attended a screening of the film* Roar, *directed by Melanie's ex-stepfather, Noel Marshall, in which a very young Melanie had a small part.*

I lived in an upside-down ranch house on a mountain overlooking the San Fernando Valley. We had a lot of land and it was very green. We had lions and tigers there for about five years so it was kind of like living in a zoo. My mom had made a movie in Africa when I was about 12, and was really taken with the plight of the animals. My stepfather wrote a screenplay about lions, tigers and all kinds of cats. I got my first lion when I was 13. He lived with me in a room off my bedroom and slept with me at night. He was my best friend.

As a child, my mother would describe me as her angel. Then I grew up. I pretty much left home when I was 14, and that must have been hard on her. That's when I met Don Johnson. I really didn't move out until I was 15½, but I spent the weekends with him a lot. He used to call me Pinky. My face looked really young, but my body was developed. I acted really silly. I was so goo-goo-eyed over him. Don was my best friend. I went to a Catholic girls' school, but I wasn't Catholic. I had some girlfriends but no one from whom I was inseparable. I graduated high school when I was 16.

For a long time, I didn't want to be an actress. When I was 16, I started modeling to make money. We're talking junior modeling, not *Vogue*. Karen Lamm, an actress friend of mine, went up for a film called *Night Moves*. She met Arthur Penn (the film's director), but she wasn't right for the role, so she recommended me. One day, I got this message on my service, and I thought it was for a modeling interview. When I got there, I found out it was an acting job, and I told them I didn't want to be an actress. I met Arthur Penn anyway, and he asked me to work on the script just for the hell of it. Don and I went over it, and I got the part and ended up doing it for the money.

When I was 22, I started to believe my own press. It wasn't what it's about for me now. I didn't have any technique. I really didn't take it (acting) seriously. I think that probably every character I played was just me. All I did was learn the lines. I played nymphet kind of roles in *The Drowning Pool* and *Smile*. I just got too caught up with the Hollywood rat race. I started to drink and do drugs. Not really bad, but I didn't take care of myself. I didn't take my profession seriously.

I got hit by a car in 1980 when I was 23. I was walking in the crosswalk from Le Dome and a driver hit me. That made me get serious. It took a year for me to go to New York and study with Stella Adler. That was a humbling experience because nobody gives a shit who you are. You really have to work and you have to be good. Being on stage is completely different. That was a wonderful time. It was Campbell's soup and knishes and the subway and hard work. It made me appreciate what I do.

If you're in a position to make somebody feel something, that's a big responsibility. If you're faking it, you're not being fair to the audience. I learned to open my heart, take chances and be someone else. I discovered acting is what I want to do, and I wanted to do it for the acting, not for the glory—because there really isn't any glory.

My goal then was to resurrect my reputation in this town. I was irresponsible and flaky and people don't have time for that. Now I want to be a good actress and to give—maybe make someone feel something. I want to give characters I play a realness, so people can relate to them.

What do I look for in a script? Some kind of through line where the character achieves something that was unreachable or maybe something people around her thought she couldn't do.

There aren't very many good scripts, and most of the good ones are about men. I don't like violent movies. I love old movies, like Cary Grant and Katharine Hepburn movies. It's not a studio system anymore. Those actresses were all groomed and nurtured and had publicity people constantly putting their names out there. Now it's an individual thing. It's whatever you do with your career and your life and how you deal with things. It must have been more glamorous then to be a movie star.

The biggest misconception about me is that I'm a sexpot. I took pictures the other day for a magazine and the photographer wanted me to wear lingerie and be sexy and show cleavage. I said to him, "Look in my eyes. That comes from them too. You don't have to use your flesh to be sexy."

Nude scenes? God, they're difficult. If you don't request a closed set and only the director, the cameraman and those people who absolutely have to be there, it seems like everyone in the States shows up! It's amazing the people who crawl out of the woodwork once there's a nude scene. It's not easy. I would never do gratuitous nudity, where I was a bimbo lying on a couch to decorate a set. My nude scene in *Something Wild* took three days to shoot. Jeff (Daniels) and I had just met and it was on the second day of shooting. It was good because it wouldn't have been as awkward if we had shot that scene later on.

How do I differ from my screen image? I stay at home with my kid. I go to the market. I read books

Shambala wildlife preserve

all the time. I work out. I don't live a fast life. When you're an actor, the roles you choose are the karma you go through in your life. Usually, people have a profession where there's a beginning, a middle and an end. As an actor, every role you do has a beginning, a middle and an end. It seems like the parts that come to you when you really have a true heart with your work are the things that you work out in your life. For me, with *Body Double*, that was kind of getting rid of or exorcising the sexpot thing. For me to do that, to be that bold and that naked and that ditsy but also give her (my character) a heart of gold and to show that there really was something there. Then with *Something Wild*, being a wild, bold woman who goes through a metamorphosis of what she really wanted and whether I have the courage to stand up for what I want. *Working Girl* takes that question one step further. I did a movie that I hope never comes out called *Cherry 2000* where I played a Mad Maxine sort of character.

Finding the right agent was difficult. I think I was with every agency in town, and no one believed in me. One of them, the agency I was with when I did *Body Double*, wouldn't even send me up on it. Brian (DePalma) called me up to ask me to introduce him to Jamie Lee Curtis. We all had dinner, but Jamie wasn't interested. I asked Brian, "What about me?" He said, "Steven (Bauer, her ex-husband) would never let you do it." I said, "Yes he would," and I tested for it and got it. When that same agency that wouldn't send me in still wanted their commission, I fired them.

Sacrifice for success? I've sacrificed a lasting relationship. It's a hard business, and the two times I've been married, it's been to actors. It's been difficult. I don't think it has to be. I'd like to have a relationship where the guy I meet is my best friend, partner and lover, and it lasts.

The whole star trip, and not wanting it but having to deal with it because you want to work, is a struggle. Where do you place your goals? How big do you want to be? You have to find a balance. I don't think you can calculate this business at all. It just sort of happens when it's supposed to happen.

I wonder if drugs and alcohol are as big a problem everywhere as they are in Hollywood. I didn't think alcohol or drugs were ever going to be a problem; everyone else was doing them too. Everyone was snorting coke or drinking. One day I felt I had to have some, and then it was a problem. I like myself now. I didn't like myself then. On drugs you're not straight and you're not who you really are. It's really painful to get straight and really find out who you are. Until you get the courage to do that, it seems a lot harder than it actually is.

My biggest disappointment is taking a long time to grow up. I don't know if I'll ever grow up, though. I think I have a different interpretation of what that means. But having a kid has caused me to look at things differently. I have a lot more patience now. I am no longer the most important thing—my kid is. I think it's important for actors to have kids because most actors are so fucking egotistical and self-involved. When you have a child that changes.

The way our country is being run scares me. I want to learn more now that I have a child. It's not about human beings anymore—it's about big business. I've been involved with issues like toxic waste, and I've gone to rallies to help raise consciousness in cleaning up the environment.

I do what I do to make a difference. I may be offbeat, but I'm not some kind of manufactured person. I'm a survivor. I'm the real thing.

Melanie Griffith, January 1988

Robert Downey Jr.

Behind Robert Downey Jr.'s bright, amusing and intelligent exterior lays a luminous old soul, one that suffered through a difficult childhood. Robert's struggle with drugs dates back to his upbringing and I hope he will emerge as the spiritually enlightened person I know is within him. Since our interview he has become one of the most respected young actors in Hollywood, winning an Academy Award nomination for his terrific performance as the legendary comedian Charlie Chaplin. Robert has always had great taste in furniture and clothes. When I photographed him at his pink house in the Hollywood Hills above Sunset Boulevard he wore an Armani suit, later changing into a Versace jacket.

I moved out on my own six years ago. I lived on Ninth Avenue and 52nd Street in New York City. There were no windows that you could see out of. I just remember it being a really depressing, claustrophobic space that I actually had a lot of fun in. I was a busboy at Central Falls restaurant. I don't think it was tough monetarily. As a matter of fact it was the best thing that ever happened to me when my dad said, "I've carried you for too long. You're 18. Don't call me up to even ask me for a dollar. I don't care if you tell me you're hungry." I remember that was the point of transition where I decided, Fuck, I really have to grow up now.

My family lived everywhere; New York, London, California, Woodstock, and

Connecticut. One day I'm going to ask my mom and dad what year we were where 'cause I'm just spacing. It seems like so much of my past I really don't remember. Maybe it's because I have these screen memories of the times that were very emotionally difficult. I grew up in a family that was doing drugs and trying to be creative. At the same time there was so much love and laughter in our family. When I was 14 my mom and dad's marriage was over. I stayed with my mom because she really needed me to stay with her. They were married and had been creative partners for 15 years and the separation left her shell-shocked. My sister went to live with my dad. While I lived with my mom I'd hang out with my friends in Washington Square Park and we'd go and watch *The Rocky Horror Picture Show*.

I'd always known that I was going to act from the third grade, from when I played the evil lord trying to take over the princess's house, to when I did *Oklahoma!*

in high school.

But it was while I was doing the play *Fraternity* across from the Public Theater that I realized that acting was something that was really good for me and that it was something I needed to do. Most of the things I pursued in my life were out of necessity, not out of desire. I had this extreme paranoia that led me to be good. I was so afraid that I wasn't going to have my shit together that I got to the theater an hour and a half before every show. I would lay down on this mat, stretch out and run over dialogue, actions and transitions in my head. Acting gave me a discipline which made me get there early and drink herb tea and really appreciate the theater. I'd help them strike sets and loved the fact that I was getting 50 a week.

At that time in my life, I was getting into all this spiritual stuff like human energy systems and auras and projections and consciousness. I almost felt like my higher self was saying, *Fuck, this kid's in trouble. We'd better surround him with a lot of good thoughts.*

I had gone through a period of being self-destructive because it's so much easier to spend every night going out getting drunk with the boys and making a thousand phone calls in pursuit of drugs than to stop and say, "All right, what am I going to do tomorrow?' Substance abuse is just a real easy way to give you something to do every day and it's something you know you'll always get the same result from; not like trying something that's artistic or not necessarily artistic but productive. Because you don't know if the results are going to be failure or whatever. I've never failed to get high from smoking a

joint, I've never failed to get depressed from doing coke. But usually, even if the outcome's negative from the drugs, at least you know it's going to be that same fucking negative every time and it's so comfortable.

While I was doing *Fraternity* I was sitting in my apartment and I was feeling potentially suicidal and the phone rang. It was the agent my dad had hooked me up with. He told me he had gotten me a reading for *Firstborn*. I went in to read for this English director and was obnoxious and he cast me. And I thought, *All right, maybe something is going to happen now.* My initial goals were external. I wanted to make a million dollars. I wanted my name above the titles and I wanted everyone to know who I was and all my friends going, "Wow, I wish I were him." It probably wouldn't have made me any happier but at least it would have given me the guise of success. Now my goals are more internal. My goals are to make myself happy and whole. Acting really helps because I feel it gives me a focus and it lets me express stuff that I can maybe relay to other people.

Lately, I think the most important thing for me as an actor is to keep working. I want to keep learning. I'm in a position to start saying no to projects. It's too easy to just

keep picking scripts that are very me and something that's so easy for me to do. Now I look for a role that I wouldn't think I can play right off the bat. What it comes down to is that I want to do roles I can learn from. The kind of films I want to do Hollywood really isn't ready for now, films about spirituality, about what's really going on in the under-current of this majestic reality that everyone is trying to suffocate and not confront.

Would I do a nude scene? Sure. What it would come down to is me saying, "I hope I don't get a hard-on." It would be distracting to the crew and I'd be embarrassed because, shit, maybe it's not as big as I want it to be. You can expose yourself in a lot more ways than taking your clothes off.

Do I consider the effect a film will have on my audience? I do more lately. I'm not worrying about money, so my struggle is more about accomplishing my goals. I was in Georgia and this lady came up to me shaking and said, "I saw you in *Less Than Zero*." I felt like saying, "You're every bit as special as I am," but I was in a pissed-off mood and I didn't want to sound like a prick, so I said my usual thanks, and started to walk away. Then she said, "Two of my friends went into rehab after seeing you in that movie." I got chills up and down my spine and thought, *Fuck, now I know why I do what I do.*

My image is of a guy who never thinks about anything, has a good sense of humor and does crazy things without thinking of the repercussions. There's a more serious side to me that sits at home, reads and is quiet. Everyone wants to feel that they're in touch with someone, and it's a great conversation piece, but me—the real me—is some-one only a few people know.

Mediocrity is my biggest fear. I'm not afraid of total failure, because I don't think that will happen. I'm not afraid of success, because that beats the hell out of failure. It's being in the middle that scares me.

My biggest sacrifice for success has been losing touch with the day-to-day reality of a modest existence. Los Angeles isn't reality, and making a movie in Los Angeles is a double-entendre of non-reality. I never get to spend time alone anymore, and that's got to change. I need time to recharge my batteries.

I love life and I would never give up. I put myself here. I'm certainly not going to cop out, and maybe I've ridden that line desperately without a net but I really feel blessed that there's some Gabriel or whatever entity that is watching over me, for whatever rea-son. Maybe it will have nothing to do with film. Maybe I'm meant to pull some kid out from under a bus who's going to be one of the major leaders in the next hundred years.

Robert Downey Jr., January 1988

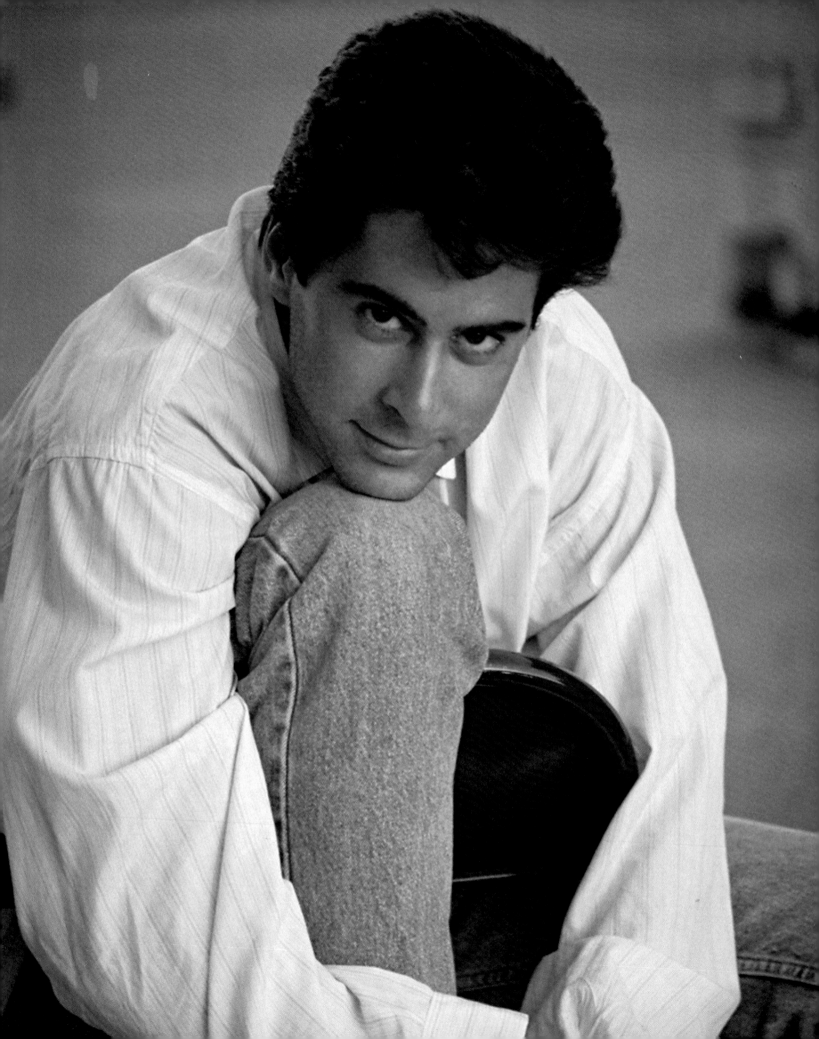

Jonathan Silverman

*W*hen he was 17 years old, Jonathan Silverman made his Broadway debut as Eugene in Neil Simon's Brighton Beach Memoirs. When I met him six years later, in 1989, he had just wrapped the hugely successful comedy Weekend at Bernie's.

Jonathan is refreshingly centered, soft-spoken, funny and a gentleman. During our shoot on the roof of my apartment, Jonathan would grab whatever prop he could get a hold of and go off on a comedic skit.

His career includes the hit NBC sitcom "The Single Guy."

I was born and raised in L.A. I'm a California native. I live here. My family's all here and hey, I've gotten accustomed to the freeway and the smog and I get homesick for it every time I'm on the road or on location.

I grew up in Westwood. I'm the baby. I have two sisters, one 16 and one eight years older than me; I felt like I had three moms growing up. I suppose I've always been pampered and spoiled but I never abused those privileges. I was surely an accident. My parents were in their 40s when they had me. Sorry Mom, I had to give it away. I grew up in a conservative home. My father is a rabbi, clergyman, preacher. We kept kosher but were allowed to do normal things. Yet when my dad left before I was 13, I rebelled against whatever I was taught, though I

still believe in God. And even when I'm in remote places, for instance last year around the Jewish holidays, I was in North Carolina where the Jewish population is all around three and I found my way to temple. Just for myself. It's what makes me feel good around the holidays. I really don't know what it is that drives me back every year. But it was the way I was brought up.

I really had no intention of becoming an actor. I enjoyed performing in high school plays and whenever baseball season ended, I would spend a couple of extra hours after school as a drama groupie, but I never thought I could make a career out of it. An agent named Von Hart, a nice guy who I owe a great deal to, was at my high school production of *A Midsummers Night's Dream*, in which I played Puck. He came backstage after the show looking for me and told me, "You're a really terrific actor. Would you consider letting me sign you and see what happens?" I thought a couple of buddies of mine had played a practical joke on me and said, "Yeah, yeah, sure, sure." He gave me his card. When I realized he was a legitimate agent, I gave him a call and within a few weeks I had an audition for *Brighton Beach Memoirs*. The audition took place in the Grand Ballroom at the Beverly Hilton. This ballroom had mirrored walls and a mirrored ceiling and Neil (Simon) sat behind this desk. I thought I was going to puke right there. I read several scenes for him. He says now that he knew within the first few words uttered out of my mouth that he was going to give me the job. I wish he'd told me that then and not years later. When I got home my agent was on the phone. He said, "Pack your bags. You're going to New York in the morning." Within six days I made my Broadway debut at 17. The first night was Tuesday, October 11, 1983, and it was fantastic. I was petrified. It was over-whelming and it was thrilling. I got through the show fine and at curtain call the buzz went around the audience, I suppose because my mother was there telling everybody her son was in the show. They gave me a standing ovation.

I transferred to a school in New York. I was working on Broadway at night and doing schoolwork in the day, pulling my hair out. I did the play for a year and graduated from high school. I wound up back in L.A. and did a television series off and on for two years called "Gimme a Break" starring Nell Carter. It was a good time. In between I managed to do a couple of movies. My first movie was called, *Girls Just Want to Have Fun* with Sarah Jessica Parker and Helen Hunt. I was able to do the movie *Brighton Beach Memoirs*, which we shot in New York. A couple of plays here, another couple of movies there. I did *Broadway Bound*, the third installment of the Simon/Eugene saga, on Broadway. After that I did a movie called *Stealing Home* and then *Caddyshack II*. I just finished *Weekend at Bernie's*, and an HBO movie with John Lithgow that I'm quite proud of about two traveling salesmen. I get to play the bad guy, this fellow from the South who totally ruins Lithgow's life. It was fun to play a guy who's basically an ambitious little shit. I never played the bad guy before. John Lithgow is the sweetest guy in the world. I want to be him when I grow up. It's so refreshing to meet and befriend someone like him, who lets you believe that nice guys don't always finish last. You can remain sweet, humble and modest while being a brilliant actor and still be respected and succeed. Otherwise, I've met people who are somewhat tough and cruel. It's not their fault. They're just told that's the way you gotta behave if you want to succeed, which I never quite enjoyed.

I always want to strive for realism and honesty in my work. I really don't want to be a star in any sense. I've come to enjoy my private life as a young adult and I would hate for it to be taken away. I want to continue as I am, doing good work and hopefully for the most part being respected for it and to be happy and maintain some sort of nice, quiet life on the side.

What drives me? Well, there's a great deal of satisfaction in portraying someone else. I suppose if I wasn't an actor and I didn't have the opportunity to explore other people's lives and find the answers to my own questions in their lives, I would need some serious therapy. It is somewhat therapeutic, taking care of someone else's problems, dealing with someone else's life rather than your own. The greatest experience I've had in terms of finding out about myself was playing Eugene. If you take my life while I

still had a complete family and Eugene's life while he still had a complete family, and Eugene's life without one and my life without one, and we both left and our fathers left, and how our mothers and our siblings and the community reacted, the similarities are remarkable. Neil asked me if I'd do *Broadway Bound* before he'd written a word of it. I accepted and when I read it a year later, I couldn't stop crying. It almost seemed like, besides taking from his own life, he took from mine. So much of our lives has intertwined meaning, Neil/Eugene and me.

It (acting) is a very frustrating profession, but like anything it's going to have its awful times. I know people who feel I haven't experienced enough of it, but rejection is a big part of this business, something you just have to accept. Various movies I've gone up for, people have told me to go fuck myself. It's hard to accept NO. I've been lucky enough where most people's reactions to my work have been positive, but no matter what the case, you do a piece of work and you try to get enough joy and pleasure out of doing it, but you're always thinking in the back of your mind, *What are they thinking? Are they going to like me? Are they going to hate me?* That's the life of an actor, always trying to please someone.

I enjoy the theater a lot more. If I could make my living solely doing plays, I would. It's almost impossible to make a living just doing theater and I certainly wouldn't be able to live in L.A. Nothing against New York. I enjoy the time there tremendously, but I'm just a California boy.

I don't enjoy that structured life, if you can call it that, of going around and pounding on doors and making yourself presentable and glamorous and you have that phony air about you. I tend to stay away from that. And I don't put on any facade when I meet people unless of course it's an audition and it's for the character. I mean, I don't have a lot. I only have what's ticking inside me, my values and my beliefs. I'm not going to change it for this. I love it (this business) but I'm not going to let it change me. No.

I never come to Hollywood unless it's for a function or a dinner. I have a home right on the beach on the peninsula in Venice Beach. I wake up and I hear the ocean and I have a little cocker spaniel puppy with whom I run five miles on the beach. He's 15 months old now but he's still a puppy in my mind. In the evenings, I sit on the balcony and have a margarita. Friends come over at night and throw something on the barbecue. I light a fire and go to sleep by the sound of the waves.

Jonathan Silverman, March 1989

Kyle MacLachlan

*K*yle MacLachlan was discovered in Seattle by David Lynch during a nationwide casting search for the film Dune.

Since first photographing Kyle in the winter of 1987, I've run into him several times around Hollywood, often dining at the now-defunct Olive restaurant and a couple of times waiting for the valet outside the Roxbury Club. Kyle is always with a beautiful actress or model, but in 1987 he was involved with Laura Dern.

There is a unique, almost repressed quality in Kyle MacLachlan that makes him very interesting to watch. I found his audacious work in "Twin Peaks" and his performance in the controversial Showgirls quite fascinating and I look forward to seeing what he'll do in the future.

If you were to ask a friend of mine from high school what I was like, she would say I was unpredictable, spontaneous and that I could laugh at myself. Also that I was talented in drama because that's all I ever did in high school. She would say I was somebody who should have let his hair down a little more. I was under the gun to be well-behaved. My parents expected a certain behavior. They insisted on their children being considerate and always aware of the other person. Growing up, I don't think I was able to experience the extremes of adolescence the way I wanted to. I realize I just wanted to tear the walls down, something which I never felt I could do. But it's something I'm discovering I can do now, at this late

date. I think it's better to discover that at 28 than at 45 or 60.

I'm trying to be aware when I hold feelings in and not feel guilty when I let them out. I'm in the process of acknowledging a certain part of me—who I really am. A lot of my repression was sexual. I was being respectable; I was being very good. Now there is a need inside of myself to kind of explode sometimes. It's a good thing. I just want to acknowledge part of me as a man. I'm exploring a different part of myself. Things have changed now that I don't feel I have to behave in a certain way because of what I learned as a child. I'm looking forward to incorporating this change in my work.

I had done plays all through high school. I went to the University of Washington in Seattle and my first summer I went away and did summer stock in North Carolina. *Dune* was my first film. I was in Seattle doing a play. The casting director had heard about me so she called me directly. We talked and she asked me to come in and read. She never saw me do anything on stage but she liked my reading enough to recommend me to David Lynch. Universal flew me down to L.A. to meet him, gave me the script and five days later I screen-tested. After I did *Dune*, people told me, "You are going to be a major star and it's going to radically change your life." But I had returned to Seattle and continued doing theater and because I wasn't a part of the whole expectation, I didn't feel the crash as bad as I might have. Still, I did think I was going to go to L.A. at a high level, but instead I came in at the same level as everybody else—at the bottom. That was tough, but then I just sort of shook it off. After *Dune*, we were supposed to go right into *Blue Velvet*, but it was canceled because *Dune* was such a failure. I didn't work for a year, but I kept trying to walk the path I wanted to walk.

When I first started out acting I wanted to be a solid regional-theater actor. Now I want to work with good directors. I want my audience to feel like they're on screen or on stage with me. I want people to be able to go through something in two hours and feel the things I feel. I want to feel at one with my audience.

I thought a lot about *Blue Velvet* before I did it. That was a big decision. I think it's important to think about what you're putting out there. I almost didn't do it, but I put my trust in David (Lynch).

How do I differ from my image? I think my image is a little cleaner than what I am inside. It's now up to me to let out that other part of myself. It's hard.

Being an actor is always a struggle—how can it not be? It's like holding a mirror to your face every day of your life, forcing self-examination. Sure, you can blind yourself with shit and you can get yourself out of yourself. But in the end, who else do you turn around to face? To me, life is about self-discovery. Acting is the greatest profession because you're dealing with yourself all the time. It supports that self-discovery process.

If I could star in an on-screen biography of someone it would be Rasputin. He was a pretty amazing fellow. There must have been a lot going on in this guy's mind to make him so powerful, and that's the side of him I'd love to explore.

I think the source of creativity is a divine thing inside of ourselves. Acting from that source of creativity is a spiritual thing. I think having a great respect for that source inside ourselves, acknowledging that divine quality and being honest and truthful to it is what's important.

Kyle MacLachlan, December 1987

Alfre Woodard

*A*lfre Woodard had just lost someone very close to her on the day we set up the photo session. Her eyes filled with tears and her pain was transparent, yet there was a soulfulness in her incredibly expressive eyes.

I had heard that Alfre Woodard was one of the most talented African-American actresses in Hollywood and got in touch with her through her publicist, Melodey Korenbrot. Extremely vocal about her commitment to help end apartheid in South Africa, Alfre had recently played the role of Winnie Mandela in an HBO film. Alfre is a woman who has a sensitivity and inner beauty rare in Hollywood.

I grew up in a small three-bedroom house in Tulsa, Oklahoma. Both my mother and father came from families of 12, and they "went forth and multiplied." My relatives were over constantly. I remember the laughter and the buzz of a million people trying to be heard. If you wanted to say something you damn well better have figured out a way to jump in there and make it interesting to get everyone's attention. If my parents had been born in another era, we would have been hippies, but they just ended up being great universal people who had strong ties to the land. It was impossible not to be real around them. I had a fun childhood. The only time I was ever uncomfortable was when I had to go outside of our house. Being a mixed socioeconomic black community, three blocks away from me were families with dirt floors. My family was well off, but I was keenly aware when I was young that things were not equal.

I was always called the "sensitive" child. I remember when I was eight years old, I walked into the living room one night and burst into tears. My father asked me what was wrong. I said, "I just read in *My Weekly Reader* that a hundred people died in a flood in India." My dad said, "Wipe your eyes—you can't help nobody by cryin'. Do your homework and maybe you can help someone someday."

I went to Kelley High School, a Catholic school. When I was 15, a sister recruited me

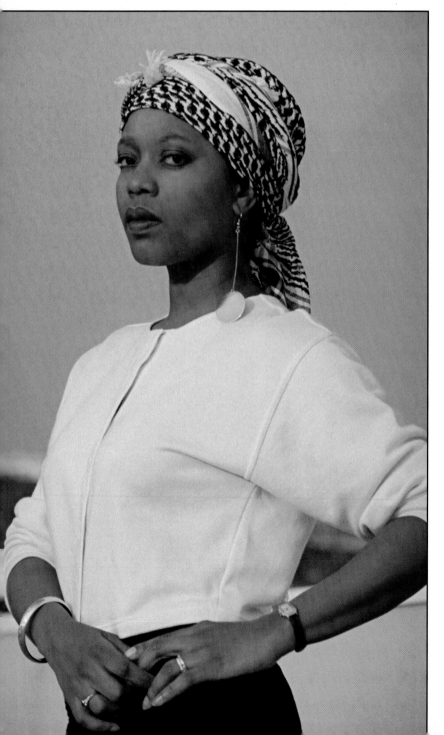

into a play. It was an original musical with a lot of Simon and Garfunkel and Led Zeppelin. The play was a hit, and the nun made me take her two-hour acting class once a week. Once I got into that class I realized that acting was my identity, it was who I was. There were no answers, no right or wrong. Acting to me was complete, absolute, infinite possibility.

When I finished high school I went to Boston University. I wanted to get a degree because there was then the mistaken notion that if you didn't have a college degree, you'd drop into a hole that goes to China.

I've known since I was a child that I wanted to live my life in Southern California. At first it probably had something to do with the sunshine and Disneyland. I went to Boston first to experience a different culture.

When I first started out in my career, I wanted to be a world-renowned classical actress who worked at the Open Gate Theater. I moved to Washington, D.C., and performed in many plays; the first was called *Horatio*. After years of training and performing, I knew I had to go to the next level. For me that meant making movies, so I moved to L.A.

I have a very deep and African look. There is a standard of what is considered beautiful and salable in this business and in this society, and I completely don't fit in. My first agent didn't send me out once in a year and a half. I left him. I am where I am today because of perseverance and my belief that good intentions and preparation win out. It's hard to get a job. You've got to deal with the social problems of people you're trying to get a job from, and then you have to consider that it is a business. It's like, "How much seasoning do we put into a Frito?" That's how they decide if someone is good for a part. Well, very black girls were just not "in." There are so many incredibly gifted actors who we will never see. For the first eight years of my career, I worked once a year for three weeks. Once I didn't work for 15 months. I didn't sit around waiting for work, though. I went on with what I would have been doing anyway. If I had focused on not working, I'd be so filled with bitterness and craziness, it would have gotten

to my openness. If that had been taken away, I wouldn't have had anything. I knew I'd eventually be doing what I wanted.

As I've gotten the things I wanted, I realize I have less of a personal need. When you get the things you want, a lot of responsibility comes with it. I realize the power of the medium in which I work, and as I've matured as a citizen of the world, I've come to realize that my personal freedom is the least important thing when it comes to the statement I'm making.

Alfre Woodard, January 1988

John Cusack

Twenty minutes before I met John Cusack in the bar of Los Angeles' Mondrian Hotel, I backed into another car. Since I had been living in New York City, I didn't have much experience driving and arrived at the Mondrian all shaken up.

John was very supportive and bought me a beer to calm me down. He was wearing a bandanna around his head because he had gotten drunk the previous night and shaved his hair off. We sat for a few moments and consoled each other. I found him articulate, worldly and a real gentleman.

An interesting, talented young actor, John Cusack's commitment to his craft is a rarity in Hollywood.

I grew up in an upper-middle-class home in one of the finest suburbs of Chicago. My parents weren't unbelievably rich, but they had enough money when they started out to buy a house in that nice area. They went through periods where they would scrape for the money to keep it but we were rich enough to have a college education if we wanted it.

My mother would describe me as somewhat of a problem child. I was very anti-establishment and discontented a lot of times. I was a very imaginative child.

High school? I didn't get along with that institution. I was very anti-high school. I hated high school with a passion. I cut as much school as I could to remain a B-/C+ student. My parents would have raised hell if I didn't at least get decent grades.

I started out going to public school but my parents were concerned about me and sent me to Catholic school. In sixth grade, I created an alternative language. It was called "Jo Mania." It was kind of an anarchy gibberish code that me and a couple of other sick little monsters thought up—a series of non-sequitur abstract paragraphs that we would spew at people. We thought it was the funniest thing. We'd call up radio shows till five or six in the morning, on school nights. We would talk about Ed Asner eating corn and we would tape it and play it back. We'd laugh ourselves into crying fits. The more absurd the better. So I spent most of my time spewing gibberish as a child. I was only interested in doing the things that interested me, as I still am. I've never had the discipline to do things other people's way.

When did I decide to become an actor? That's strange. I think people fall into it because that's what they are. People who I know that are good at it are social psychological mutants in a way. They're either shy, introverted people or they have a great need to express themselves so they don't explode. They're not like regular people who are happy being themselves and happy with ordinary pleasures. They have a much deeper want.

I was doing theater very young. My parents were hip in that

way. They exposed us a lot to the arts and culture. When I was ten I got into a theater group called the Pivot Theater Workshop. We did a lot of different Greek tales and improvisations. Through my teens we were adapting Singer, Salinger and Bradbury. We'd take short stories and put them in a form where you'd speak out to the audience. It was good training.

I wonder sometimes why I had this drive at the age of 13 to be in films, and why I wasn't content to go and play. I got my first role in an industrial film when I was 14. I went and shot it and got 700 bucks. I did one where a city boy goes to the country and discovers the wonders of dairy products. He meets his cousin Tracy and his uncle Jim and they talk about dairy products. It just doesn't seem right to me now that I was doing that, but, um, you know, so be it. Then I did some commercials. I did one for Nightlight. My lines were, "Look, flick this switch, it's a flashlight. Flick this switch, it's a wild strobe." So you tell me what I was—some weird fucker. It's equally strange to see eight-year-old kids with glossy eight-by-tens. I think it's kind of a sick thing.

I first started out wanting to do roles in films, probably motivated by a little jealousy of other people and wanting attention, and also ambition and drive. I really did think that I could do it. When I was eight I had this weird pragmatism that no, I couldn't be a football player, but I could be an actor. I thought, *Yeah, I can do that. Sure I can bullshit*. That's what I thought it was in a way. The people I hooked up with taught me respect for it (acting). Then when I was 16, I walked into my agent's office, Ann Geddes in Chicago, and I said to her, "If you get me an audition I'll get the part." I was just a real cocky 16 year old. The next day she sent me out for *Class* and I got the part.

My goal today is to do no more bad films. One of the things that got me in trouble in the beginning is that I improvise a lot in theater and I thought I could fix holes in scripts, improvising cool lines and coming up with stuff. What I learned is that the holes don't fix themselves. It's in the play or in the script. So you have to look for a good script first. Then of course you want to work with great directors like Alan Parker, Stanley Kubrick or Woody Allen.

What kind of roles am I looking for? I didn't want to do any more love stories where I fall in love with a girl, because I feel like I keep doing that and I keep graduating from high school. That's kind of my dream and my nightmare. Then I read a script that was really well written and I said, "Fuck, man, I don't care. I'll do anything as long as it's good." Most important to me is to be in a good director's film, to be a part of a good vision. I'd fucking foam for him. Just work as hard as I can.

Everything is going the way it should. I have a good understanding now of what's good. Over the last two years I've learned a lot about the business since I did *The Sure Thing*. You have all these people coming at you from all these different angles. Slimy fucks. Agents and producers who are really good at meeting in the office, who talk a good game and then don't produce. I've done some of these films and made a lot of money and then been really depressed after they came out.

I have a lot of really good friends in L.A. but I don't want to live here. I like snow. I like wearing a nice overcoat. I like the look. I like roaring fires and around Christmastime

I like to be with my family and friends who I grew up with. L.A. is not really seasonal to me. I also like to go out and meet someone who's not in the business. You can't do that here. In L.A. you go out and only meet actresses, people with scripts and stuff. I guess L.A. is the capital of the film business so that's normal. But I've done three films and a play here. So it's not as though I don't ever go to L.A.

Acting for me is instinctual. I just try to put myself there and start imagining. I spend time thinking about it. I think studying things other than acting is important to my growth as an actor. At NYU I took a law class and an ethics class. I feel, the more I grow as a person, the more I learn about new things and meet cool people with good visions and ideas, the cooler I'll be on film and on stage.

What do I look for in a script? I think that it's either got to be funny or it's got to make people think. So far all I've done in my career is make people laugh a couple of times. Or maybe make them think—ugh, probably not, probably just made them laugh. But I will, I'll try to do all those things in the next years.

The only weird thing even at my modest level of success is when people you don't know come up to you and want to be a part of your life. You try to be courteous and stuff. It's strange because by them actually seeing you, it makes them feel better. It's a weird kind of responsibility. But you know at times it gets tiring. I'm trying to start some theater in Chicago and see my family and find another girlfriend and these people kind of just want to talk to you about your films and what you've been doing.

There was a lot of me in *The Sure Thing*. When I do a role, I bring as much of myself into it as I can but I also take on the characteristics of the role. In *Tapeheads* I got a chance to do something that I hadn't done. I got to play this sleazy white trash would-be video producer and when I was doing that film man, I started talking like that. I started taking on a lot of characteristics of that character. You spend two months talking, discussing and thinking about this character in this film and before you know it, you walk off the set and you've still got your pencil-thin mustache and long hair. You find yourself talking to women in clubs and saying these ridiculous things.

After you finish a film it is strange. You go out 10, 12 weeks and you're just going boom boom boom, hauling ass, trying to make all this stuff work. Then you finish it and you look around and there's nothing to do. Your regular life can't possibly be as exciting as those 12 manic weeks you spent with that new group of people. It's like you become a family and you have affairs and you do all these things on the set. After it's over you just go out and drink beer and stare for a couple of days. There is a kind of a letdown that way. When making a film there's a fine line between being in the spirit of partying with your fellow actors and your commitment to the work. That's a struggle. Fuck man, I'm 21, I'll work it out.

I've never had an image of myself being like James Dean or Marlon Brando. I relate more to actors like Dustin Hoffman and Jimmy Stewart, who were never into being unbelievably introverted superstars.

My biggest fear is that I'll waste my potential. I'm just starting off my career and I don't think what I've done so far has been all that impressive. If you recognize that I'm a good actor, hard-working and trying to do better projects then that's all I ask for. All I can say is that I will do a lot of good work in the next 10 years because that's what I want to do

Jason Priestley

*W*hen Jason Priestley came over to my place in May of
1991, "Beverly Hills 90210" had been on the air only nine
months, yet Jason had already become a star.

During our interview I made him a cup of tea which,
being Canadian, he thoroughly enjoyed. He was bright,
forthright, charming and quite grounded despite a quirky
appetite for thrill-seeking. I would never have pictured
Jason Priestley bungee jumping off a bridge in the
Angeles Forest, but at the time I met him that was
his favorite pursuit.

The day after we met, Jason was off to England to be,
as he said, "raked over the coals by the British press."

I grew up in Vancouver, Canada.
My mom works in real estate and my dad
is a manufacturer's representative. They
are both very down-to-earth people. I
hold my family very dear to me.

I spent most of my childhood in
the hospital. I kept getting hurt. I was a
very active and reckless child. I was never
afraid to do anything. There was a river
next to my house and I used to inner

tube down it. One year a friend and I
went down when the river was flooded.
We almost got sucked down to sea but
we both got thrown off the tube. I went
under and smacked my head on a rock
and started bleeding. I was 10. That
didn't teach me a lesson. I've always
been somewhat of a thrill-seeker. I think
the moments when you feel most alive
are the moments when you feel closest to

death. I enjoy that feeling, but because I'm older and supposedly wiser, I do a lot safer things now like bungee jumping. It's great. I jump up in the Angeles Forest. There are lots of bridges up there. My mother got really bored of taking me to the hospital all the time. She hated it. I broke my neck in a skiing accident and I was a hockey player too, so I'd always get pucks in the face, breaking my nose.

Yeah, every Canadian wants to be a hockey player. It's the national sport. And at some point you realize you're not going to make it and so you say, "All right, what else am I going to do?" I have a sister who is 18 months older than me. We fought a lot. It's that gap. If it's any shorter you're friends. If it's longer you're fine, but 18 months, forget about it. I first thought I wanted to be an actor when I was a little boy. I used to watch TV as a kid, and I decided acting looked like fun. When I told my mom I wanted to be an actor, she said, "Well, you're going to have to take a bath every day." And that was whoa; that was rough. I had to think about that. Finally I said, "OK, OK!" I think that was the first sacrifice I ever made to be an actor, to take a bath every day. Something (laughs) that I don't do anymore. I'm an adult, goddamn it. My mother made me pay her to drive me to auditions, as well she should have. She said, "Look, I'll drive you or you're going to have to take a cab." That was cool. She wasn't a stage mother. She didn't push me. Then I quit about five years later when I was 10. I said, "I don't want this anymore." I was never not a normal kid. Growing up in Vancouver and working in Vancouver isn't like growing up in L.A. and being a working child actor in L.A. Thank God.

I did one play in high school. But I wasn't an actor in high school. I was just a guy. I was a pretty good student. I was an honor roll student, actually. I found it to be easy. I never had a problem with reading comprehension. When I read something, I remembered it. I could memorize things very easily. High school was very frustrating for the most part. I found it boring. It didn't hold my interest very well. Still, I wanted to do well, because what are you going to do without a high school diploma?

I got back into acting in my last year in high school and started taking acting classes at night. I also taught an acting class to eighth-grade kids. That was fun. The year before, I started thinking about what I was going to do with my life. It wasn't so much an external thing. It came to me that this (acting) would make me happy; that this was a career that I would enjoy, that would satisfy me. I did toy with going into the military and being a pilot but there's something about washing the soap after washing your hands that didn't appeal to me.

I studied with June Whittaker, one of the founding members of The Neighborhood Playhouse in New York. She had a kid who she didn't want to raise in New York, so she moved to Vancouver and started a school there. I got really lucky to find her. She taught me so much. I learned about Method acting and then I went to another coach and learned about technique and then to another coach and learned about characterization. I took from all of those different coaches what I found worked really well for me.

While I was still in school, I did an episode of "Airwolf." Shortly after I did an episode of "21 Jump Street." I played a punk rocker who lived in a Goodwill box. I was working in Vancouver and I was doing some theater and some guest spots and a Canadian feature, and I was approached by a manager from L.A. who asked if I wanted representation in the United States. I said, "Of course." So I got an agent in L.A. and started going back and forth between Vancouver and L.A. After a while I got fed up and said, "This is stupid. I'm going to move to L.A." I made the big move to North Hollywood and didn't work for a year. Then the writers' strike hit and I thought, *What am I going to do?* The phone rang and it was my old acting coach from Vancouver. She wanted me to come up and do this play for her. So I said, "Cool." Boom. I was on a plane back. I moved with three friends into a three-bedroom apartment in South Grandville (a dubious neighborhood in Vancouver). Our rent was about 300 bucks. We lived on Oak and 21st Street and became known as the 21st Street Gang. That was my second starving

actor phase. The play was a strange adaptation of the film *The Breakfast Club*. After that a friend and I wrote a short film called *One Single Rain Drop*. We got it produced by a cable company in Canada. We wrote it, acted in it, edited it and scored it. It was about two friends, one of whom gets killed. The focus of the story was on the other guy and what you can do to alter your destiny. I was the one who got killed. It was very artsy and esoteric and strange. But taking an idea and turning it into a film, from the nebulous to fruition, was such an incredible experience. I learned so much, not only about acting but also about the whole filmmaking process.

In the fall of 1989, I came back down to L.A. to read for an independent film called *Nowhere to Run*. Afterward they said, "How long do you need

to wrap everything up in Vancouver?" I said, "Ah, a couple days, I guess." So I went back up, put all my stuff in storage and moved back down to Hollywood. And I haven't left since. Next I did a cable movie for Disney called *Teen Angel*, where I play an angel from 1959. Then I got a pilot called "Sister Kate" starring Stephanie Beacham. After that I did an episode of "Quantum Leap" for which I dropped down from my normal weight of 140 to 125 pounds to play this guy called Pencil. It was a great experience. "Sister Kate" got picked up and I did that for eight months. When I got released, I didn't know what I was going to do next. And then the pilot for "Beverly Hills 90210" came around. When I found out I was going to read for Aaron Spelling, that was scary. I mean, what was ABC in the '70s? Aaron's Broadcasting. The next day, a Friday, I went in to read for the network. On Monday we started filming. It was very quick. The whole cast had been in place except for Brandon and I went in and got it. That's what I've been doing ever since.

How has the show changed my life? I still live in the same little house and drive the same car and wear the same clothes. The money hasn't changed my life, except that I don't have to worry about where my next meal is coming from, thank God. But I don't go out and spend it because I remember all too well what it was like not to have any.

I enjoy doing television. I like the show because we deal with controversial issues that are relevant. At least we try to accomplish something. "21 Jump Street" was the same way and if we can attain the success they did, I'll be very happy. I hung out a little with Johnny (Depp) in Vancouver, but never on the set. I was hanging out with him in the bars. That was back in the first season (of "21 Jump Street"). Nobody knew who Johnny was. He was just another swinging dick like the rest of us. I'm really happy for Johnny, he's done great. He's achieved success in feature films, which is what he wanted. Hats off to him 'cause we all know how tough it is.

I think as an actor it's important to know what everybody on the set is doing because you can give the greatest performance of your life but if you don't play to the camera, no one is ever going to see it. You have to understand the way the camera works and that's where technique comes in. I have learned more about that on the set than I could ever learn in a classroom. A lot of what you can do as an actor depends on what you have gone through in your life; what you've seen and experienced. You need to be able to draw from those experiences. I think actors have to live.

Which character in history would I most like to play? Rommel, the Desert Fox. He tried to kill Hitler 'cause he knew Adolf was out of his mind. I read autobiographies about Rommel. I always thought he was the coolest. The other person I thought about was Attila the Hun, but I'm a little too old for that. He was 13 when he started taking everything over. I don't look that young.

I respect a lot of guys around my age. I respect Jason Patric. I respect Johnny Depp for what he's done. I think Christian Slater's very good. Gary Oldman is awesome. Leading women I'd like to play opposite? Most of them are older than myself. I'd love to work with Gena Rowlands and I'd really like to work with Jessica Lange.

Right now I'm concentrating on the show, but I am looking somewhat into the future and I'd love to move into features. I'd love to do some theater too. There's something about being on those planks. I really love the stage. Going back to the stage is almost like going home and it really brings me back to the roots and what I'm in it (acting) for.

There's something inside me that is quelled when I'm acting that when I'm not working is not. It drives me crazy and it makes me just want to keep working and not stop. It's a good feeling to be acting, to become someone else for a while.

I don't follow any one organized religion. I find some things in Buddhism that I like, some things in Zen that I like and some things in Christianity that I think are OK. I don't feel that I need someone to tell me what's right and what's wrong because I know in myself what's right and what's wrong for me and I'm the only person that I have to wake up with every morning. I listen to my own voice.

Jason Priestley, May 1991

Before They Were Famous

Photo Gallery

Over the years I photographed many actors and actresses for books, magazines and advertising campaigns.

Nicolas Cage

Drew Barrymore

Chazz Palminteri

Sean Young

Michael J. Fox

Andy Warhol

I. Jimon

Elizabeth Perkins

Patrick Swayze

Chris Isaak

144

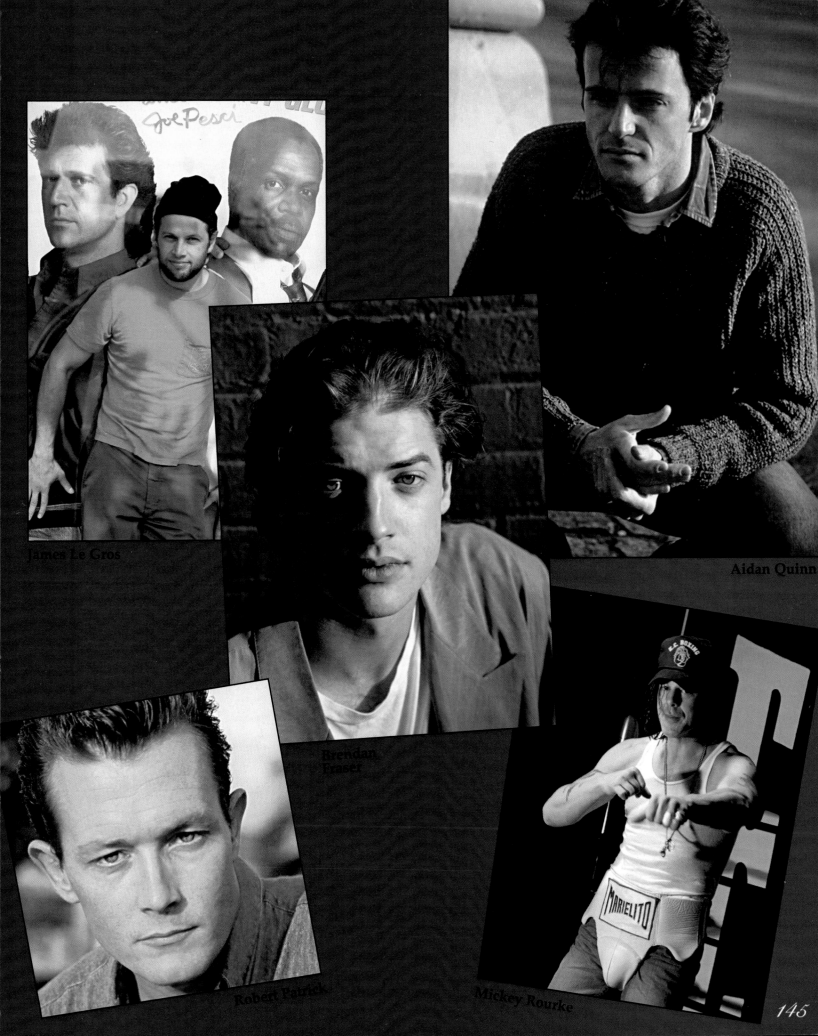

James Le Gros

Aidan Quinn

Brendan Fraser

Robert Patrick

Mickey Rourke

145

Jared Leto

*I*n the summer of 1993, Jared Leto was sitting at a table outside one of his favorite hangouts, Kings Road Cafe, which was also one of my haunts. I was having lunch with my mother, Charlotte, when she pointed Jared out to me. She said, "You should photograph that guy. He looks like one of your actors." When I turned around and saw Jared I knew she was right and went over and introduced myself. His penetrating eyes bore right through me as he told me that yes, indeed, he was an actor.

For a while, we hung out together, going to screenings and parties and for coffee. Another one of Jared's favorite places to eat was Jan's Family Restaurant on Beverly Boulevard. I got the idea that he ate dinner there frequently, mostly alone. He also liked to go to movies alone.

At the point when I met him, Jared was doing well financially. He had just scored a Levi's commercial and was driving a new red Isuzu Trooper with a killer stereo from which he blasted assorted rap music.

$\mathcal{J}$ared leased a room in a modern apartment building on Detroit Street. He is not only blessed with beautiful looks, but he is also incredibly focused, smart, talented and creative. He showed me some photographs he had taken of some 17-year-old models he had worked with. The photographs were really wonderful, kind of new wave.

One day, he called to tell me he had found a great location for our photo session. He picked me up in his red Trooper and we drove to an area in downtown Los Angeles which reminded me of New York's meat district. The light was beautiful. It was fun to photograph Jared because he really participated in the process.

I haven't seen Jared in a while, but his career has begun to take flight. He starred as the confused but intense Jordan Catalano in the acclaimed but short-lived TV series "My So-Called Life," and has recently been cast in Disney's film *Prefontaine*, about the life of the late runner Steve Prefontaine.

Photos of Jared Leto taken in the fall of 1993.

Balthazar Getty

In March of 1989, when I met Balthazar Getty at Triad Agency, he was a precocious, energetic, worldly charming 14-year-old who brightened up the lives of everyone he interacted with. At his young age, he had seen more of the world than most Americans do in a lifetime.

Balthazar had just finished filming the remake of Lord of the Flies, *in which he played Ralph, the hero who refuses to descend into the primitive behavior of his shipwrecked schoolmates. When Balthazar wasn't hanging out at his agency, he attended Excelsior, a school for kids who are in the performing arts.*

A year and a half later, in 1991, I saw him on a plane to New York and brought him a dessert from first class. Several months later I interviewed him again. He had grown into a young man, had a live-in girlfriend named Lala and was more introverted and into rap music, tattoos and hanging out with his friends.

I was born in the San Fernando Valley and I lived there for about two days. Then I moved over to Brentwood and then over to Munich, Germany. I lived there for a few years and then moved to San Francisco and ended up living there for seven years. I went through a whole bunch of different schools. Then we came back to Los Angeles.

My mother and father just got divorced. They were separated for a long time. They're really good friends, though.

I have a 16-year-old sister who's trying to act also, Anna Constantine. Everyone in my family is Paul. There's my great-grandfather, J. Paul Getty; my grandfather, Paul Getty; my dad Paul Getty; so I'm just Paul Balthazar Getty. But my name is Balthazar.

If it wasn't for Robin I wouldn't have anything. She's from a casting company. She's the best. She was looking for kids for *Lord of the Flies*. After class, she pulled me and some other kids aside and I went to an audition and got called back ten times. Then I flew to Scotland to go to summer camp and right before I got on a boat there, someone said to me, "Quick, you're flying to New York." So I flew to New York, met the director, auditioned and got it. I was packing, getting ready to go to Jamaica to shoot the film when I climbed up a tree, slipped and fell 25 feet and broke both my wrists. I was in the hospital for six days. We called them and they made arrangements for me and wrote my accident into the script. Then I flew to Jamaica with two casts on. Oh, God, it was a big mess. By the time they started filming, my right cast was off. They covered it with a T-shirt to make it look like it broke in the plane wreck.

Everyone thinks we just relaxed in Jamaica for four-and-a-half months but it was hard because we worked long days. It was raining and we had the hurricane which lasted for 53 hours and that ruined us and we had to wait for a week and a half without doing anything. After a while we just started to go crazy, running around in our underwear, just total savages. We lost track of the time, of which day and even which month it was. When I first started *Lord of the Flies* I wasn't very good. Now I'm getting better and better at it. I watch people. My favorite actors are Jack Nicholson and Robert DeNiro. I think Christian Slater's good. I watch a lot of films to get tips. If I have to cry or something, I'll think about my dad. Eight years ago he was taking drugs hardcore and he tried to get off of them and the doctor gave him too much medicine and he fell into a coma. We sued the doctor. They thought he was going to die five years ago but he's getting better and better. Someday he'll be able to do more than he does now. He's paralyzed and in a wheelchair, but that doesn't stop him. He still goes to concerts and gets chicks. He can move a little and talk a little. He's awesome. I look up to him. He was an actor and so was my mom. My dad did a Wim Wenders movie and my mom did a Shakespeare play.

What makes me different? I'm someone new who nobody's seen and so far people are interested. Whatever the role is I'll do the best I can. I've been all over the world and seen a lot even though I'm only 14. I've been to Russia and Spain and Portugal and Saint Tropez.

Balthazar Getty, March 1989

*I'*m getting into music. I DJ and I've been doing a lot of experimental stuff with my four-track and my records. I DJ sometimes on Thursday nights at Roxbury. I play a lot of Ice Cube and some of the other hardcore rappers. I like what they're talking about and I like the beat. James Brown and Marvin Gaye are cool too.

I just finished *Where the Day Takes You*, about street kids on Hollywood Boulevard. I met a couple of street kids and talked to them. They're not much different 'cause they're just kids. They have a little attitude 'cause they're on the streets and stuff. They hung out a lot on the set and we used them as extras. They asked me to come to their squat. They find an abandoned building and 200 of them will live in it and they invited me to stay there for the night. Me and Dermot (Mulroney) are going and Dermot's going to bring his video camera and I'm going to be the tour guide. The film I did before that is called *December*, about five kids in boarding school during the Pearl Harbor bombing in 1941.

I'm 16 now. My birthday is January 22. I'm an Aquarius. What do I do for fun? I hang out with my girlfriend Lala a lot. Me and some friends just got some automatic paint guns and we go paint gunning every couple of days. I'm still going to Excelsior. I'm in grade 11. I like English. I like creative writing.

Balthazar Getty, August 1991

Neve Campbell

Neve Campbell is part of a new breed of actress in Hollywood. As Julia in Fox's award-winning series, "Party of Five," she emanates an intelligence and strength combined with a vulnerability which makes her so refreshing to watch. After I arrived on lot 18 at Sony Studios, where she was shooting her series, Neve greeted me warmly with a smile that lit up her face. She is very grounded and real, crediting her spirituality to her Dutch mother, who now teaches yoga in Vancouver.

I'm from Toronto, but I was born in a town called Guelph, which is about an hour outside of Toronto. My mother is Dutch and my father immigrated from Glasgow. My parents divorced when I was a baby. I lived with my mother until I was four and then I lived with my father in Mississauga until I was eight. I would spend every other weekend with my mother in Guelph. I moved to Toronto when I was nine with my dad because I was accepted to the National Ballet School of Canada. I started dancing when I was six years old. I saw *The Nutcracker* ballet and fell in love with it and wanted to be a ballerina. By the time I was nine, I did *The Nutcracker* at the O'Keeffe Center with the National Ballet of Canada. I've been dancing ever since. Dance is by far my biggest passion. It's only in the last few years, since I've been working so much in film, that I haven't really continued my dancing. I've got hip problems so I had to quit but I did do *Phantom of the Opera* when I was fifteen for two years and some classical ballet. So I'm lucky because I was able to do what I loved for a while. I'll probably choreograph at some point in my life.

I have a bid on a house right now that I'm so enthusiastic and excited about. I really hope I get it because there is a 1,400-square-foot space downstairs that I can turn into a dance studio. Then I'll be really, really happy.

I take classes when I can but it's been difficult with the show ("Party of Five"). For the first two years we were doing a lot of publicity to get the ratings up, which meant traveling to different states on the weekends to do mall signatures so there wasn't much opportunity to take dance lessons.

How did I get into acting? My father and mother met while doing a play at the University of Windsor. They both had the aspiration to be actors. They got married

and had my older brother, Christian, and me at an early age and didn't continue their acting. But my father has been teaching drama in high school for the last 25 years and throughout my childhood directed an amateur Scottish theater group. My brother and I were always in the plays. We had a blast doing pantomime and theater. My mother owned a dinner theater. I'd sit in the back a lot and watch the play and watch people's reactions.

While I was doing *Phantom of the Opera*, an agent picked me out of the audience. They wanted me to model, but I absolutely hated it. I think a big part of the reason is that I'd trained since I was six years old and standing in front of a camera doing nothing didn't intrigue me that much. I took on a commercial agent and did about ten commercials in a period of five months. I did Tampax and Coke with Bryan Adams. I got a TV series called "Catwalk." I did that for a year and left because of a dispute with the producers. Six months later I moved to Los Angeles. I knew I needed to come because you get to a certain point in Canada, unfortunately, where you can only get so far and then you have to move to the States to get big. Canadians really don't acknowledge their stars until they get big in the States, which I think really needs to change. Producers on this movie of the week that I'd done for NBC suggested that I fly to L.A. to meet the network. I flew out a week after the Northridge earthquake so none of the agents were really willing to see me because they were picking up their houses. It was difficult, but a week after that I met a manager, Arlene Forester, who said she would help me out and get me a few auditions while I was looking for an agent. Within a week I had an audition for "Party of Five" and got it.

I am married. My husband's name is Jeff Colt. We've been together for five-and-a-half years. We met when I was in *Phantom of the Opera*. He was a bartender at the Santageous Theater. We hit it off and fell in love. Jeff is extremely supportive of me and has been wonderful for me. This career can be very difficult to carry on your own. How would he describe me? He'd say I'm intuitive, street wise, very giving and sometimes too trusting, gullible and vulnerable.

Ever since I was a child I have believed in future and past lives. I was never brought up on a religion per se. So I was very open to choose my own spirituality. I believe that everyone should have faith in themselves and faith in the diamond that they have within themselves. It's about strength and believing in energy and believing that whatever you put out will come back to you and whatever you ask for can come to you if you ask for it nicely and if you're positive. It's about growth and everything in life being a learning experience whether it be negative or positive, and therefore it becomes positive.

In terms of the future I definitely want to move into feature films. I love doing television and I love doing a series but I'm at a point now where I'd like to be doing other characters. Also, you can do three months on a feature and then take as much time off as you want and have time for your family and friends. Right now I'm working 14 hours a day every day and on Saturdays and Sundays doing a lot of publicity. I definitely want to get to a point where I don't need to be working that much and I can enjoy my life as well.

I just finished a film which I did on my hiatus called *Scream* with Drew Barrymore and Courteney Cox. It was a wonderful experience to be carrying a film alone, to be the lead this time. (Neve's previous films include *The Craft*.)

Neve Campbell, July 1996

Tate Donovan

Tate has been my neighbor for four years. When I first met him in 1991 through Sandra Bullock, he was subletting a room in a house in the Hollywood Hills and had just returned from a monthlong trip to India. Tate is considerate, sweet and humble. He was also a wonderful daddy to his Jack Russell terrier, Luigi, who was tragically stolen from him one day outside his apartment. He was devastated.

Sometimes, sweet music spills out of Tate's window. He plays violin in a pop Irish folk band called The Descendants. A large following, including the "Friends" gang, gathers on most Thursday nights to hear the band play at Molly Malone's on Fairfax Avenue.

Tate has the talent, looks, magnetism and persistence it takes to be a star and I believe his time will come.